Praise

The Brok‹

"*The Broken Fife* by Gary Demack is a beautiful tale of forbidden love at the start of the American Civil War. Demack masterfully weaves the history of the era with engaging characters struggling against the bounds of societal norms as Junius, the son of a Jewish merchant, hides his faith, as well as his feelings for Ruby, the family's slave. What will Junius do when the war, and all its implications, lands squarely in his small town in Missouri? Demack's story will leave readers wondering what they would be willing to do for love. A must-read for historical fiction fans."
- Teri M Brown, author of *Daughters of Green Mountain Gap*

"Gary Demack's character driven story reacquaints us with a historically remarkable period in our history. It brilliantly continues to draw us into Junius' world as his rollercoaster life takes a multifaceted journey with twists and turns impossible to predict!"
- Brant Vickers, author of *Fedor* and *Culver City*

The Broken Fife

A NOVEL

GARY C. DEMACK

atmosphere press

To Radolfus

for making it all possible

Chapter 1

June 1856

It was a deceptively glorious early summer afternoon in the northwest corner of Alabama as the country edged toward civil war. Whispers of secession grew louder as everyone awaited the day when the heat and humidity would blanket the region unmercifully. Friends, neighbors, and even relatives started taking sides openly on the issue that divided the country and would render it irrevocably broken over the next several years.

Junius Hart, who had just turned thirteen and was the son of one of the few Jews in Alabama, remained largely unaware of the impending crisis. His concerns were far more immediate in nature, and he struggled with how best to deal with them against what he knew were considerable odds. Chief among those were how to deal with his stepmother's opposition to just about anything he planned and his growing discomfort around Ruby, the daughter of Jim, his father's slave. While she had once been a favorite playmate when they were much younger, things were different now that he was becoming a man. He was having trouble understanding what it was he felt toward her now that he saw her in a new light.

All in all, however, Tuscumbia wasn't all that different from La Grange, some fifteen miles to the southeast, where the family had lived until a few years ago. Junius's paw, Radolfus, had decided to open up his new store in a different town where he could have a small farm nearby as well. Paw had explained to Junius's stepmother, Sarah Anne, that La Grange was not likely to grow much more while Tuscumbia would, given its proximity to the Tennessee River and the railroad that now came to town. In addition, the growing town of Florence lay just across the river to the north, and a smaller town called Sheffield was springing up just to the north and east of Tuscumbia on the same side of the river. He believed he would have a much greater clientele in the new location in Tuscumbia, which had proved to be true.

At least, Junius thought, he no longer had to attend La Grange Academy, and he could spend more time practicing his fife, the one thing he really enjoyed. Plus, his studies were more to his liking without the focus on the classics that he had endured at La Grange Academy. Why his father thought he needed to learn the classics of Rome and Greece was beyond him. "Cicero, Xenophon, Virgil, Livy? What do they have to do with anything, Paw?" he would say. As Paw had said repeatedly, he hoped Junius would make more of his life than being a tailor, even if his establishment—R.H. Hart, Fashionable Tailor—kept the family in decent comfort. He thought that a gentleman's education was the way to help Junius do more.

Once Junius had completed his chores at home—the ones that couldn't wait until tomorrow, anyway—he debated between practicing his fife and walking into town to discuss something he had been wanting to mention to his father. Lately, he had been spending all his free time on the fife and wished he could spend even more time practicing on it, but school and his chores prevented that. At the same time, the chances of hearing anyone playing music were rare, and he needed to be in town to have any chance of that. The churches would have music playing on the weekends, of course, but Radolfus wouldn't consider allowing him to go to a church. His only chance to hear any music was to walk into town to talk to his father. Then, perhaps, he would be able to hear someone practicing an instrument along the way. The walk into town won over practicing on his fife due to the beautiful weather, and besides, Ruby wasn't around to listen to his playing.

"Where are you going?" Sarah Anne called out to him as he walked away, but he pretended not to hear her. He had grown as tall as she stood and no longer felt compelled to do as she said. He had never warmed to his stepmother even after all these years, nor, as far as he could tell, had she to him. She went about life always bent slightly forward at an angle from her waist, looking as though she was searching everyone's souls to find out what they were thinking. Junius couldn't understand what had attracted his father to her after his first wife, Junius's mother, died. Maybe he had been desperate to find a decent woman to look after Junius and his baby sister, Lizzie. But then, Radolfus and Sarah Anne had several more children in the following years, so there must have been more between them.

Junius flirted with the idea of briefly taking a detour down to the swimming hole to take advantage of the beautiful weather but changed his mind when he realized that some of his schoolmates would already be there. Even though he couldn't swim, he could at least wade in the shallow part, but he would have to strip to do that; otherwise, Sarah Anne would be upset if he came home with wet clothes. Stripping meant exposing himself to the other boys, who would point at him, laughing at the fact that he had been cut. None of them were, and that set him apart from virtually everyone else his age.

As far as he knew, there were no other Jews in Tuscumbia. Paw even occasionally remarked on that fact when he was sure Sarah Anne was out of earshot after she mentioned anything having to do with churches. Junius supposed it should trouble him as well, but he wasn't entirely sure why that should be the case. He just knew that it was an issue.

As he drew closer to the central part of town, Junius saw

a group of older boys milling around near the Baptist church, laughing amongst themselves. He quickly decided to walk on the opposite side of the street. Paw's store was still a few blocks away, and he had no desire to have to deal with their taunts and jokes—jokes about his religion and the fact that he was the smartest boy in the one-room school.

The shop was on Main Street near Mechanic's Row, just north of R.B. Alexander's dry goods store. A pair of golden scissors hung outside the entrance off to the side through an alley. Why his father had never gone to the trouble of installing a door that opened on Main Street was a mystery to Junius.

Most of Paw's customers came to the store on foot or on horseback. But that day, a handsome carriage drawn by two matched horses stood waiting out front. As Junius was about to enter the store, a gentleman with a top hat and heavy wool suit, sweating profusely, charged out of the door past him and let it slam shut. The man, who wore expensive, well-shined shoes, looked vaguely familiar to Junius, but he couldn't quite place who he was or how he knew him. Jim always told him that you could tell a lot about a man by the way he wore his shoes.

"What are you doing going in there, son?" the man asked, stopping to mop his brow. He spoke with an accent not unlike his father's. Then Junius remembered. It was Mr. Lehman, the banker from Montgomery he and Paw had met a couple of years ago.

"It's my paw's store," he stammered.

"Oh, yes, of course, you are the young Master Hart. My goodness, how you have grown, young man. Before too long, you'll be taller than your father, I reckon! Well, I'm sure your father will be happy to see you." And with that, he doffed his hat and climbed into the waiting carriage, smiling back at Junius.

Junius wasn't so sure his father would be pleased to see him. He had an agenda, one that his stepmother disapproved of. He wanted to learn how to swim, and Jim was eager to teach him. Sarah Anne held strong views against swimming, considering it too dangerous, so he had to talk to his father alone, which meant confronting him at the store.

Steeling himself, Junius entered the store. Gentlemen spoke to each other in small groups without drawing attention to themselves. He was unaccustomed to wearing any of the finery he saw displayed about the store. Even Paw rarely wore anything beyond his modest work suit as he kept his own finest clothing confined to Saturdays and the occasional Sunday gathering.

There were bolts of gray and black and brown fabric here and there in large cupboards against the walls of the shop, but rarely any color other than the very occasional white or beige. Many of the garments his father sold he had made himself, but there was also a goodly number that he had acquired from merchants in New York and New Orleans. There were many different fabrics, cassimeres, and vestings of every material imaginable.

Junius spied Jim, busy as usual, bent over a carton that contained new bolts of fabric that needed to be displayed. Jim knew the business as well as Radolfus did, having been with the family for well over ten years now.

The store attracted a clientele of notables. The former governor, Henry Collier, had visited the shop on more than one occasion, coming all the way from Tuscaloosa to do so. Rumor had it that the current governor, John A. Winston, would also be visiting Tuscumbia soon, and that he planned to talk to Radolfus about new suits as well. Junius had heard Radolfus say that he looked forward to discussing issues with Moore inasmuch as he had publicly stated his vehement opposition to secession on more than one occasion. The governor was already known as a Unionist, which caused some catcalls from older residents of Lauderdale and Franklin counties when he was out of earshot.

As Junius scanned the shop, he recognized the mayor of Tuscumbia in one corner of the store holding court while a man he was reasonably sure was a member of Alabama's House of Representatives did likewise in the opposite corner.

In the back of the shop, two gentlemen were having an animated conversation. Something to do with "Fremont" and "secession." To Junius, it sounded like they were disciples of the firebrand secessionist fire-eater like William Yancey, who had recently spoken in Tuscumbia to rile things up. Based on what Yancey had proclaimed, it was obvious that the new Republican Party's nomination a few days ago of the anti-slavery John C. Fremont of California for president in the upcoming election had gotten their attention. Junius had heard Paw whispering to Jim how he thought Fremont might be just the thing the country needed right now, but that was something he would never say openly.

While Junius waited to catch his father's attention, he crept closer to where the two gentlemen were discussing politics.

The taller one seemed more agitated than the other man. "Fremont? He doesn't want slaves? Why doesn't that son of a gun go back to California? They don't have slaves there because they don't need them. They have Injuns and Mexicans to do everything our slaves do. Ain't no difference as far as I'm concerned. Jack, here's a man who won California from Mexico, and now he has regrets about what he did? Bastard!" he said loudly.

"I know, Colonel. I don't think we have to worry about him winning the election. And if he does, well, we know what to do about that, don't we?"

"Secession is a drastic step, Graham. A drastic one indeed," the man referred to as Colonel said. "And do you really think your native Maryland would secede if it came to that?"

Before Major Graham could answer, Radolfus approached them. "Colonel Cochrane, Major Graham. How good to see you, sirs," Radolfus said before noticing Junius standing nearby. When he did see him, with a brief nod he indicated that Junius should leave the men alone.

Junius walked away disconsolately. Radolfus was always trying to shield him from anything that would result in a controversial discussion.

Not wanting to appear disobedient to his father, Junius slowly ambled to the door, still looking for Jim.

It didn't matter what the task was; Jim seemed to be able to carry it out effortlessly. Junius thought it amazing that a man so big and powerful could perform any task with such ease and grace. Jim knew so much about so many different things. Occasionally, he would hum to himself songs he must have learned in New Orleans years ago, because Junius didn't recognize them. He had tried to explain to Junius that he spoke both Creole and Cajun but the differences between the two were lost on Junius.

Just before he reached the door, Jim returned from putting things away in the storeroom.

"Hi there. Are you busy right now?" Junius asked, looking back over his shoulder.

"No more so than is usually the case on a summer's day," Jim said, smiling.

Junius stepped back a few inches as Jim spoke. He usually had a serious expression, muttering under his breath about how some of the customers missed the spittoon or why they dropped their cheroots on the floor before leaving the store. But he wasn't complaining at all about customers this afternoon. In fact, his mood seemed strangely buoyant.

"I'm going to talk to Paw about swimming today," Junius said to Jim.

"Don't you worry. I'm sure he'll approve, and I'll be able to teach you. We'll go down to Spring Creek late afternoons before supper. Shouldn't take too long to teach you," Jim said. "You just tell your paw that's what we're going to do, all right?

But if I were you, I would wait a bit longer before talking to him. Tomorrow might be a better day."

"Tomorrow? Why not today?"

"I think your father will have something to tell you and the family once he gets home. I'd just wait a bit longer if I were you," he said, smiling even more broadly now.

As Junius went to the door to leave, Jim called out to him. "Did you talk to Ruby this afternoon?"

"No, I didn't. I guess maybe Sarah Anne sent her off to one of the neighbors to help out. Why?" He wondered again why he hadn't seen her before he left the house to come to the store.

"Oh, probably nothing. I asked her to come to the store if she had a chance. There's something here, a new arrival, that I wanted her to see. It's not often that ladies' things come in that I think she might like, and your father is being very generous. And that dress of hers is getting old. She has sewn that old thing up so many times that it can't have much life left in it. It's going to be a surprise for her, so don't say anything if you see her."

Junius nodded and made for the doorway. A new dress for Ruby. She'd like that.

Deciding to take the short way home rather than walk through town, Junius cut through side streets. He would still have to pass the Baptist church but figured the boys who had taunted him earlier would be gone by now. As he walked, he kept thinking about why both his father and Jim had smiled so much and about the hoped-for swimming lessons, and he forgot about the boys.

Although the boys he had seen earlier on the way to the store were no longer in front of the church, their voices carried from somewhere behind it. Junius was tempted to pick up his pace so he could go past them quickly and avoid them, until he saw something out of the corner of his eye. The boys were all there, and there was someone else there, too.

A slave girl. They stood in front of her, backing her up against the wall of the building behind the church. She had her arms crossed in front of her as the boys grabbed at her arms, them laughing as they did so. One of them was pulling her hair from the back, forcing her head up as two others were trying to force her to her knees.

Ruby!

The boys were trying to move her away from the building, further down the road, further away from the church and the main part of town. As they steered her away, she looked back in the direction of the church and tried to scream, but the one Junius recognized as Buford covered her mouth with his hands while she struggled. Two others pinned her arms behind her back as Ruby kicked and thrashed.

"Ruby!" Junius yelled and sprinted across the street. "Ruby!"

Just then, the front door of the Baptist church opened, and the parson walked out. He saw Junius and ran with him around the corner. When they turned the corner and realized what was happening, the parson yelled, "Stop!"

At that, the boys let go of Ruby's arms and ran off toward the river.

By the time Junius and the parson reached her, Ruby was sobbing, her eyes wide with terror. Junius fought an urge to reach out to her. "What happened, Miss ..." the parson said.

"Her name is Ruby. She's my paw's slave's daughter," Junius said.

"Your paw's slave's daughter? That makes her a slave too, now, doesn't it?" The parson frowned at Junius as he said that, then turned to Ruby. "Well, what happened?"

She didn't say anything but just kept staring after the boys and breathing hard. Finally, she turned back to the parson and Junius and said, "They said they wanted to have some fun."

The parson nodded. "Who were they?"

Ruby glanced at Junius before answering, and he shook his

head ever so slightly.

"I don't know. Never seen them before," she lied. "I only come into town when my paw summons me."

The parson turned to Junius and asked, "Do you know who they were, young man?"

Junius wasn't sure how to answer. Weighing the probable consequences of answering truthfully and the certainty that the boys would make him pay, Junius decided to lie and said, "I'm not sure, sir."

Junius was sure the parson saw right through him as he told the lie.

"I see. I don't recognize you, young man. Does your family come to my church or another one? You aren't Catholic, are you?" the parson said, a note of disapproval in his voice.

"My name is Junius Hart. I'm Radolfus Hart's son."

"Ahh, that's why I don't know you. I do, however, know your mother, a fine God-fearing woman. Regularly attends services," he said as he looked toward the heavens.

"My stepmother. My paw is God-fearing, too. It's just that there isn't a church for him in town. No rabbi here, either."

"Of course. For now, I suspect you probably ought to get your slave girl home, don't you? Do you wish for me to accompany you in case the boys come back for more fun?"

"No, sir. We'll be fine," Junius said.

Ruby looked up at Junius. Even though she was a few months older than Junius, he was now taller than she was.

Before leaving them and going back into his church, the parson had something else to say. "Young man, was your deceased mother a Jewess?"

"What?" Junius asked. The question had never been posed to him before.

"If your father is inclined to marry outside his faith, as he obviously did, then I wonder if your deceased mother was also perhaps a Baptist."

Junius had never considered this before.

"Was she of the same faith as your father, R.H.?"

"I, I don't know. I guess so. Why?" *Where was this leading?*

The parson was quiet for a long moment. "It's actually an important question. If your mother was a Jewess, then you are too. If, however, she wasn't, then you are not one by reason of birth. I have studied other religions in depth, young man, especially the Hebrew faith. After all, our faith stems from that one. With certain changes for the better, of course."

Junius just stared at the parson, not knowing what to say. He had never actually conversed with a parson before and was surprised by his gentle and curious questioning.

"If you find out that you aren't a Jew, then you would be welcome to accompany your mother, I mean your stepmother, to church," the parson said. "You'd best get the girl home to her parents now. She's had quite an experience today and needs to rest."

With that, the parson walked back to the church entrance.

Junius asked himself why the question of his mother's religion had never occurred to him before. Radolfus and Sarah Anne hardly ever discussed religion, even when it had come time to baptize his siblings at Sarah Anne's insistence. His father hadn't attended these ceremonies, and now Junius wondered whether his mother had tried to have him baptized before she died if she was a Christian too.

Ruby was whimpering a little bit as she walked. Junius looked down at her knees, and there wasn't any blood that he could detect, but they must have hurt her.

"How did your knees get scraped?"

"Two of the boys tried to force me down. I got up, but they kept trying. One of them started to undo his pants. That's when I started to scream loudly, and then you and the parson ..." she said.

He could only imagine what would have happened had he and the parson not shown up when they did. His cheeks reddened, and he felt an indescribable anger rising inside him.

How could they even consider harming her and doing whatever they intended with her?

"Junius?" Ruby said, interrupting his thoughts.

"Oh, yeah, I guess we'd better be getting on home. Tell me, has that sort of thing happened to you before? What those boys were doing?" he asked, afraid of how she might answer.

"No, not really. But I know of other girls who have had things like that happen, and some of them have, well, some of them haven't been so lucky," Ruby said.

Junius had overheard some of the boys at school talk of their exploits and understood what she meant. His cheeks flushed again. "How unlucky were they?"

Looking away from him, Ruby said, "I don't really want to talk about it."

Sensing her discomfort, he dropped the subject. "Well, I guess Jim will be mighty angry when he hears about it."

"No!" she said. "You can't tell him! Please promise me you won't!"

"Not tell him? Why not?" Junius asked.

"Because he'll be so angry that he'll want to teach the boys a lesson. And then ..."

"And then?" What did she mean, he wondered.

"Please, please, just promise me you won't say anything to anyone. This has to be our secret," Ruby said.

She was probably right, Junius realized. Jim was big and strong and could do some real damage to those boys if he was provoked. But the fact that he was just a slave would make things hard on him and the whole Hart family if he took any action whatsoever.

"All right, I promise," he said.

They started walking home in silence. After a while, Ruby said, "I didn't know Missus Hart isn't your real maw."

"Well, she isn't. And I only remember a little bit of my maw. Paw never really talks about her anymore."

"My maw died when I was a little girl, too." Ruby's eyes

grew sad, but she didn't cry.

"I know. That's when Paw bought you and Jim and brought you here from New Orleans," Junius said.

"What did you say?" she said, stopping suddenly.

"Paw. He bought you and Jim after your maw died," Junius said.

"In New Orleans?" she asked.

"Yes, that's what Paw told me."

"You mean I was born in New Orleans? Not here in Alabama?" she asked.

"Yeah, New Orleans." Junius wondered how she never knew.

They walked the rest of the way home in silence.

Junius kept wondering about what the parson had said. Had his dead mother been Jewish? If not, what had she been?

The list of questions he had for his father continued to grow, but he wouldn't be able to ask Radolfus any of them while Sarah Anne was within earshot. Like so many other things, the questions would have to wait.

Chapter 2

Junius and Ruby walked the rest of the way home side by side, with Junius occasionally glancing behind to make sure no one was following them. He was careful not to get too close to Ruby because people would talk if they thought they were touching. Besides, he had no idea how Ruby would react if they even accidentally brushed against each other.

"Are you sure there's no tear or dirt on my skirt?" Ruby asked.

"No, you look fine." Junius understood that she didn't want her father to suspect anything had happened.

When they reached the Hart family home, Junius said, "Goodbye. I'll just wait here to make sure you're home safe."

She gave him a small smile and walked away toward the cabin behind the Hart house she and her father shared. Before she entered, she turned to Junius, smiling, and called out, "Are you going to play your fife?"

"I just might. Would you like that?" he asked.

"You know I would," she said.

Junius smiled and looked down, embarrassed.

"I know you can't hear me," Ruby said, "but I try to sing along with what you're playing when I recognize the tune."

She likes it when I play the fife, Junius thought and walked slowly to the front porch.

He had started practicing on a tin whistle so he could get his mouth right, his embouchure. It had been months since he had needed the whistle, since he had finally figured out how small the hole in his lips needed to be to produce the right sounds. He rolled the hole this way and that just a little bit while his lips were pursed together until, finally, he could play up and down the scale. Each time he did it, it got a little easier. Would Ruby have noticed the improvement over the past several months? He hoped so.

Still grinning, he walked up the three steps of the front porch. As he opened the front door, he nodded briefly toward the center of the room where he expected to see Sarah Anne seated at the piano, but she wasn't there. That was odd since it was the time of day that she normally spared herself a few minutes to practice when things at home were relatively quiet.

Radolfus had only recently given her the piano for their anniversary, and from what he heard, Junius suspected his stepmother was having trouble remembering what it was like to play the instrument she had learned as a child in Moulton, Alabama. Her playing was full of mistakes and jarring discords. She just needed more practice, he thought.

He gave a quick glance to make sure no one was watching and then sat down at the piano and tentatively struck one of the keys. He softly struck yet another key and another. Finding a rhythm wouldn't be that difficult, and as he experimented with the other keys, he found that he could make out the right ones to sound out one of the tunes he was learning to play on the fife.

As he pushed key after key, he marveled at how different the piano was from the fife. Anyone could make a sound on it simply by pressing down on a key instead of having to work to develop the right embouchure. He remembered when Paw had taken him to Montgomery the year before and there had been a piano in the restaurant of the hotel where they stayed. Instead of just one note at a time, a piano could play entire chords, like a whole band on its own.

Suddenly, he felt a presence behind him. Sarah Anne. He

didn't even need to look up from the keyboard to know that his stepmother was at the entrance to the room staring at him. He slowly stood and turned around to face her. He had seen her look angrily at him before, but this expression was a new one. The anger was there, but there was something else he couldn't quite distinguish in her look. He didn't think it was sadness that he saw. It couldn't have been jealousy, could it?

Without even looking at Junius, Sarah Anne stared straight ahead at the piano and said, "Don't touch this instrument again."

He started to protest but decided against it. Arguing with her about it would be a lost cause. The piano belonged to her.

Junius brushed past his stepmother as he headed for the staircase and climbed the stairs quickly. Reaching the alcove he shared with his younger brother, he retrieved his fife from under his bed. The fife was the only family heirloom his father had managed to bring with him when he traveled from Germany to America over twenty years ago. It had been given to his grandfather Jacob by his grandmother Lilly, who had nursed him after he had been wounded during Napoleon's retreat from Russia. What he understood was that she had done so to make it seem like he hadn't been a belligerent but rather a reluctant soldier in the event he was captured by the Russians or any of Napoleon's other enemies.

After he retraced his steps downstairs, Junius went out the back and sat down on the top step of the back porch. Placing the case behind him on the wooden barrel that served as a table, he then snapped open the case and carefully lifted out the fife.

I am going to make you sing one day. With that thought, Junius took a deep breath and put his lips above the mouth hole, covering a few of the other holes with his fingers. Then he blew his breath out over the edge of the hole just as he had before, starting to play one of the simple tunes he had managed to teach himself, and as he did, Ruby emerged from her cabin. He waved at her as she turned to face him. She smiled, and after looking around to make sure no one could see her, quickly waved back. He motioned for her to come over to be nearer the house, but she shook her head no. Then she put her hands up to her mouth and face as if she were going to play an invisible fife, and he realized she wanted him to continue.

Not long ago, they could play together just like all the other children, but that changed when they each turned thirteen. Before that, he would talk to her about what he had learned at the La Grange Academy, and she would listen to him, totally engrossed in whatever he had learned that day. But now, although Ruby was just a few months older, she had already developed into a young woman with creamy skin and greenish eyes that seemed to dance. Other boys looked at her with expressions Junius didn't like, and it suddenly felt awkward for them to spend any time together. It was as if some sort of barrier that hadn't existed before was now ever-present.

After a few minutes, Ruby disappeared, and Junius lost interest in continuing to practice. He crept back upstairs, staying out of Sarah Anne's way. As he placed the fife in its case and under his bed yet again, out the window, he saw Jim walking briskly toward the cabin he and Ruby shared. Normally, Jim would be smiling at this time of day, but Junius thought it odd how fast he was walking. Jim said something he couldn't hear to Ruby, who cast her eyes downward before following her father into the cabin. When father and daughter were that close together in bright sunshine, the contrast in their skin color was stark. Her mother must have been what Paw referred to as high yellow—an octoroon—down in New Orleans, he thought.

Junius wondered again how Jim wound up a slave when there were so many free Blacks in New Orleans. Paw had often commented on that peculiarity as if he, too, had been surprised by Jim's station in life before he bought him. The man was intelligent, hard-working, industrious, and obviously not destined to be a field hand like so many of the other slaves who worked the cotton fields. What curious set of circumstances had thrown him into slavery? And not only him but Ruby too?

After he finished putting the fife back into its case, Junius retreated downstairs and went out on the back porch, more to stay away from Sarah Anne than anything else.

When Radolfus came home and entered the house, Junius hoped that he might find out what the purpose of Mr. Lehman's visit to the store had been. He decided his best option was to stay on the back porch while Sarah Anne complained to his father about Junius's behavior and let him tell her whatever news he needed to share with her. Before too long, he heard the two of them go out the front door to the porch, where Radolfus spoke for several minutes. Occasionally, Sarah Anne would say something, but after a few minutes, all was quiet.

Then his father opened the back door briefly and said as he held the door open to the house, "Come inside. I have something to tell you."

Chapter 3

As Junius entered the house, he could tell something wasn't sitting well with Sarah Anne by the expression on her face. It was more pinched than usual, and her eyes were red, and she had a far-off look. Radolfus stood near the fireplace several feet away from the kitchen table, where Sarah Anne sat holding the baby in her arms, rocking back and forth. The younger children were arrayed around the room in various postures, looking bored and anxious to get whatever was coming over with so they could return to playing with each other. Only Junius's sister Lizzie, gangly at the age of eleven but constantly smiling, seemed to be interested in the proceedings that were about to start.

"I had a visitor at the store today who made me an interesting proposal," Radolfus said as he looked directly at Sarah Anne, who turned her head away.

"Mr. Lehman of Montgomery, whose brothers from Bavaria joined him in business here, wants to expand his business dealings and has suggested that I might be able to assist him in this regard. He has entered into a partnership with another man from Bavaria, Mr. Levi Strauss, who is setting up a business that involves tailoring in California."

California! Junius thought.

"The business opportunities there are truly amazing ever since gold was discovered several years ago. And there apparently is no end in sight to the amount of gold to be found. Mr. Lehman thinks that we should move there, where I would become the chief tailor to Mr. Levi Strauss."

Sarah Anne gave an impatient sigh as she glanced around the house and at each of the children. Her children, anyway.

"Mr. Lehman expects me to give him an answer one week from today when he will return from Montgomery. If we are to go to California, there will be a great deal to do before we can depart," Radolfus said.

Trying to control his excitement, Junius asked, "How will we get to California, Paw?"

"You mean, how would we get there should the decision be made to go? We would have to travel by train to Memphis, where we would take passage up the Mississippi on a steam-boat to St. Louis. Once we reach St. Louis, we would have to then transfer to another steamboat, which would take us up the Missouri River into Kansas Territory near the Missouri border where we would join a wagon train across the plains to California. To San Francisco. The journey would take sev-eral months and includes traveling over mountains, so there is no time to waste because the mountains would be impassable during the winter. We need to leave sometime next spring at the latest."

The room was silent with the exception of the baby start-ing to cry a little. Sarah Anne quickly hushed him, and they all just looked at each other. Junius tried to read the reac-tions on the others' faces, but the only one that was clear was Sarah Anne's look of disapproval, if not downright disgust. He couldn't decide what Lizzie was feeling.

The Mississippi was a river everyone knew about. Junius was less certain of the exact whereabouts of Missouri and Kansas, but figured they must lie up north somewhere. He wasn't even sure that Kansas was a state. There had to be Indians out there, too, not like the ones that used to live in Alabama before most of them were removed from their ances-tral lands. He was sure that the Indians in Kansas and Missouri and further west would be real Indians. Ones that hadn't been forced to give up but were still fighting for their way of life.

Paw had said something about mountains they would have to cross, too. Ones that were even higher than the Great Smokies. Those would make for an even more exciting trip. He couldn't wait to get started.

Why was Paw hesitating?

"If we undertake this journey, it means a total change to our lives," Radolfus continued. "Not just temporarily, but forever. I've been through this before when I came here from Germany. The dangers on this trip are nowhere near similar to what I experienced crossing the ocean, but nevertheless, they are real." Radolfus had never spoken to Junius about why he had chosen to leave his home in Swabia at the age of eighteen and what exactly he had endured on his journey to America.

"I believe that our family will benefit from this change, so I am prepared to undertake it. Before we leave, however, there are things that we have to accomplish. Your mother has professed a desire to see her parents in Moulton one more time, and that will take some time, but it needs to be arranged quickly," he continued. Sarah Anne wiped her eyes with her sleeve, and Junius thought she might burst out in tears any second.

"I also have two or three commissions to finish, and the store has to be sold, but Mr. Lehman has promised to help in that regard."

"What about Jim and Ruby?" Junius asked.

"What about them?" Radolfus answered.

"Are they coming with us?" Junius asked.

"Of course they are; what else do you think would happen to them?"

"I don't know. Maybe you had a notion to sell them."

Radolfus stared at his son for several seconds before he answered. Sarah Anne looked up at Radolfus, too. Radolfus stepped away from the fireplace suddenly and glanced at Sarah Anne before turning his attention to Junius.

"Why would you even think that? I couldn't sell them

even if I wanted to," Radolfus said.

Junius wondered what his father meant exactly. They were slaves. Why couldn't he sell them? But he was relieved by his answer.

At the same time, Junius could only imagine what Jim would think when he learned what was in store. Or did he already know? Had Radolfus told him before returning home? It would be just like him if he had done so.

The man back at the store had said that there weren't slaves in California. That must mean that Jim and Ruby would be free. But not until they were safely through the journey.

Chapter 4

May 1857

The entire trip to California would take several months. Just getting to the trailhead in Missouri would take at least three weeks, and then after that, a lot would depend on weather and timing. How quickly would they be able to join a wagon train once they reached Independence, and what obstacles would they encounter along the way? Sarah Anne said she didn't feel well, and Junius wondered if she wasn't pregnant again.

Junius couldn't sleep for three days prior to their departure for Memphis. He tried to tell himself it was because of the oppressive heat and humidity that lingered into the wee hours of the morning, but was well aware that he was lying to himself.

As they began their journey from Tuscumbia to Memphis, he had been enthralled by the sight of the locomotive, the A.E. Mill, the newest locomotive on the line, which the company had fitted out with its best passenger carriages. Everything had a new smell to it. Except for the last two cars, that is. They appeared to have been used for hauling freight before being converted to passenger cars. Their condition was also in stark contrast to that of the caboose, which gleamed in the sun. The route to Memphis had only been completed the previous year, making it the first railroad to link the Atlantic Ocean with the Mississippi River.

Most of the passengers who waited to board the train at the station were well-heeled. The men mainly wore top hats and black suits and stepped forward to inspect the engine as they waited, while the ladies who accompanied them tended to remain in the background, away from the cacophony and the steam the engine produced. Junius caught a glimpse of the engineer in the locomotive as he surveyed the station, looking every bit the master of his domain.

As they were about to board, Radolfus asked the conductor, "Where do they sit?" pointing to Jim and Ruby. Junius decided to stay close to his father to hear what would be said. He sensed that the conductor was going to provide some valuable information based on his experiences on the railroad.

"These two are your slaves?" the conductor asked.

"Yes," answered Radolfus.

The conductor studied Jim and Ruby carefully. "You have papers to prove that?" he asked as Radolfus started to reach into his valise for them.

"Of course I do. Why?"

"Oh, I don't need to see them. Where are you headed?" the conductor said, waving his hand at the papers as Radolfus started to produce them.

"California," Radolfus answered.

"I take it you'll be heading for the California Trail then," the conductor said as he looked at the entire family, shaking his head.

"Yes, indeed," Radolfus said.

"You'll need those papers when you book passage on the steamboats you'll be taking upriver," the conductor said as his eyes searched the platform. Junius wondered what else he was looking for.

"Why is that?" Radolfus asked.

The conductor raised his eyebrows and first glanced at Jim and then back at Radolfus before answering.

"You don't know about that uppity slave up there in Missouri? The one who claims he's a free man because his owner moved to the territories? Where slavery isn't allowed?"

the conductor asked.

"No, can't say that I have," Radolfus said.

"I see. Well, there's a slave up there, name of Dred Scott. He's been arguing in court for years now about how he's supposed to be free. And his woman too." The conductor spit a wad of tobacco onto the tracks, being careful to avoid the platform.

Jim and Ruby were standing behind the entire family but close enough to hear the conversation, and Jim leaned in close to the conductor as he spoke.

"Wouldn't he be free if they were in a state which didn't allow slavery?" Junius asked the conductor as he rushed up to stand beside Jim and Ruby.

"Depends. Why, is your paw intending to free your slaves once you get to California? If you do get there, that is?"

"But California doesn't allow slavery," Junius said.

The conductor laughed. "No, they don't, I suppose. Thanks to Fremont." He spit a wad of tobacco onto the ground. "But that doesn't mean that it isn't practiced there. Not just with Africans. But with the Indians there too. Lots of Indian slaves."

"What do you mean?" Junius asked.

"That's enough, son," Radolfus said, also waving his hand at Jim as he spoke.

Junius glanced at the valise holding the papers again. He had never really thought about them before and wondered what they actually said.

Finally, the conductor said, "They'll have to ride in the rear car. The other one reserved for coloreds is already full."

Junius started to protest, but one look from Radolfus was enough to get him to keep quiet.

They reached Memphis after an eight-hour journey covering the one hundred and fifty miles. By the time they arrived at their destination, Junius had had enough of trains to satisfy his curiosity for a long while to come. Opening the windows to let fresh air in was a chore in itself, and keeping them closed meant that they sweltered in the wagons. The wooden benches were practically upright and even less comfortable than the desks at school. Sleeping for more than a minute or two at a time was out of the question, given the heat and the bumps along the tracks.

Once they reached Memphis, Junius accounted for their luggage while Radolfus gathered Jim and Ruby. Then he asked the station manager for directions to the harbor, Center Landing, which was just over a mile away, and Radolfus hired two cabs to take them there, with Jim and Ruby riding in the second one along with the luggage. It would take several days to reach St. Louis and a similar length of time to reach Kansas City on the second steamboat.

Once they arrived at Center Landing, Radolfus quickly found the harbormaster and asked, "When does the next boat leave for St. Louis?"

"How many people?"

"Seven."

"Paw, what do you mean?" Junius asked.

"I mean nine," Radolfus said, correcting himself.

The harbormaster asked again, "Seven? Or nine?"

"The seven of us and those two over there," he said, pointing to Jim, who placed his arm around Ruby.

The harbormaster explained that Jim and Ruby would cost extra but would at least have space to sleep on the floor of the boiler deck, where the Harts would have their own accommodations. That was in contrast to the slaves on board who were chained together on the main deck, beneath the boiler deck, and who remained exposed to the elements for the duration of the trip. There weren't that many slaves on board, and they were shackled together on the port side, the side that could be closer to the middle of the river, instead of the starboard side, which was closer to land.

"Best to avoid that side of the boat. Tends to get messy, and the smell will get you if you venture over there," the captain said.

"Why are they on that side of the boat?" Junius asked as he watched the boat being loaded with its cargo. He chose not to comment on the slaves' shackles even though he had never seen a group of men tied together and looking so morose.

What were Jim and Ruby thinking?

"Sometimes these darkies will take their chances with the river. Just to get away. Once the boats get up there near Cairo, they jump in even if they don't know how to swim. Most don't make it, but they try."

"Cairo?" Junius asked.

"Town in Illinois. Got a railroad station. No slavery allowed. After that, the boats are back in the middle part of the river, and it starts to get rougher," the harbormaster said.

Their boat, a side-wheeler, wasn't the grandest. Looking a little worn from its previous trips, it nevertheless was ready to sail later that day. As they boarded the boat, the captain proudly told Junius that she was only four years old and had lasted a lot longer than most of the side-wheelers that plied the river.

Radolfus said, "She's not the prettiest ship on the river, I'm sure, but as long as she gets us to St. Louis ..." Junius was relieved that Sarah Anne didn't complain about the ship.

"The journey shouldn't be that difficult," Radolfus said. Junius thought he was just saying that to make sure Sarah Anne stayed calm. "After all, it's just a river. Not like crossing an ocean."

Junius saw Jim react out of the corner of his eye. He looked down and shook his head. Junius walked over to him and asked, "What do you think, Jim? Is Paw right?"

"Your father is right in most things. But the Mississippi isn't like other rivers. No telling what will happen around the next bend in the river," Jim said.

"Is he right about it being easier than crossing the ocean?"

"I suspect your paw's voyage across the ocean was a lot different than the way my grandparents came here."

Junius didn't know how to react to what Jim said, so he just smiled.

It didn't really matter how pretty the ship was. The boat looked fine to Junius, and after all, this was all part of the grand adventure. Besides, they were off the train.

"Do you think you'll be able to teach me how to swim in the river along the way?" Junius asked.

Jim laughed. "No, there's no swimming in the Mississippi. You'll see what I mean when we start going upriver."

Jim was probably right. The distance from the main deck to the water was only a few feet. A man could jump in the river and climb out with only a little bit of assistance from someone standing on the deck, but the waters flowed by quickly.

Junius explored the boat as much as he could, and early the second evening, he heard music coming from the parlor on the main deck. Curious, he stepped inside the entrance to the saloon, where he saw a piano considerably larger than the one Sarah Anne had had at home in Tuscumbia. He approached cautiously, hoping none of the adults would shoo him away as he strained to get closer to the piano.

An African sat on the bench, striking the keys and swaying to the music. Occasionally, he would close his eyes, and it seemed as though he knew instinctively which keys his fingers should hit. He noticed that the man worked the pedals beneath him quickly and without hesitation as well. What emerged was a sound unlike that which Sarah Anne produced when she labored at her instrument. After several minutes, Junius tore himself away to rejoin the family for dinner.

Once they reached a place called New Madrid, the steamship actually lifted up and down a bit. It dipped a little this way and then that, and the few people who braved the elements retreated from the railings, which were barely sufficient any-way. To Junius, it was as if something below the surface was causing the river to flow in awkward directions. On one side of the river, the water would flow one way, while on the other side, the river seemed to reverse itself. So that's what Jim meant. How would anyone survive in the river? Even an experienced river pilot might not be able to anticipate its flow and know how to maneuver these massive boats.

"The Mississippi isn't like I had imagined it. It's not like the Neckar, or the Rhein, or the Seine outside of Paris that I crossed before coming to America from Le Havre. Those flowed evenly. They were blue. Or green. This one is just brown. And muddy," Radolfus said.

It was just like Paw to revert to names of places that Junius didn't recognize at odd moments. The Mississippi didn't look that much different than the Tennessee River did back in Tuscumbia, and Junius had difficulty imagining what his father was seeing.

Finally, they reached St. Louis and found passage on the next steamboat, which would take them up the Missouri to a port near Kansas City. Then, they would proceed to Independence, where they would begin their trip across the continent by wagon.

Once they boarded the next steamboat, Junius walked around the entire main deck. Jim and Ruby appeared to be relatively comfortable, at least, and it wasn't unbearably hot. Besides, they had some cover in contrast to the other unfortunate souls not too far behind them. As he strolled, keeping a watchful eye on Lizzie and Lalea, he saw another young man about his age who appeared to be traveling with his father. *Can't hurt to be friendly. Maybe folks in Missouri are friendlier than the fellows in Alabama. Besides, they don't know who we are.*

As the other boy and his father stared out at the river, Junius sidled up alongside the boy.

To his relief, the boy said, "Hello."

"Hello. Where are you going?" Junius asked.

The young man grinned. "All the way to Kansas City. You?"

"The same."

"You live there?" the young man asked.

"No. We're from Alabama, and Paw has decided to go to California. Something about business opportunities there."

Junius wanted to continue talking to the young man. Someone other than his family and Jim would be refreshing. Jim and Ruby were standing off to the side, not too far away, engaged in conversation.

"California, hey? Are these your family's slaves?" the young man's father asked, straining a little to view the other side of the boat toward the stern.

"Yes, sir."

The boy's father studied him carefully. "I see. What is your father's profession, if I might ask?" the man said.

"He's a tailor. He owned a store back in Tuscumbia where he sold men's clothing. A man from Montgomery offered him a chance to be the firm's representative in San Francisco, and Paw accepted. There's a businessman there who is waiting for Paw to arrive and expand his business."

"He makes clothes himself?" the man asked.

"Mostly, yes. Sometimes he buys the latest imported fashions from New York and New Orleans."

"Interesting."

Junius wanted to start talking with the other boy, but the man appeared to have something else on his mind before he could do so.

"My name is Younger. H.W. Younger. This here is my son, Thomas Coleman Younger. Everyone calls him Cole."

"Don't like the name Tom," Cole said.

Mr. Younger laughed. "What's your name, young man?"

"Junius Hart."

"Nice making your acquaintance. Perhaps I'll get to meet

your father while we're on the river. Are your accommodations satisfactory for your family?"

"Yes, sir. Paw didn't want to repeat our experience on the boat that brought us to St. Louis, so we have a cabin on the hurricane deck. Jim and ... our slaves don't, of course, so we go down to the main deck to say hello to them. It's really too hot, loud, and smelly for my ... mother ... so she only comes down for a minute or so," Junius said.

"So, your father intends to take his slaves to California with your family?" H.W. asked.

"Yes, sir, indeed he does," Junius said.

H.W. shook his head as Junius awaited his family. "Does your father know that slavery isn't permitted in California? And actually, just past Kansas City, in the Kansas Territory, it isn't permitted either. He'd best be careful when this boat gets to Kansas City because some abolitionists settled in a townsite called Quindaro just over the border with Missouri. Rumor has it that they have already been helping slaves escape."

Junius hadn't contemplated the possibility that slaves could escape, and he couldn't imagine Jim feeling the need to do so. "I don't think that Jim would even consider escaping, sir," Junius said.

H.W.'s eyes widened. "No, why not?"

Junius couldn't decide how to answer H.W.'s question. There was something special about his family's relationship with Jim and Ruby. Nonetheless, he decided he should share the discussion with his father as soon as he could.

"I just don't think he would. It's like they are family," Junius said.

"I see," H.W. said. "Interesting that someone would think that," H.W. said as he walked away.

By the next morning, they were about halfway to Kansas City. The family had just come down to the main deck after breakfast to check on Jim and Ruby, whom they found on the starboard side after a few minutes upwind of the animals and the other slaves, which today meant at the stern of the boat.

While they chatted with Jim and Ruby, an explosion rocked the boat, followed by a whooshing sound and then another explosion. Junius had no idea what had happened until several of the deckhands rushed to the railing, pointing at the paddle-wheeler in front of them.

"The boiler blew! Look out!"

Junius followed the deckhands to the railing. The steamboat ahead of them listed to its side with a lot of smoke billowing and fire raging across its deck. There were people in the water, some moving, some not. Fiery objects rained down on the water, and the boat stood stockstill. The boat they were on was slowing, and larger waves were headed their way. Some people retreated into their cabins, and crew members hastened to secure the bales on the deck more tightly in the scant seconds they had before the first waves would strike the boat.

"Wave coming! Big one!" one of the crew yelled as he braced against the rail, and others leaped forward, hanging on to the railing too.

A sudden swell in the water rocked the smaller boats ahead, and even the larger ones moved up and down a little. Backing away from the railing, Lizzie stood stock-still, obviously petrified. Junius was oblivious to anything as he went forward on the deck with Lizzie tugging at his shirt. Suddenly, they were engulfed by spray. Junius was knocked off his feet by the shockwave and looked up and saw everyone in his family lying on the deck. He started crawling back to them desperately, holding tight to a crying Lizzie.

Another brown wave struck amidships, covering Junius, who had managed to get back on his feet, with brownish water. He brushed the water away from his face and wiped his eyes. It took a minute before he realized he was still on the ship.

Sarah Anne rushed toward Radolfus, screaming, "Lalea! Where is Lalea?"

Then a deckhand yelled out, "Girl overboard!" Junius rushed to the port side of the ship and looked into the water. The girl was Lalea. She was thrashing about, and each time she did, her head stayed underwater a little longer than the last time. Junius thought her dresses were pulling her under as the waves continued to pound the ship.

One of the deckhands was at the stern, and then suddenly, he was gone. He reappeared, and they could see him in the water trying to reach Lalea, but she kept getting farther away from him and the boat. The deckhand's head bobbed up and down, and he spread his arms wide, but he lost ground.

Then Jim appeared out of nowhere, shoveled Ruby toward Radolfus, and hurled himself into the water. Ruby pulled her hand away from Radolfus and, not sure where to turn, reached out for Junius. He took her hand and then put his arm around her shoulder.

"The African's gone and jumped in!" one of the deckhands yelled out, laughing. While the Hart family retreated to the stern to avoid getting any wetter or going overboard, Ruby rushed forward to get to the rail, and it was all Junius could do to hold her back. He had to put one arm around her waist while holding on to the railing to keep her from falling overboard. She dropped her arms until her hands were touching his and she held them close to her sides.

When Jim reappeared, his arms flailed in the water, first one arm out front and then the other, but he quickly caught up to the deckhand and then passed him as if the deckhand were standing still.

"Throw him a line!" another deckhand yelled, and quickly, a rope was thrown back in the general direction of where Jim was headed. Then Junius made out Jim swimming toward a little thing bobbing in the water. Lalea. Jim stopped occasionally to make sure he could still see Lalea's head and then resumed swimming toward her.

After what seemed like an eternity, he reached Lalea, grabbed her with one arm, and then swung around to capture the rope with his other arm. The boat slowed, and slowly, he was pulled toward the boat by two deckhands. He went under a couple of times but always took care to keep Lalea's head above water somehow. When he reached the boat, he raised Lalea out of the water as the two deckhands bent over the rail and hoisted Lalea aboard and, in doing so, let the rope go. Junius grabbed it before it completely disappeared and began pulling with all his might. After the deckhands handed Lalea to Sarah Anne, they joined Junius and, after several minutes with additional help, managed to get Jim alongside the boat. Sarah Anne was staring hard at Radolfus as Jim was dragged out of the river. Junius let go of Ruby, and she rushed to Jim as they pulled him over the ship's rail.

At first, they couldn't tell if Lalea was breathing. "Baby, please, baby! Don't die!" Sarah Anne wailed. Finally, Lalea spewed muddy water all over Radolfus's shoes and convulsed several times. Jim started to approach her, but two deckhands held him back. He tried to protest and break free, but they blocked him from getting any closer to her. After another minute, Lalea began breathing regularly. As Radolfus picked her up to carry her back to their cabin, Sarah Anne stood in front of him and, as calmly as she could, said, "Radolfus, I won't go any further. This California idea is too much. We have to stop!" Her eyes weren't begging; they were demanding.

Radolfus carried Lalea upstairs back to their cabin as numerous other passengers voiced their concerns and slapped him on the back. Sarah Anne and the rest of the family followed along into the cabin.

Once he laid Lalea down on the larger bed in the cabin, Radolfus said, "Stop? Stop where? We are somewhere in ... Missouri?"

"My baby. I don't want to lose my baby," Sarah Anne cried as she gripped her stomach.

She was pregnant! That explained her moodiness, which was excessive even for her. No wonder she was short with everyone.

After that, Sarah Anne mostly slept the rest of the trip upriver. It only took another day, fortunately, because every time she ventured out of their stateroom, she vomited. When they docked near Kansas City, Sarah Anne simply arose from her sickbed and walked off the ship.

"We'll figure out how to continue the trip once you've rested a while. Maybe we can wait until after the baby is born," Radolfus said.

She turned to him and stared at him with her mouth wide open.

"What?" she asked.

"We'll rest a while somewhere here before we continue. California is our goal."

"I don't care. I am not going any further, and neither are my children. I'd rather go back to Alabama, but that probably isn't worth it now that you have done what you have done. Selling the store and everything we owned. We would have to start all over there, and the way you left ..."

Junius feared that she was right and suspected that his father did too. Going to California had been a grand dream. A glorious one.

Radolfus turned to his son and said, "I can't imagine three or four more months of traveling with Sarah Anne in the state she is in and the possibility of Indian raids and a cholera outbreak along the way."

"You don't have to explain it to me," Junius said, swallowing his disappointment.

California will have to wait, Junius thought. *I'll get there, but not just yet.*

Just then, H.W. Younger approached Radolfus. Junius waited nearby, curious to see what Mr. Younger might say.

"That was remarkable."

"What was?" Radolfus asked.

"Your boy there. He just jumped in the river. In the Missouri! To save your daughter."

Radolfus sighed and ran his fingers through his thinning hair.

"Yes, I suppose so. But he has been with us a long time," Radolfus said.

"Do I understand correctly that you are a tailor, Mr. ..."

"Hart. Radolfus Hart."

"A pleasure, sir. Henry Washington Younger. Folks call me H.W."

Radolfus explained that he had had a store in La Grange and then moved his family to Tuscumbia, where he had opened an even larger store, which he had run until Herr Lehman had offered him the opportunity in California.

"I see. Well, it does appear that you and your family have a dilemma, no?"

"Dilemma?"

"If I understand your son correctly, you intended to go to California. But it appears that you will now be changing your plans, if I understand the little lady's concerns," he said, pointing to Sarah Anne.

Radolfus had to acknowledge he was right. "Yes, I suppose so."

H.W. considered Radolfus carefully and then took in the rest of the family one by one before continuing. "I own considerable property in Strother, just south of Kansas City, and need a good, reliable man to help me. I'm planning on expanding my business. My family needs more room. Don't know when the little woman will stop having babies!" After a chuckle, H.W. said, "Thing is, you might be just the man for the job."

Taken aback, Radolfus said, "Why me?"

"I need to have a good, God-fearing family man in my employ. Just looking at you and the way your family behaves, and with a loyal slave to boot ... why, it seems I have found just what I am looking for in you. In these perilous times, Mr. Hart, it is important to have the utmost trust and confidence in your associates. Wouldn't you agree?"

"But you hardly know me," Radolfus said.

Junius looked back and forth between his father and Sarah Anne, who had been hovering nearby, taking in every word. Junius's life, their lives, were changing dramatically in that brief moment in ways none of them could have anticipated. He didn't know what to think of the sudden change. It was as if his life, which had already been turned upside down, was now being turned upside down all over again.

"True. I tell you what. Why don't we get to know each other better on our way to Strother? If one of us discovers that it isn't meant to be, you can go your way with no issue."

One look at Sarah Anne, who had overheard the conversation, convinced Junius that Radolfus had no choice.

Mr. Younger motioned for Radolfus to join him for a private conversation. Junius was just close enough to hear most of what they had to say.

As he listened to H.W.'s proposal to his father, he looked up and down the river, studying it carefully with new respect. Paw was going to accept H.W.'s offer; that much was clear. The trip was over, at least for now. California would have to wait.

The river had won. For now, anyway.

Chapter 5

At first, Sarah Anne insisted that they needed to return to Alabama once the baby was born. She wouldn't listen to anything Radolfus had to say to her until he explained that they would have to take two more steamboat rides back to Memphis or else travel overland for several days.

"We'll discuss this again after the baby comes," she said. "But for now, I simply need peace."

The Harts went along with H.W. Younger and his son, Cole, to Strother, where Radolfus was able to practice his trade and learn about the market for fashion in Missouri, which was, in fact, different from what it had been in Alabama. There was less of a premium on high-quality suits since the gentlemen here worked the land and raised animals more than Radolfus's customers in Tuscumbia had needed to do. There weren't as many slaves in areas where cotton wasn't king. Even the gentlemen, such as they were, needed clothing that would withstand all kinds of weather and outdoor work.

Not too long after they all arrived, H.W. decided to move to Harrisonville, a small town further south along the Kansas–Missouri border, where he opened a larger dry goods store and offered continued employment to Radolfus, who had become indispensable to him. He was soon elected mayor of the new town and relied even more heavily on Radolfus, who in turn counted on Jim to help him with most of the tasks involved in running a store.

Junius figured that being elected the mayor of a small town that showed no promise whatsoever of ever amounting to anything must have been small consolation to H.W., who had larger ambitions. If Strother was depressing, Harrisonville was simply pitiful. A body couldn't walk through the City after the occasional rainstorm without sinking up to his ankles in a mixture of mud and horse manure.

In the ensuing months, Sarah Anne gave birth to another daughter, Allene, and mother and child were healthy. Lalea had suffered no ill effects from her near-drowning months earlier except a fear of any body of water, and Leon was now approaching his fourth birthday. Radolfus told Junius that he was biding his time until they could continue on to California, and Junius remained anxious to continue the westward journey. As the months went by, Radolfus shared with Junius how they would resume their journey once Allene was old enough to travel.

Then, one day, everything changed.

Junius was just about to take his fife out to practice on it some, hoping that Ruby would hear him, when he saw his father trudging up the road toward the house after work that day.

"Good day today, Paw?"

"Good enough, I suppose," Radolfus answered, but Junius could tell something was bothering him.

Junius was aware that Radolfus was exhausted. He had seemed worn out ever since they had landed in Missouri. It was as if the disappointment of not reaching California yet weighed so heavily on him that he found little to enjoy in life. He usually bantered with the children and would joke with Junius about becoming a man in a frontier since he believed that Western Missouri was still just that. He claimed Missouri didn't compare to Tuscumbia in terms of culture and society.

Radolfus said that back in Tuscumbia, everyone knew his place, while here in Missouri, everything was always in a state of flux, constantly changing as events along the border with Kansas unfolded, which was sometimes a daily occurrence. The fact that the Jayhawkers in Kansas, those who advocated the abolition of slavery by any and all means necessary, kept mounting raids across the border into Missouri to kidnap slaves and hunt down slaveowners was becoming a real problem, and no one seemed to have the will to do anything to stop them. Then, each time the Jayhawkers raided a settlement or a homestead, some of the locals—always secessionists—would launch reprisal raids, and the violence escalated.

Junius could hear Sarah Anne wailing at night once everyone was in bed, lamenting the fact that they had ever left Alabama and swearing she would never forgive Radolfus if any of the children got sick with cholera and died. She swore that facing yellow fever with its occasional outbreaks wasn't as bad as a cholera outbreak since the frontier doctors didn't seem to be able to deal with anything serious.

Once in a while, when only Junius and his father were still awake and Junius was putting his fife away after practicing on it, he would look at his father and say, "What about California, Paw?"

On one such night after Allene's birth, Junius decided to bring up the subject again, hoping that it would cheer up his father to think about resuming the journey.

"A letter came from Mr. Lehman in Montgomery today," Radolfus said.

"You wrote him a while back, didn't you?"

"I wrote to him a while back explaining how we had to interrupt our travel there due to Sarah Anne's condition and what happened on the river. I have been waiting for his response. I asked him to give me time until after the baby was a little older before we continued our journey."

"What did he say?"

Radolfus's shoulders slumped, and he raised his eyes to the heavens before he answered. "He said he's found someone else to take my place in California. And that there is no point in returning to Tuscumbia because he has already sold the store to someone else. We're on our own."

"But he can't do that, Paw. You had a deal," Junius said, hardly able to believe what was happening.

"He can, son. Because he already has. I should have known better."

Junius had never seen his father look so defeated. So utterly lost. There had to be a way to salvage the situation, but he didn't know how. Looking at his father now, however, he realized that any further talk would have to wait.

Radolfus's chin dropped into his chest. "You have to forget about California, son. It just isn't going to happen. I suspect things are going to change for the worse soon, not just here but throughout the country. We have to be prepared to defend ourselves from any threats that may be brewing."

Junius forced himself to stop thinking about the disappointment of not continuing on to California and focus on what his father was telling him.

"You think it's going to be that bad, Paw?"

"I think it's going to be even worse than that. I don't know if we'll be able to recover."

Paw had often remarked that they would have been better off staying in St. Louis after they got off the steamboat that had taken them from Memphis to that city, but since California had been the goal back then, stopping at that point wouldn't have worked. "You thinking about St. Louis, Paw?"

"No, I'm just remembering places. And people."

Chapter 6

While the family tried to adjust to life in Harrisonville that summer, Junius found himself spending time at the store trying desperately to find something to do that kept him out of Sarah Anne's view. It seemed like whenever he decided to practice on his fife, she would invent some chore for him that was new and, in his view, unnecessary. So, he would pack up his fife and steal out of the house when she was otherwise occupied with one of the children and whistle when he walked past Jim and Ruby's cabin so Ruby would know not to expect to hear him playing. When he tired of practicing the fife, he would walk to the store to see if anything was going on. The more often he walked into the store, the more he noticed the newspaper office a few doors down on Main Street, and his interest in a possible job there continued to grow.

"Why don't you and your family come to church, Radolfus? There are a couple of good options right here in town?" Junius overheard H.W. ask his father as he entered the store one day.

"I prefer to keep our prayer services private, H.W. What with Sarah Anne and the children and the work that I have to do on the weekends too, it's not easy to gather everyone together all at the same time."

"Well, just so you know, some folks are wondering whether you might not be practicing one of those religions that profess to be God-fearing but are anything but. Like them Mormons we had to run out of the state a few years back. They were planning on setting up their new Zion here in Missouri, of all places, until the governor got wise to them and ran them out.

There was a good bit of fighting before they were run off back to Nauvoo. Then they left there, and I hear they have settled someplace out west."

"I can assure you, H.W., we're not like them folks at all. Anything but."

"I surely hope not. But mark my word, it might do you good to at least show your face occasionally in church. That's all I'll say on the subject."

Junius listened intently to the conversation but acted as if he was focused on the book he was trying to read. He knew that going to any church would never happen, not as long as Radolfus had his way, even if Sarah Anne were to insist on it. He doubted that would happen, though, especially since she made it clear that she wasn't happy about even being in an area that she considered to be populated by a bunch of low-lifes.

"At least back in Moulton there was a sense of style, of class. Even Tuscumbia had more class than this place," she had said on several occasions.

Junius watched his father's reaction to the things she said and would notice that whenever he read the newspaper, he would shake his head and only very rarely nod. Sarah Anne would glance at what he was nodding at and walk away frowning and muttering under her breath.

Junius at least had made a good friend in Cole Younger during their time in Strother, and the friendship continued once they arrived in Harrisonville. Even though Cole was a year younger than he was, Junius thought of him as a big brother. He seemed to get a handle on situations more easily than Junius did. Cole always knew his mind and was determined to see things through no matter how difficult that task might be. Not that he cared that much for schoolwork. His smarts lay elsewhere, in more commonsensical things. Like shooting a rifle and riding a horse, things that Junius didn't have the chance to do that often and wasn't very good at.

The one thing that Junius was good at was running. That he could do, and he could beat just about anybody in a foot race, including Cole. He suspected that was because of all the running he had done back in Tuscumbia, running to and from school and then, after school, back to Radolfus's store before heading home. Occasionally, schoolmates would challenge him to a foot race, but as he grew older, there were fewer and fewer challengers. People would even stop and stare at him as he raced here and there, and occasionally, they would ask him if someone was chasing him and, if so, why. Questions like that usually spurred him on to run even faster as he looked back to see if they were still watching him. It didn't really bother him what people thought; it was just his way of being free.

There were two things that really separated Junius and Cole, though, and both of them bothered Junius more than he acknowledged even to himself.

One was the way that Cole reacted whenever Junius would beg off of going to the swimming hole or trying to play that game that involved a stick and a ball and running around a field. He would much rather practice his fife. As he played, he would look across the road to where Jim and Ruby's cabin was in the hope that he would catch Ruby looking out the window, listening to him play.

The other thing that bothered Junius was how Cole reacted whenever Ruby's name was mentioned. He never said anything one way or the other, but instead, he would get quiet, which was totally out of character. And his eyes would light up and sometimes it even seemed his face would flush at the mere mention of her name. Junius learned quickly enough not to discuss home life with Cole as a result, no matter how hard Cole tried to pry information out of him.

Cole and Junius made a friend of another boy their age, named Buck, who appeared and disappeared at random intervals. No one seemed to know where Buck actually lived or was even interested in finding that out. Buck seemed to be interested in nothing other than riding his horse and getting into scrapes with other fellows his age simply for the sake of testing his courage and perfecting his wrestling and boxing skills. Junius couldn't stop admiring Buck for all the things that Cole wasn't. While he suspected that Cole was someone whom he couldn't trust, he felt that Buck was someone he could trust in any situation. He found himself wanting to spend more time with Buck and less with Cole, but had to keep his father's employment by Cole's father in mind.

One late spring day when the weather was turning warmer, Cole launched into what, for him, was a long inquiry about Junius's plans.

"You still thinking about going to California, Junius?" Cole asked.

"Yeah, one day I'll get there. It may take me a while, but it's been on my mind for quite some time now, so I reckon I will one day."

"Just because you reckon you will won't make it happen. I could reckon on a lot of things, but it takes a lot more than just reckoning to make things happen. Paw says that a man has to make a name for himself somehow, then make a little bit of a fortune, find the right woman to stand behind him, and then set out to fulfill his ambitions. Whatever they may be."

"Is that what your paw says?" Junius asked, and Cole nodded.

That made sense to Junius, and he figured that was what Radolfus had had in mind when he had decided to accept Herr Lehman's offer to go to California. Maybe that explained why he seemed more frustrated these days, having been unable to fulfill his lofty ambitions.

"It is."

"How does your paw think a man might make a name for himself, Cole?"

Cole hesitated before answering, and Junius thought he had a strange look about him when he finally did.

"A man's got to stand up for himself, for his family. For his woman, if he has one or wants a certain one. Or for an idea."

"Stand up how?"

"Paw says everyone is going to have to take a stand afore too long, Junius. It's gonna come down to that over states' rights. And Paw says that will be soon enough."

"What about states' rights?"

"Ain't no business of the government if a man wants to provide for himself and his family any way he can. Even if there are them abolitionists up north who want to free all the slaves don't make it the right thing to do. People out here need slaves. What would we do without them? And being a slave ain't all that bad, is it? That Jim and Ruby of your paw's, they have it pretty good, don't they?"

Jim and Ruby did, in fact, have it pretty good, when Junius thought about it. He had never seen them treated like other slaves who worked the cotton fields or labored in the elements regardless of the season. He hardly thought of them as slaves, actually. They were more like another branch of the family.

"I guess the folks up north decided they don't need slaves, though. How come they don't and everything seems to work fine for them, Cole?" he asked. And from what he had witnessed, especially since leaving Tuscumbia, he wasn't all that sure that it made sense for the colored folks to do whatever their White masters told them to do.

"How do we know that things work all right up there, Junius? You ever been there? No, I didn't think so. My paw has been to these cities on business several times, especially New York, and he says it's just a mess of confusion where no one knows who's in charge of things and the colored folks don't have to do what us folks tell them to do."

Junius doubted that New York was a mass of confusion. It was hard to imagine a city that big would function the way

New York did if it was all that confusing.

"My paw spent time there when he first came over the ocean years ago. He says it was an exciting place. I'd surely like to see that one day, too," Junius answered.

"Maybe too much excitement going on up there," Cole said. "Paw says that the day will come when all them slaves that have been freed will take over those states. And then they'll come after all our women. It's bad enough that some slave owners who take slaves as their mistresses decide to free their offspring. Then they try to pass themselves off as White and darken the whole race of people that we are. Just goes against God's will, Paw says."

Junius thought about Ruby's skin color with that and decided to drop the subject. He hoped that Cole wouldn't bring her into the conversation and was pleased when he didn't.

Junius also realized that before making any plans for the future, at some point, he would have to discuss things concerning California and the future with Jim, too. Without Jim's approval, putting the embryonic plan he had been contemplating for weeks now would be nigh impossible. He had hardly allowed himself to form any conscious thoughts about it, given how daring it was. He and Ruby simply had to make their way to California. And sooner rather than later. He sensed there was little time to wait if he was to be successful.

In the meantime, the school year was about to begin, and Junius wasn't sure how he would handle it.

Junius grew nervous as his first day of school in Harrisonville's one-room schoolhouse approached. Perspiration from his palms ran down his arms as he tried to practice on his fife, forcing him to stop repeatedly to wipe his hands on his trousers and leave wet prints. No doubt Sarah Anne would complain about them, just as she did about everything else he did.

Radolfus had told Junius that the teacher was of German stock, although he doubted he was Jewish. Junius wasn't sure any longer why this was so important, but for some reason,

Radolfus continued to view everything through that particular lens.

Junius debated taking his fife with him to school the first
day but decided against it when he ran into his friend Buck.

"What are you doing bringing that infernal thing along
with you to school?" Buck asked. "It's not something you'll be
able to learn to play any better than you already do, is it? You
think that bringing it along will make you appear to be that
much smarter than the rest of us?"

"Not at all. Paw told me that the teacher might be able to
help me learn to play it better," Junius said.

"Well, I think you'd best leave that possibility for another
day sometime down the road. For now, you'd be better off just
trying to fit in and not seem to be too uppity," Buck said.

No point in being seen as too uppity before he met any of
his new schoolmates. Besides, he would only have to tolerate
the schoolhouse and his mates for a year, perhaps two at most.

With any luck, he would see Jim in the town laboring to
get the newly arrived goods into the store before the rains
came, if any would ever come. If Jim wasn't too busy, maybe
he would have a chance to chat with him briefly, and Junius
could see how Ruby was faring back in their cabin. Plus, he
needed to somehow get a job that paid hard cash if he was
to finance his plan concerning Ruby and California because
he knew Radolfus wouldn't. Jim could provide Junius with
good advice without him having to spill the details of what
he was planning just yet. The most viable option that he was
considering meant going to work at the newspaper. Learning
the printing trade would be useful whatever unfolded in the
future, and Jim probably knew something about how the
Gazette functioned just from listening to different conversations in the store as he went about his day.

The only problem with that part of Junius's developing
plan was that Paw was suspicious of the newspaper editor's
political leanings and tended to discount whatever he heard

being bandied about after another edition of the paper was published unless he heard it repeated several times. It was true that any political discussion anywhere ultimately revolved around one issue alone, and that was secession. When Junius passed by the store, he didn't see Jim, so he continued trudging toward school.

Although he had passed by the building on numerous occasions, he had never really contemplated what it would mean to be a student there. He guessed that was because of how detached he felt about life in Harrisonville. When he arrived at the small building, a number of younger boys were milling outside. Not surprisingly, no girls were present, something that vexed him when he thought of Lizzie, and Ruby, too, for that matter. Weren't they just as much in need of some basic learning?

After a few minutes, a man whom Junius supposed must be the teacher exited the building and blew a whistle. Apparently, that was the signal for everyone to go inside. Junius fell into what passed as a line and, keeping his head down, joined the line heading toward the entrance. As the last boy in line ahead of him started walking up the short flight of stairs, the teacher stepped in front of Junius and blocked his progress.

"Hart?" the man said.

"Yes, sir. Junius."

The teacher eyed him for a few seconds and then said, "Your father has some aspirations for you. I understand you're something of a musician."

"I am trying to learn how to play the fife, sir." How did he know about his musical bent? When had his father had a chance to talk to the teacher, and why had he chosen to do so? Was he trying to ensure that he wouldn't choose to pursue his passion at some later stage, or did he actually want him to keep playing?

"I see; not an easy instrument to learn, is it?"

"No, sir. Not easy at all."

Junius looked away from the teacher, trying hard not to tremble. There was no reason for him to start a teacher-student relationship that way, was there?

"You read music, Master Hart?"

"I do," Junius answered the teacher, but was already beginning to feel like this was going to be a long year.

"Sharps and flats?" the teacher asked with a raised eyebrow.

"Yes, sir." Junius wondered why he was asking him such a simple question.

"So, you know the best way to play the fife would be in the keys of C and B flat major?"

"What?" Junius had never even considered that before.

"Ah, you have much to learn, Master Hart. Perhaps we can make time to work on that as the year goes on," his new teacher said.

Junius nodded, and the schoolmaster stepped aside so he could proceed to enter the schoolhouse.

He took a seat at a desk that barely looked like it would support him, toward the rear of the room. Several younger boys were standing around toward the front of the room.

"Seats!" the teacher said, and the boys who weren't yet seated immediately hastened toward the desks that were still unoccupied.

So, that would be the tone he would use with them? They were practically grown men, not children. This was ridiculous. Why were they all willing to be subjected to this kind of treatment?

Not only that, but what could he possibly learn that would serve him in any capacity? Surely there had to be some reason why the teacher had to explain how important it was to be educated in the classical subjects if they were to be truly successful in life. Junius, however, saw no redeeming reason for him to have to be subjected yet again to lessons that had nothing to do with real life.

Yet the teacher's questions about his fife made him hope he might get more out of school than he anticipated. The best thing to do would be to see how the first day and the first lessons would go. It was up to the teacher to make it happen.

The teacher strode to the front of the room, looking this way and that as if he were sizing up each individual child. When he reached his lectern, he spoke softly to the younger boys seated near him. Then, in a booming voice directed at the students Junius's age, he said, "You older fellows, it's time to learn the classics. We'll start with Julius Caesar's *Commentaries*."

Junius groaned.

That settled it. There was really no point in continuing this charade any longer than necessary, even if there was a thought that the teacher would help him improve his fife-playing.

Junius needed to get a job and start earning a living. Maybe he would be able to start saving money for the inevitable trip to California that the family would undertake soon. As soon as he could, he would get a job at the *Gazette* since he already knew how to read and write better than any of his contemporaries.

Chapter 7

One Sunday afternoon in late September, Jim was speaking with Radolfus out back of the cabin. They were engaged for several minutes in what seemed like a serious discussion. Finally, Radolfus summoned Junius over to where they were standing.

As he walked closer to where they were standing, Jim was smiling at him.

"Jim wants to know if you want to take a ride with him on the wagon this afternoon, Junius," Radolfus said.

A ride to where? He was planning on practicing on his fife, and an afternoon ride, even with Jim, would disrupt his plans.

"You want to go down to the crick where the fellas and I go fishing, Junius?" Jim asked.

Junius shook his head. "I don't want to go fishing today," he said but couldn't keep from smiling and started to laugh.

"I don't mean fishing, Junius. You know what I mean," Jim said.

Junius helped Jim get the wagon ready for the ride that would take them past the place on the outskirts of Harrisonville where the slaves gathered on Sundays for their praise sessions. Ruby had told him that she enjoyed attending those when they were able. She said it was the closest thing to going to a regular church service that she could imagine. She loved the parts of the service where the congregation would sing. She said that sometimes, some of the members of the makeshift choir would stick around after the praise sessions and harmonize if they didn't have to hurry back to work.

Once they were seated in the wagon, Junius felt a freedom that he often felt when he and Jim could spend time together. He could talk with Jim about anything.

"How did you get him to agree to the swimming lessons, Jim?" Junius asked once they were in the wagon and well on their way to the creek.

"I told your paw that you needed an outlet aside from that crazy thing you call a fife. Got to do something physical, not just moving your mouth and your hands. Boys becoming men need to know things, how to do things, in case they have a reason."

"A reason?"

"No man can tell you what comes tomorrow. All may seem nice and gentle one day, and the next day, that can all be snatched away from you. And with what is going on these days in these United States, there is no telling how many more peaceful tomorrows we're going to have. If indeed there are some left."

Jim was talking about what everyone who visited H.W. Younger's store talked about these days. It seemed like everyone would swing by the *Gazette* office to catch up on the latest rumors before heading to the store, where they could freely gossip about what passed as news. And from what Junius overheard the men saying, it surely looked like the problems with the Jayhawkers coming over from Kansas to make trouble were just getting worse, with no end in sight.

Once they reached the creek, Jim climbed down from the wagon and strode to the bank. He waited while Junius gathered his thoughts together to focus on swimming before he said anything.

"All right, let's see what you're made of here. In the water you go."

Junius stepped out of his clothes cautiously and peered at the water for an instant. Making up his mind that he really wanted to learn how to swim, he stepped on a group of rocks that weren't completely submerged and lay next to a pool of water that looked safe enough to step into. To his relief, the water wasn't as cold as he feared it would be, and he let his body relax as it slid under the water.

Swimming wasn't easy. Every time Junius would try to do what Jim told him to, he would raise his head out of the water and spit out what he was sure were gallons. He was amazed that there weren't any fish swimming around in his mouth. Jim said it would be easy to open his eyes under the water, but he saw no reason to do that. Why have to look at what terrified him?

When he surfaced, he could hear Jim laughing from the bank of the river where he waited.

"Again, Junius! Again! Swing your arms and kick your feet. Breathe out the side of your mouth. You don't have to swallow the whole river, and the fish won't bite you!"

Thus encouraged, he would try again, and gradually, he relaxed to where he thought he was doing an admirable job of it.

"That wasn't too bad for the first time, Junius. Not too bad at all. But you got work to do if you don't want to drown the first time you get into a real river," Jim said, and then he laughed again.

After an hour of what was a bittersweet first encounter with all that Neptune could throw at him in a small creek, Junius had had enough. Jim sensed that and told him to get out and dry off before putting his clothes back on.

They climbed into the wagon, and Jim started back toward town. Instead of taking the fork that led to the Hart family homestead, however, he went the other way. He was going in the direction of where music was coming from.

"What kind of music is that, Jim?" he asked.

"It's our praise session music. Just not White folks' kind of church music. We take our old African songs that we learned as children with the songs that we heard coming out of the churches where we were slaves and blend them all together." Neither of them said anything to the other. Both just listened, with Jim humming and Junius straining to hear if any singing accompanied the music. Mainly they heard singing with an occasional drumbeat added into the mix. Junius thought that it would be fairly easy for a piano to mimic the sounds he was hearing. Not so much a fife, though.

As they approached a clearing, Jim doffed his hat at several of the men they passed by, all of whom did the same while staring at Junius. The music got louder, and Junius could make out there were a lot of people singing, but the words were hard to understand at first. And at first, he thought there were drums, but it turned out it was just clapping.

He couldn't move from his seat in the wagon. He dared not breathe, either, for fear of breaking the spell he was under. The music was magical, and he could only imagine what it would sound like if there were an instrument to accompany the singers. Not his fife. His fife would be lost amidst the cacophony that would result. But Sarah Anne's piano. That would be a different story. He could feel it.

Then he heard the strains of one of the hymns that Sarah Anne would sing to herself whenever Radolfus wasn't around. Except that it was different. There was life in these hymns the slaves sang as they rocked back and forth with their eyes closed and arms outstretched. This was the way the songs should be sung.

Listening to the music the slaves created was even more exciting than surviving Poseidon's best efforts to keep him submerged.

Chapter 8

Every day, as he walked home from school, Junius would glance over at the small cabin Jim and Ruby shared, hoping to get a glimpse of her. Often, he would see her looking out its only window toward the road that led out of town, guessing that she was on the lookout for Jim to return home. On those occasions that Cole or Buck would accompany him home, he managed to avoid looking in her direction, concerned they might guess what was on his mind. If they guessed, they could tease him mercilessly and probably spread the word amongst their classmates. That would undoubtedly lead to adults learning about his feelings, and it would eventually reach Radolfus and Sarah Anne. Or, worse, Jim. And then Ruby would suffer for his carelessness.

Junius saw her come out of the cabin whenever he took out his fife to practice on it, and he figured that she was doing her chores when she did. When he made the occasional mistake, she would look up from whatever it was she was doing and wait until he played the note correctly and then resume her work. Sometimes she would laugh when he got frustrated with a particular note. Her laughter didn't bother him; instead, it just made him try harder the next time. And then, when he succeeded, her smile stayed just that and didn't turn into laughter. When she laughed, it made him feel somehow like they were a team. Without that connection, his notes were so lonely no one could appreciate them.

Occasionally, she would take one of the two chairs they had inside the cabin and sit in it on their front porch, fanning herself with a straw fan. At some point, before it got dark, she normally would go around to the back of the cabin. When she suddenly stopped doing that, Jim explained that she stopped because she heard something moving back there. He said that she swore up and down that the sounds were unlike any of the varmints that normally were in the area. When Junius asked her about it on one of the rare occasions that they could talk to each other privately, she told him that she thought she heard men's voices more than one time, and they didn't sound like slaves' voices.

What would a White man be doing sniffing around the back of a slave's cabin? Junius could only imagine why that would be the case and tried to erase those thoughts from his mind, but couldn't. He was afraid to guess what Ruby's ghosts might have been scheming.

When Junius arrived home one day not too long after Ruby told him of her concerns, Sarah Anne was standing on the front porch of the Hart household. He slowed his steps, hoping against hope that she would withdraw inside the house before he got any closer.

She didn't.

"Junius, could you come help me for a minute, please?" she called out to him as he slowly approached the house.

"Yes, ma'am." He sighed, knowing that she only spoke to him that way when she had something on her mind. It wouldn't do any good to try and beg off because any delay would just make her that much more determined to talk with him on the next occasion. He resigned himself to having to listen to what would likely be a sermon and promised himself he would at least try to look like he was listening to her.

With her hands on her hips, she stared at him. "Boy, I know what you're thinking, and it'll come to no good."

He was afraid that she had noticed how he played a little more loudly and a little longer when he knew Ruby was listening. "What I'm thinking?"

"Junius, have I told you what my daddy learned back in Mobile before I ever even knew your paw?"

"No, ma'am. I don't believe so." Might as well just endure it rather than protest. The lecture was coming regardless.

"Well, let me share some things with you. I suspect you're going to need to hear these things sooner rather than later, and it's probably best they come from me. Here, come inside and sit down over there, young man."

She motioned to Lizzie, who was attending to the younger children, in such a way that Lizzie understood she should take the children upstairs, which she did hurriedly. Once Sarah Anne and Junius were alone, she put her hands on her hips and motioned with her head that he should sit down.

"My father is a learned man, Junius, and I miss his wise counsel at times. I wish you had had a chance to get to know him better. He would be able to guide you in ways that even your father can't."

This was going to be worse than ever before. He regretted his decision to endure what was coming and now desperately sought a way to avoid the coming lecture but couldn't conceive of an escape plan, so he sat there shifting back and forth.

"Your grandfather used to do business in Mobile quite often when he was younger. It was there that he became acquainted with Dr. Joseph Nott. A brilliant surgeon, I might add."

More to humor her than anything else, Junius said, "What did this Dr. Nott have to say that was so important?" Maybe acting curious would spur her on to shorten the sermon. It had worked once or twice in the past, and maybe it would this time too.

"He developed the idea of phrenology."

So, Junius listened to Sarah Anne explain why the races shouldn't mix based on the lumps on their skulls and what would happen to their way of life if mixing were to occur. She told him how lucky they were that Radolfus hadn't succumbed to the temptations that must have been presented to him on his trips to New Orleans.

Lumps on their skulls? What could that possibly have to do with anything? This whole lecture sounded like so many other cockamamie arguments he had heard over the years from people he thought would and should know better. All he had to do each and every time he heard a different argument was talk to Jim and Ruby to dispel any notion that Africans were destined to be slaves due to their inferiority.

How often had Radolfus had to listen to her spew this nonsense? And how had he managed to carry on once he knew how she felt?

Chapter 9

June 1860

Now that he was seventeen, Junius thought there wasn't anything else the teacher could add to his knowledge on the subjects that mattered, and he had already stayed in school longer than most of the other young men his age. Even Radolfus had come to appreciate that. And when he told Junius that there was an opening for a printer's apprentice at the newspaper, Radolfus actually smiled. Sarah Anne said it was a bad idea and that he should concentrate on learning his father's profession. He wasn't sure whether she meant tailor or farmer and had no interest in inquiring.

Being a farmer meant being outside far more than he wanted to be in all kinds of weather, doing what could be back-breaking work and leaving him little time or energy for the fife. Being a tailor meant having to listen to Radolfus critique his work, listening to customers who thought they knew far more than he did about anything and everything, and constantly being nice to people who didn't deserve such courtesy. Being a printer's apprentice meant he could actually learn something useful while appreciating what was happening in the world, at least from a distinctly frontier perspective. Yes, he would get ink all over his hands and his dungarees, but he could always wash up before getting his fife out of its case. Sarah Anne would probably want to inspect his hands before they sat down to supper anyway.

The conversations that he would overhear in the newspaper office that would result from some bit of news would also be interesting, and Junius was sure that Radolfus would love to hear his summaries of them. Jim, who was otherwise deprived of knowing much of anything that went on except what he heard through the slave networks, would be equally interested. Whenever Junius could, he would summarize for Jim and Ruby and thus keep them informed of whatever was important, a fact she would certainly appreciate.

"You just be careful who you talk to about politics, Junius. Let them keep thinking we are states' rights supporters. Might be dangerous otherwise," Radolfus told him on the first day of his new job.

After that, Junius worked three days a week at the *Gazette* since it was only published twice a week. Radolfus would wake him up at 6 a.m., and he would be at the newspaper by 7, working until at least 5 p.m. He usually got off early on Saturdays, but the rest of the days, he stayed busy arranging and rearranging the next issue as new items came in and local merchants paid for new ads to be run. Richard O. Boggess, who had bought the paper from Nathan Millington and enlarged it to a seven-column paper instead of the usual six, changed its politics from the dying conservative Whig Party to Democrat as soon as he purchased it, in fierce opposition to the nascent Republican Party. Even after Boggess had sold the paper to Thomas Fogle in 1857, he continued to write its political editorials. All decidedly Democratic.

"This Lincoln fellow is even worse than Fremont. And the damned Democrats can't come together to support one candidate. Instead, there are two, three even! We've got to pull together behind Douglas. Why can't they see that?" Boggess would fume in the months leading up to the election.

Every time he started on one of his rants that would invariably become impassioned speeches to anyone who was forced to listen, Junius pretended to tend to the printing machine more closely.

"Hart! Your father, he's a tailor, isn't he?"

"Yes, Mr. Boggess, he is."

"Works for Mayor Younger, right?"

"Yes, sir."

"How can he stand working for that man? A Republican who bought himself the mayoralty with the help of some Kansans whom he claimed had just moved to Missouri. Can't have no Lincolnite Black Republicans working on this newspaper now, young man," Boggess said. Junius wondered if the other side didn't buy votes just the same, and he suspected that they did. He could guess what being a Black Republican meant.

The job wasn't that demanding once Mr. Fogle had managed to acquire a new printing press, and he had a lot less ink to clean off at the end of the day. Once he mastered the new machine, he found he had lots of time on his hands, which he wished he could spend practicing on his fife.

His father's excitement hearing whatever news he came home with usually elicited a sharp reaction, if Sarah Anne wasn't around. That, in and of itself, made him even more curious about what it was they disagreed about so strongly, and as he considered the divergent views on the main issue, he found himself appreciating the Republican candidate's views even more. Of course, that issue was slavery.

Lincoln won the presidential election when the Electoral College met in mid-December. The outcome was obvious before that, based on the popular vote, but the Electoral College hammered the final nail in the coffin that had been Missouri's forlorn hopes that Stephen Douglas, their favored candidate, could win. Junius shuffled between the *Gazette*'s office and H.W.'s store after school to convey the results to his father as they were announced.

Mr. Boggess was particularly displeased. "The wrong

Illinoisan won! The Democrats brought it on themselves," he said repeatedly to anyone who would listen. Junius watched as his father chose not to respond, trying to keep his happiness with the outcome from being too obvious.

"They couldn't decide which candidate would best represent their goals, and now we're all going to pay for their idiocy. There is going to be a reckoning, and it won't be easily resolved. There is going to be violence on a scale that will make the border wars here look like child's play," Boggess continued.

Tension was indeed rising in and around Harrisonville and all of Cass County and the surrounding counties. Every day, Junius heard rumors of what happened to slaves who were taken by the Jayhawkers from their farms and learned that most of them withdrew from even casual contact outside the cabin out of fear. Ruby would hardly leave the cabin after thinking she had heard even more strangers behind the house while she was alone. Jim had to practically force her to go to the religious services on Sundays, but she wouldn't talk with anyone or sing the psalms and would dash into the cabin when they returned home.

Returning home from work early one Saturday afternoon, Junius found Ruby outside the cabin washing clothes. When he halloed her, she practically jumped away from him.

"What is it, Ruby?" he asked as she covered her face with her hands. She was obviously close to crying.

Her eyes darted this way and that before she could look directly at him. "Oh, Junius, I'm sorry. I should have realized it would be you. It's just that, I don't know, I keep hearing people. Jim thinks it's all in my head, but I know I hear them. And I'm scared."

"You don't know who they are?" Junius asked her.

"No, and even if I did, what could I do about it? You know no one would do anything to help me. Not really."

She was right, of course. Besides, who would believe her?

And if anything did happen to her, it would be considered a minor event compared with everything else going on in the region. Even if she were harmed by someone, nobody would think it worth the time to investigate it.

With that, a bold plan began to take shape in Junius's mind. He would have to be very careful how he arranged it, and it would take time, but that was the one thing he wasn't sure he had very much of. As he mulled his fledgling plan over in his mind, something his father said the next day accelerated his planning.

"War is coming; just about everyone knows that. Although some people think that Missouri will side with the other slave states, that simply won't happen," he announced after dinner to no one in particular. "No one knows, however, what will happen in the Kansas Territory, should it become a state, with its competing pro-slavery and abolitionist legislatures," he continued.

He was right. That sentiment confirmed what Junius heard at the *Gazette* offices. But, of course, the majority of those voices disagreed with what happened in Kansas. And most of them advocated secession.

A few days later, South Carolina seceded, followed by Mississippi, and Florida followed suit in mid-January. Then Alabama seceded, followed by Georgia and Louisiana in late January. At the same time, Kansas was finally admitted to the Union at the end of the month, making it the thirty-fourth state. Except now, there were only twenty eight still in the Union, and then when Texas seceded in early February, there were only twenty-seven. It was just a question of time before the other slave-holding states would go.

"Go wash up, son. Get all that ink off your hands and then tell us what is going on," Radolfus said as Junius entered the cabin shortly after the news came that Texas seceded.

"All right, Paw, but things are getting, I don't know, they

are becoming a little tense at the paper," Junius said.

"Because of all the states seceding, I reckon."

"Yes, sir. And now even Mr. Fogle is talking about publishing a list of Black Republicans in the paper."

That comment stopped Radolfus in his tracks. Junius pretended not to notice that his father was obviously scared now.

"Why would he do that?" Radolfus asked.

"It seems that the secessionists want all Republicans to leave the county. And not just Cass County either."

"I knew we should never have left Tuscumbia," Sarah Anne said as she joined them on the front porch.

"What do you mean, woman?" Radolfus asked.

"I heard what Junius was telling you. We wouldn't have any problems if we were back in Alabama, where we all belong. Danged fool idea of California is what got us into this mess."

When Junius brought home a copy of Alabama's secession ordinance, Radolfus read it with great interest.

"Now, that doesn't surprise me at all. A convention to be called in Montgomery to organize the states that had seceded into their own country. I figure Yancey, that old fire-eater, is no doubt behind the effort. And they expect that the border states—Missouri, Kentucky, Maryland, and Delaware—will soon follow suit, and I suspect they will," Radolfus said.

Junius continued to keep Radolfus abreast of the news whenever he worked and, at the same time, wondered how his former classmates would respond to the states that had seceded and now were in the process of forming their own country. Rumors persisted that all the states would be asked to provide a certain number of men to a new army and that the states like Missouri, which were expected to secede in the near future, would do the same. He especially wondered what Buck, his adventurous classmate, would do if he were still in Harrisonville.

As soon as he had finished his last school year, a few months earlier, Buck had ridden off to St. Joseph to get a job with the Pony Express, which had just begun to deliver mail all the way to California. Buck could ride a horse better than anyone else, but he was headstrong and didn't like being told what to do. Buck's father wasn't all that happy with his son's decision, but he couldn't stand in his way. Harrisonville was far too small and mild a place for his boy.

Then, one day in early February, Buck reappeared out of nowhere. He looked older, his quick smile was no longer present, and he had obviously lost a lot of weight.

"Buck, you're back!"

"Yeah, done with that Pony Express."

"Why, what happened?"

"Junius, I'll tell you. Those mountains. The Rockies. They'll kill a man. I know of two other riders, and I actually met one of them, who froze to death trying to cross them. Almost lost my own horse in a heavy snowfall too. I suppose I could tell ya that it was fun, but overall, it was just too much to deal with. And the Indians. Made me some money, though."

"What are you going to do now, Buck?"

"Well, I don't rightly know just yet. Got to do some thinking about things."

Maybe it had been a good idea to stop in Missouri rather than continue the trip to California after all. When Junius decided to complete the trip, hopefully sooner rather than later and with Ruby, he'd have to take all these things that Buck had mentioned into consideration.

Junius and Buck ran into each other again a few days later, not too far from the Hart homestead, somewhat unexpectedly. Junius was tending to the field with a hoe and didn't really want to be interrupted because that meant that much more time away from the fife, but it was Buck. Normally, Buck wouldn't have had any reason to be on that road out of town, but he also had a penchant for going places just to explore, so Junius figured that was what he was doing.

Buck reined in his horse and asked, "Didja hear the news?"

Still wondering what it would have been that Buck was exploring this far out of town, Junius studied him carefully as he walked up the muddy road toward the farmhouse.

"What news would that be?" Pausing over his hoe, he looked to his left. "You know I've been helping Paw get the fields ready for planting when I'm not working the presses at the paper."

Buck looked around carefully. With a tug at his belt, he pulled down his pants enough to piss on top of a pile of horseshit in the middle of the road. "That Jayhawker, name of Colonel Anthony. The one who raided Pleasant Hill a couple of times last year. He did it again last week and stole some more property and money and took another fifty-five Negroes along with him and his boys."

"Fifty-five?" That seemed like an awful lot, and he figured that Buck was exaggerating what he had heard to make the news seem that much more impressive.

"Yeah, whole bunch of 'em. Mainly young'uns."

Junius considered what Buck had said. Maybe he wasn't exaggerating after all. He seemed to know what he was talking about this time.

It could have been Harrisonville they had come to. They could have taken Jim and Ruby if they had, and what could have stopped them? Junius wondered why that information hadn't yet made it into the local news and suspected it was because Mr. Bogguss didn't want to scare everyone.

"What do they do with them? They don't need any slaves in Kansas, do they?" Junius asked.

"They set 'em free," Buck said as he spat out a wad on the muddy ground and put his boot on it.

"Free? Where would they go once they were free?" Now his interest was piqued. He wondered how he would ever find

Ruby if the Jayhawkers took her someplace.

"Dunno. Folks up in Pleasant Hill and other towns are trying to figure out how to get 'em back. But once them Jayhawkers get them darkies into Kansas ... they get them to that Underground Railroad, and then they're good as gone forever."

Harrisonville was more or less in the middle of Cass County and less than thirty miles from the border with Kansas, and it wasn't so far from Pleasant Hill that the Jayhawkers might not try the same thing there.

"Whatcha thinkin'?" Buck asked Junius.

"Nothing much." After a pause, he asked, "What's going to happen, Buck?"

Buck looked away, back down the road. "You know where this is headed."

Junius glanced over at the shack that Jim and Ruby stayed in and let his gaze linger. Buck watched him for a couple of minutes before interrupting his thoughts.

"You taste that yet?"

Junius snapped out of his thoughts. "What?"

He looked at Junius amusedly. "The darkie's daughter ..." he said, smiling oddly.

"I ... I ... haven't tasted nothing. I mean ... no one." He forced himself not to look back at the shack, half-afraid Ruby would walk out to fetch water or check on Jim.

Buck turned to walk away.

"Well, Junius, I don't know if I'll be back this way again anytime soon. I have half a mind to join up once I see how things go. The Missouri State Guard. You should think about it too. The Guard will need a band," Buck said.

"Join up?" Junius asked, his mind still focused on the shack.

"Yeah, the governor said he'll probably need some more men to join the militia," Buck said.

"What for?" asked Junius.

Buck looked at him curiously. "You know there's going to

be a convention soon, right? The one where a bunch of delegates are going to meet in Jefferson City to decide whether Missouri is going to stay in the Union or leave."

"I know about that. But the governor said Missouri was going to stay in the Union when he was running, didn't he?" Junius said.

"Yeah, but now that he is the governor and he's seen what other states have done, and what others are likely to do ... besides when Mr. Lincoln becomes president, assuming he does, who knows what he'll do with the states that have already left the Union? Even Maryland is going to secede, and then how will them Yankees be able to stay in Washington? They'll be surrounded by rebels." Buck seemed pleased with the notion.

"What do you mean, assuming he becomes president? He's been elected and all," Junius said.

"Yeah, he's been elected all right. But that doesn't mean that he'll live long enough to assume the office, now, does it? If you get my meaning," Buck said.

Junius wondered what Buck could possibly mean by that and decided it was just him mouthing off his wishes that had no basis in reality.

Junius thought some more before asking Buck any more but decided to hear him out more out of curiosity than anything else. Even though Junius didn't believe the governor would support Missouri seceding, he decided to play along with Buck's train of thought. "What would the state militia do if Missouri decides to leave the Union?"

"I suspect that since it is the Missouri State Militia, we'd be duty-bound to protect us and our families from any Yankees trying to invade."

"Yankees?" This sounded serious. More serious, in fact, than what he had heard being discussed at the newspaper and more serious than even Paw had suggested might be the case.

"Hell yeah, just like them Jayhawkers been doing for the

past couple of years. Only maybe Mr. Lincoln might get an army together and have 'em come down here to make sure Missouri don't leave the Union. Hell, the militia might even be ordered to go retrieve the slaves that the Jayhawkers have kidnapped," Buck said.

They looked at each other for a couple of minutes, each lost in his own thoughts. Finally, Junius asked, "What are you going to do in the militia if you join up?"

Buck smiled. "I got me a rifle, and I knows how to use a knife right good, and you know I can wrestle anybody my size to the ground. Even some fellers a bit taller than me, too. So, if anything gets started, I'd be able to have some fun."

Junius was inclined to agree with Buck's self-assessment and thought he probably would have some fun. In contrast, Junius was several inches shorter, slighter of build, and had a different temperament. He wasn't sure how he would fare in any fight with anyone on either side if there was a war. Besides, carrying a rifle with a pack and all seemed like it would be a pretty heavy chore.

"Doesn't sound like anything I would be interested in doing. What else could I do in the militia?"

Buck wondered the same thing. "I don't think you have to worry about fighting no Yankee, Junius, cuz I doubt they would even get this far once we get the militia organized. But you could still join up, and you know, be in the band. What about your thing, what do you call it, a flute?"

"You mean my fife?" Junius hadn't thought about that.

"Yes, your fife. All right, Junius, I really better be going now. Wanna be home before dark."

"But why would you think I would join the Missouri Volunteer Militia?" Junius asked.

Buck gave him a backward glance. "What other choice do you have?" he asked.

Junius decided to let him think that. That way, Paw couldn't get in any trouble for his political views. Maybe Buck had a point. And it's bound to be for only a few months, and being in the band would mean he would be safe from harm.

Junius stared after Buck as he trod down the path, wondering if and when he would see him again.

A band. Might be a good way to spend a few weeks. Maybe he would get to know some other fellas who liked to play different music and instruments, too. Plus, if Buck was right, he wouldn't have to go too far away from home, neither. And he sincerely doubted that Governor Jackson would really support the secessionists. After all, he had promised Missouri would stay in the Union. Buck had to be wrong.

There was one thing Junius had to do before joining any band, though, and now it seemed like he had to do it sooner rather than later.

Chapter 10

Radolfus accompanied H.W. to St. Louis on business soon after the news of Alabama seceding reached them. It was a long-planned trip to get more clothing that H.W. had had shipped from New Orleans. In the meantime, Jim had fallen off a ladder, hurt his back, and was confined to bed for several days. According to Ruby, he was in a great deal of pain and drifted in and out of sleep all day and night.

The day after H.W. and Radolfus rode off to St. Louis, Junius walked into town to work at the *Gazette* just as he normally would. The new printing press really sped things up, but Junius found himself covered in ink most days. He had a hard time getting the ink out of his hands, and before his accident, Jim would laugh at him, saying, "It ain't so bad having a little black in you, is it, Junius?"

The *Gazette* office was only just over a mile from the Hart home, and Junius could cover the ground in less than half an hour. Paw couldn't spare either horse, so he had no other choice but to walk. H.W.'s son, Cole, who was still in town pretending to go to school, made a habit of intercepting Junius on the outskirts of town on his way to work to see if he could get him a job at the newspaper. A word from H.W. should have sufficed to do just that, but Cole already had a reputation for being something of a rascal and a ruffian. Junius half-expected to see Cole waiting for him every day that he went to work, and he couldn't avoid him on foot.

When he got to town that day, there was a well-dressed man with a handsome wagon and horse outside the newspaper office. He had never seen that man in town before.

As Junius approached the newspaper office, he heard the well-dressed man say something to the effect that he would be going to St. Louis with his cargo later that week. When Junius entered the newspaper office, Cole was already inside, smiling at him. He'd obviously decided it was no use talking to Junius on his way there, which suited Junius just fine.

"Hey, Cole, I don't really think I can ask Mr. Boggess or Mr. Fogle about giving you a job again," Junius said.

"Don't worry about that. I actually came to give you some news. Besides, Paw says I don't really need to work here. He'll find something for me to do at the store if he needs help." Cole glanced out the window to where the well-dressed man was continuing his conversation.

Junius followed his gaze. "Who's that?"

"Oh, he's a trader. That's what I wanted to tell you."

"A trader?"

"Yeah, in precious ... commodities."

Junius could well imagine precisely what Cole meant by commodities, and it sent a chill down his spine. He started to ask anyway but, at the last second, bit his tongue to keep from doing so. No point in letting Cole know that he would be concerned.

"I hear he may be headed to St. Louis at the end of the week. Maybe I'll hitch a ride if I can," Cole said.

Junius knew full well what Cole had in mind to do when he got to St. Louis, and it bothered him to think that he might have set his eyes on Ruby for the same reason. He couldn't get angry at Cole because that would just lead to questions about why he was so concerned, so he swallowed hard and tried to force the thoughts from his mind.

After a long day on the press at the *Gazette*, he walked out of the office only to find the same well-dressed man still there, slightly wet from the drizzle that had fallen all day and obviously exasperated. While Junius debated whether to wait out the rain, he stood in the doorway assessing just how wet he might get if he went now.

Another man approached the stranger as Junius continued debating his options and deliberately slowed his gait.

"I understand you're taking a cargo to St. Louis this week."

"I am, if it seems like it might be profitable, that is."

"How many you got so far?"

"Only four worth selling. But tomorrow, I think I'll get another one, and she should fetch a good price."

"Where?"

"Outside of town a mile or so. Fella owns a small spread and has a shop here in town down the street."

"Fetching?"

"So I hear."

Junius didn't know of anyone else just outside of town who had any slaves except for his father. *They're talking about Ruby.*

The other gentleman reflected for a moment. "How long will you have her here before you head to St. Louis?"

"Couple of days at most."

"Suppose the fella who owns her won't sell her?"

"I'll do my best to persuade him, and if nothing works ... Well, there are other ways of obtaining slaves in these parts, aren't there?"

They both laughed.

They were planning to kidnap Ruby and take her to St. Louis to sell her. And they were going to do it in the next couple of days. Junius forced himself not to panic and think clearly, but he couldn't concentrate. He had to act fast. There was no time to lose.

Chapter 11

Junius needed to get home quickly and let Jim know what the slave trader was planning and that he had an idea of how to get Ruby to safety.

"Kansas?" Jim responded incredulously when he heard what Junius had to say.

"Yeah, Jim, to the Underground Railroad we heard about. You know more about it than I do, I'm sure. Folks in town keep whispering that there is a place up near Kansas City called Quindaro where escaped slaves go to get to Canada. There's even that book about it published by some lady back east, and more and more and more slaves are fleeing their masters with the help of lots of folks who help them along the way. Causing all kinds of ruckus, it is. White folks, too. Seems like quite a few of them have gone there," Junius explained.

When Jim nodded, Junius knew he was right. Jim had heard about it and probably knew as much as anyone in town would know about it, too.

"How would she get there?" Jim asked. "I can't take her. My back would never let me ride that far."

Junius swallowed hard. "I could take her."

"You?"

"We could leave after supper tomorrow night," he said, the words coming out in a rush. "I could ride until dawn, get her to safety, and then be back before Monday morning."

"Quindaro must be at least fifty miles from here! And that is as the crow flies."

"But if I ride at night, I could do it in two nights, then

75

leave her there in safe hands, and ride back all day and all night if need be."

"Junius, the horse ... you can't ride that far that fast. It would kill the horse."

He had never ridden a horse that far before and hadn't thought of that. It would take longer than he thought, and he'd have to be even more cautious. He could still do it, though.

"Well, if I don't make it back by Monday, I could be back by Tuesday. I don't have to be at work before Wednesday anyhow," he said.

"Junius, there are things you don't know."

"Those things don't matter right now, do they, Jim?"

He couldn't read Jim's mind but had to get him to agree to his plan regardless of what he was thinking about. There was no time to lose.

"You should wait until your paw gets back from St. Louis. You'll understand why."

"Your daughter's life is at stake. We can't wait," Junius said.

As Junius left Jim and Ruby's cabin, he was surprised to see his father approaching the house in a wagon.

"Paw, what are you doing home so soon?" he asked.

"We got through in St. Louis sooner than expected, son. Why, are you sorry to see me?" Radolfus said, laughing.

"No, sir. Of course not. It's just that ..."

"Just what?" Radolfus asked.

"Nothing, Paw. We can talk later," Junius said, deciding that he needed a little more time to get everything arranged before telling Paw what he had a mind to do. He really wasn't sure he was even going to tell Paw after the way Jim had responded. What didn't Jim understand?

Once Junius had thought through everything he needed to, he decided he could broach the plan with his father. He stressed that there was little time to waste given the discussion he had overheard in town and tried to impress upon Radolfus that they had to act fast. He sensed hesitation in his father's reactions, much the same way that Jim had reacted, and couldn't understand why they both failed to grasp the need to act immediately. He chewed his nails for the first time in a long time as he pondered what about the situation either he or they didn't comprehend and came up empty. If they didn't agree to his plan soon, he might have to take matters into his own hands. That would make everything that much more difficult to carry out because there would be no one to make his excuses in his absence, but that couldn't be helped. He had to save Ruby.

Much to his surprise, his father agreed with his assessment of the situation.

"Although this is a complicated matter, you're right. We can't risk Ruby being kidnapped. I'll discuss the matter with Jim," Radolfus said.

"I've already mentioned it to him, Paw. He told me to wait until you returned, so I did. But there's no time to waste."

Radolfus looked like he was about to say something else, but instead, he merely said, "I'll talk to Jim."

Junius awoke earlier than usual the next day. He hadn't slept that much, only nodding off shortly before dawn. He awoke with a start, but forced himself to stay calm. Much to his surprise, his father was waiting outside for him with Jim standing alongside.

"Jim's agreed," Radolfus told Junius under his breath, trying to make sure Sarah Anne didn't know what they were discussing.

Junius reeled. Paw had stayed up to talk with Jim, and they had agreed to the plan. Both of them. Suddenly, the enormity of what he had proposed struck him. He was relieved, excited, and then afraid. Afraid of failing Paw and Jim and Ruby, though in what way, he didn't know. But afraid.

Still whispering, Radolfus continued, "You two leave after supper as soon as it is dark. Don't say anything to your maw either. You'll have to pack up what you need to take right after dinner, so you'd best be planning now. I took the liberty of sketching out a rough map of the area based on my business trips up there and what I remember from when we arrived in Kansas City a few years ago. You may find it useful."

Junius thought quickly. Some food, water, a blanket or two, his knife, and his rifle.

"You need to get to the Kansas border as quickly as you can. That's a good twenty miles from here. So, you will need to ride almost due west, and then once you're at the border, you'll need to head north," Radolfus said.

He was waiting for Junius to say something, but he didn't know what to say. He just knew this had to work.

"Can you reckon how far twenty miles is? The border won't be marked, and there is no telling what kind of fellows you'll run across before you get there, but any chance meeting won't be good. Different story once you're into Kansas, of course. You'll need to ride at least five hours to make the twenty miles, probably more like six at night."

Six hours? He could do it. Could Ruby handle that much time on a horse at night? She had to. He'd put her in front so there would be no danger of her falling asleep and falling off the horse.

"We can handle it, Paw. I'll make sure of it."

"Once you think you're inside Kansas, just keep riding due north until you see a big town. If you get to the river, you'll know that you need to turn to the west to get to Quindaro."

"Yes, Paw."

"Probably take you at least three nights riding to get there, and then who knows how much longer until you find the right folks. Sleep as much as you can during the day. You may need to light a fire if it gets too cold, which it can do this time of year, but only do that if it's really necessary."

"Right."

"And Junius, you're of an age now. And so is Ruby. Best be careful. I know you know what I am talking about, too."

Junius didn't answer. He wondered how Paw would react if he really knew how he felt.

Junius couldn't concentrate on anything after arriving at the *Gazette* that day. Mr. Boggess commented that he was making more errors than he normally did and admonished him to be more careful in setting the type.

"Boy, what's gotten into you today? Normally, I can trust you with just about any job there is, but you seem a bit distracted today. Something eating at you?" Mr. Boggess asked.

Junius shook his head and went back to work, but now he was even more troubled.

He tried unsuccessfully to focus more on his work, but nevertheless somehow found himself able to finish the day. He hurried home and reconsidered yet again what else he might take with him and decided there was nothing more. He tried to eat slowly while Paw acted his normal self, but Sarah Anne watched both of them very carefully.

After the plates were cleared, Junius looked over at Paw, who simply nodded in his direction, a gesture Sarah Anne noticed. She started to say something, but with one look from Radolfus, she kept quiet.

With that, Junius went upstairs and grabbed the few items he had gathered from under his bed. He considered taking his fife as he returned downstairs, too, but decided that wouldn't be wise. When he returned to the area where they ate dinner, he managed to avoid looking at his stepmother, whom he knew would be searching his face for clues as to what was about to happen, and then he left the house.

Slowly, he walked the horse that Paw said he would loan him down to the cabin. When he arrived, Jim, still on crutches, stood outside the cabin with Ruby. She was clutching her hymnal.

"Baby girl, you've practically grown up with Junius. You know you can trust him. I certainly do," Jim said to Ruby as Junius approached.

Slowly, she nodded through her tears.

"I want you to promise me you'll let me know when you have reached Quindaro. I've even written a letter for you to give to Junius to bring back to me. Then, when you get to Canada, I've written another one for you to send to me so I know you're safe. As soon as I'm able to, I'll come find you. Junius doesn't need to know what is in the letter, in case it's intercepted. That way, no one will know where you are headed," Jim said. With that, he pushed her gently toward Junius. Glancing at Junius, she then turned to look at her father again with tears in her eyes.

Jim took her in his arms for a long moment and told Junius, "You take good care of her, Junius; you take good care of my baby girl. Now go on, girl."

"Did you bring your fife, Junius?" she asked.

"No, why?"

"Please get your fife. I think we may need it," she said.

Rather than let him go back into the house, Radolfus retreated inside and upstairs. After only a couple of minutes, he returned with the fife in its case.

"Be careful with that, Junius. Make sure no one can hear you if you decide to play it," his father said as he handed him the instrument case. "And make sure you bring it back with you."

With that, Junius hoisted Ruby onto the horse and then mounted behind her. As Junius slowly turned the horse around, Jim called out, "Godspeed, baby girl!"

At first, they rode slowly, more slowly than Junius would have preferred, but he sensed how tense Ruby was while riding in front of him. He had to put his arms around her to hold the reins and wound up touching her arms, elbows, and even the sides of her dress. After an hour or so, as it grew quieter and darker and as they rode further into the woods, she relaxed just a bit. After another hour, she seemed even more comfortable, and he could ride a little more easily.

About midnight, by his reckoning, they must have made at least fifteen miles, if not a little more. He pulled the horse to slow it a little more and, at the same time, realized that the trip to Quindaro might take longer than he had anticipated.

"Ruby, I've been meaning to ask you something for a while," he said.

"What's that?" she asked.

"How did you get your name? It's not one that's all that common, is it?" he asked.

"Oh, I don't know about that. But I know in my case it's because of my momma. She loved rubies," said Ruby.

"Why is that?" he asked.

"Her pappaw was a rich man. Did some sort of business in Barataria. Involving ships and precious cargoes. Apparently, he did a lot of trading. Jim says he helped that general they called Old Hickory when the English tried to take New Orleans in the Second War of Independence, too. I didn't know anything about it until you told me I was born in Louisiana and I asked Jim about it," she said.

"You call your paw Jim?" he asked. He marveled at the other information that she related to him, never imagining that her family history could be so interesting. It all made her that much more appealing to him for some reason. Was it normal for Africans to have their children call them by their given names?

"He told me I should a couple of years ago. Says he prefers that. He says that sometimes it's better if people don't think he's my father. Not sure why. It's not really that strange, though," she said.

Shortly before dawn, Junius found a good, secluded spot near a stream where they could spend much of the day unobserved and wait for the safety of darkness to return. He spread the blanket on the ground on top of a bed of fallen leaves. Ruby watched him and slowly dismounted. She looked at the blanket and then back at Junius.

"Are we both going to sleep in that?" she asked.

"I'm sorry, Ruby. I don't know what else to do. It's liable to get colder, and if we're close enough, maybe we can keep each other just a little bit warmer."

"I suppose you're right."

"I'll make sure to keep my back to you, and you can do the same, all right?"

She nodded.

Junius slept fitfully, unused to trying to sleep during the day. When he awoke, it was mid-afternoon, and he looked over to where Ruby should have been sleeping, but she wasn't there. At first, he panicked, thinking she'd been captured or even run away. Then he heard a splashing sound and turned to see her by the stream, scooping up water in her hands and drinking it.

When she returned from the stream, he said, "We have to stay here until close to dark. There won't be much to eat, and we have to keep quiet. I'm not sure whether we are still in Missouri or if we are already in Kansas now, but no matter, we got to stay quiet."

Ruby said nothing, but her discomfort was obvious. They'd never been alone like this before. She wouldn't look at him but instead kept glancing all around at nothing and everything.

It was cold for an early spring day, and he decided they could use a fire. Once he gathered enough wood, he started a fire, and gradually, she approached, taking the blanket and wrapping herself in it. After a while, he took out some hard tack, warmed it a bit over the fire, and offered her some. She took little bites, her eyes still searching all around them.

Eventually, Junius fell asleep again. When he awoke, the sun was still high in the sky, with its rays shining through the remaining leaves of the surrounding trees, but it was already getting cooler. He looked over, and Ruby seemed to be sleeping, albeit lightly. When he moved to get up, she instantly sat bolt upright but relaxed when she realized that there was no one else around. He went to the stream, and Ruby followed him with the blanket still wrapped around her.

When he realized that he, too, was fidgeting, he took a deep breath, washed his face, and then refilled his canteen. Returning to the clearing, he told her, "We're going to need to get some more sleep if we are to make it all the way tonight."

"I wish you could play your fife," Ruby said.

"So do I. But it would be too loud. Someone might realize that we are here."

She sat back against a tree trunk opposite him and pushed some twigs out of the way. Then she picked one up and lazily scratched her back with it.

"Did you really sing when I practiced on it back home?" he asked.

"Whenever I recognized a tune, I'd sing the words. And when I didn't, I'd just make them up."

She hummed softly. It was one of the tunes that he played regularly, and she carried the tune perfectly. Slowly, she stopped humming and began to sing softly. He hadn't realized she had such a beautiful voice.

As he lay down, she continued humming while glancing here and there and then back again. Junius started to drift off, and as he did, he felt her lie down next to him, this time closer than before.

When he awoke in the late afternoon, it took him a

moment before he realized she had her head nestled in his arm and her arm was across his chest. Rather than get up immediately and risk waking her, he lay there for several minutes, luxuriating in her touch and scent. Even though she appeared to be sound asleep, her fingers clasped and unclasped one of the buttons on his shirt, and she nuzzled ever closer to his cheek with her face.

Suddenly, she went still. Then she lifted her head up off his chest and sat straight up.

"Junius, I'm sorry. I didn't know ..."

"It's all right. I didn't mind at all. I was just trying not to wake you up just yet," he said.

At dark, they mounted the horse and started riding west. Junius wanted to make sure they were well within Kansas before they stopped again prior to daybreak. Looking to the west at the setting sun, Junius turned north, thinking that he didn't want to get too far west of Quindaro. The weather had turned even colder than the night before, and the moon was plainly visible in the clear sky.

Ruby had moved behind him on the horse because she said it would be less uncomfortable that way, and she was right. While they had been riding with her in front of him, he had merely thought of their closeness as being a necessity. He realized that her hands around his waist was a completely different feeling than the other way around.

And on occasion, when she grew tired, she put her head against his back, and he imagined she closed her eyes. Being this close to her felt good, unlike anything he had felt before. Except for the time on the steamboat when Lalea had been in the river and he had put his arm around Ruby, he had never been this close to her.

When they stopped just before daybreak, he began to gather wood but, after hearing noises in the distance, decided to abandon the idea of another fire. Whether the noises were from farm animals or otherwise, he couldn't tell. He spread the blanket again and beckoned Ruby to lie down while he selected a spot a little further away. She waited until he was lying down and then crept toward him on her knees until she was right next to him. Startled, he sat up, but she lay down and covered them both with the blanket.

"We'll be warmer this way," she said, "back to back."

At first, she fidgeted some, and after half an hour, she said. "Junius, it's colder than it was last night."

With that, he turned toward her and rubbed her left arm while he slipped his right arm underneath her head and around her shoulders. She tensed at first, but gradually, he could feel her muscles loosen.

"Is that better?" he asked after a couple of minutes.

"Yes, that's better, thank you," she said.

He didn't know what to do or say next. He couldn't let go of her and, at the same time, couldn't think of anything to say to break the growing tension.

"Ruby, you're ..." he said finally.

She turned back to him again and asked, "Yes, Junius, I'm?"

"Beautiful," he said.

She smiled at him, her green eyes dancing.

"Ruby, we can't," he said.

"Can't what, Junius?"

"It's just, it's just that I have to get you to Quindaro. To make sure you're free." He forced himself to concentrate on what he was saying.

"I know. And when will we see each other again after Quindaro?" she asked.

"I ... I don't know," he said. He tried to come up with an answer that sounded reasonable but couldn't.

"It could be a very long time, Junius. It could be months, maybe even a year," she said.

Feeling her close to him like this made him want to turn

around and ride back to Harrisonville. Quindaro could wait, or they would come up with another solution. He couldn't stand the idea of being away from her now.

"Junius, please."

"Please what, Ruby?"

"Don't you know? I thought boys knew what to do."

He didn't have a clue what to do, but his body was telling him all he needed to know. Was he betraying the trust that Jim had placed in him by acknowledging how he felt? Acknowledging what he had wanted longer than he had even admitted to himself?

She moved her mouth toward his. He didn't know what had hit him. He let her kiss him until he had to respond just as fervently.

His left hand found her breast, and she moaned. He propped himself up with his right arm, and she pulled him toward her. When he rolled on top of her, it was as if their bodies knew instinctively what to do. She had closed her eyes, and he did, too. He rocked back and forth and then moved faster, and she responded in kind. He heard her making little noises as she breathed deeper and deeper.

Suddenly, he shuddered, moaned her name, and collapsed on top of her.

She was quiet for a minute and then began crying.

"Ruby, are you all right? I didn't hurt you, did I?"

"No, Junius. These aren't sad tears at all."

She let him draw her closer and then rested her head against his shoulder, and he reached for her hand as she did so. She laced her fingers through his.

"Junius, what are we going to do?" she whispered.

He tried to gather his senses and focus on her question. He had to look away from her and pull back a bit. "I am going to deliver you to people who will make sure you are safe. That's what this journey is all about."

"You know what I mean, Junius. About us."

"About us?" She felt it, too.

"Yes, Junius. Us. You must know how I feel about you. And now ... I know you better than anyone, and I feel like I know what you're thinking. I think it comes out when you play the fife. It's so different now than it was when you first played it." She laughed. "And now. After what we just did."

He couldn't think of anything to say to her and tried to get up, but with her hand on his chest, she pushed him back down to the ground. He didn't protest. He couldn't. He felt like he needed to clean them both off somehow, but couldn't move.

"Junius," she said.

"Yes," he gasped.

"I felt it. It was powerful."

"I probably shouldn't have, but I couldn't stop myself. I'm sorry; I hope that—"

She interrupted him. "I know, but I wouldn't have let you stop even if you had tried. I wanted to feel that as much as I wanted to feel you inside of me. That was a wonderful feeling, Junius. I feel like a woman now. Your woman."

He didn't know what to do or to say. He finished dressing quickly, put his boots back on, and stood up, trying to gather his thoughts.

"Junius, play for me," Ruby said.

"Play?" Junius looked around as he said that, deciding whether to honor her request. "All right, but just a note or two; we can't risk being discovered."

He slid the instrument case out of the saddlebag on the horse and whisked the fife out. Placing it against his lips, he smiled at her as he played two random notes softly.

Hearing him play, she smiled. Quickly, he placed the fife back in its case and into the saddlebag.

She was so quiet he thought she was asleep. After a few minutes, however, she turned toward him yet again and caressed his face, whispering his name. Then they fell asleep in each other's arms.

When he awoke hours later, Junius lay on his back staring at the sky. The clouds looked puffier than ever, and the wind whistled past him and swirled about them with a wonderful softness. Occasionally, he would hear a bird squawking, searching for its flock or calling out to its parents for more food. He hadn't ever thought about how touching those sounds were. He lifted his head up to study Ruby as she slept and watched her breathe in rhythm with the sounds of nature all around them. She seemed so at peace with herself while he felt an urgency he hadn't known before.

He had to get her to Quindaro as quickly as possible to make sure she was safe. That much he was sure of. He would find her again as soon as he could, but in the meantime, she had to be away from Missouri. If any Jayhawkers crossed into Missouri from Kansas to free more slaves, they would eventually get to Harrisonville and make off with her and Jim, and who knows where they would take them? He would never be able to find her. She had to be safe. He had to make sure she was safe.

Canada couldn't be all that difficult to get to during normal times. Why, hell, he knew Paw had gone all the way to New York City with H.W. Younger to buy goods to sell at the store, most of which they had had shipped, but some of which they had even brought back with them. New York City had to be farther away than Canada. He tried to remember what he had learned in school last year about geography and remembered Canada being sort of to the northeast. It was cold in Canada, but it couldn't be cold the entire year. He wondered if seasons in Canada were the same as seasons in Alabama and Missouri. Probably not.

How would he know where she would go to in Canada? The letters. The ones that Jim had written for her. She would send one once she got to Canada, and then he would know where he had to go to find her and take her to California. Everyone would help him find her. He was sure of that. As long as they didn't know what he was planning for them, that is. If they knew what he had in mind, they might reconsider and try to keep him from finding her. If that were the case, he might never find her. What would happen in the meantime? Would she find someone else before he could reach her if, indeed, he could reach her?

He reminded himself that if he succeeded in getting her to safety in Quindaro, it would be a long time before they would see each other again. Or maybe they would never see each other again. No, that couldn't happen. But if it did, that meant that the first time they had made love would be the only time that they did.

He sighed, the weight of responsibility heavy on his heart.

Whatever happened or didn't happen, they would both have to deal with the aftermath of their decision to have been as intimate as they had been. And they wouldn't have much time to do that if they were as close to reaching Quindaro as he thought they were. He should talk with her, at least raise the subject when she awoke. The world was a different place now in more ways than one.

Should he tell her that he was going to miss her? Should he tell her that he was uncertain about what to do, or should he just dismiss his fears and proceed as if nothing was bothering him?

He had propped himself up on one elbow to get an even closer look at her when he heard them. He reached his hand out to her so he could quickly lift her up on their horse and then scrambled to mount the horse.

Chapter 12

Suddenly, there was a rider in front of him, then another appeared to their right, and one to the left. He held out his hand to Ruby, thinking they could quickly spur their horse, but a fourth horse and rider blocked his way. There was no way to even move their horse forward.

Ruby sat close behind him, and he could smell the fear in her breath. He began to put his hand on top of hers, but thought better of it at the last second and held back. No point in letting them think that there was anything between them, he thought, although he couldn't imagine how that wouldn't be obvious to anyone who saw them together.

The riders' clothes were somewhat worn, and their boots had seen better days. One of them had what Junius thought at first was a lopsided permanent grin on his face until Junius realized it was a deep scar that ran from the right corner of his mouth up the side of his face toward his ear.

The rider in front interrupted the tense silence, saying, "Where you headed with that darkie, fella?"

Junius said, "Are we in Kansas or in Missouri?"

The rider replied, "Well, you'd be in Kansas, son. Why, you from Missouri?"

Ruby's grip tightened just a bit.

"Yes," Junius said, "I'm taking our slave's daughter to Quindaro so she can go free, away from Missouri."

Now Ruby fidgeted.

"Oh, I see. Quindaro, you say? I'd guess that's up near Kansas City, probably on the river. Where in Missouri you from?"

Junius didn't want to say exactly where they were from. Something was telling him to be careful. "Down Cass County way."

"Cass County? There's a lot of secesh down there, ain't that right?"

"Why, yes, I suppose there are."

"But you're not one of them, I guess?" the man asked.

"No, no. Not even my paw. He doesn't like being a slave-owner," Junius answered. He wondered if they would believe him. Were there other slaveowners who didn't like being sla-veowners yet kept their slaves anyway?

"That right? How many other slaves he got?"

"Just her father."

The other riders, except for the one who stayed behind Junius and Ruby, gathered around the one in front, who seemed to be the leader of the small group. After a quick, hushed conversation, the one whom Junius presumed to be the leader said with a broad smile, "I think we can help you out, son."

The hair on the back of Junius's head tingled. Ruby pressed her forehead into his back. "Help? How?" Junius asked.

They must be Jayhawkers, he thought. Why else would they offer to help him out? Surely, they weren't in league with any slave-catchers, not here in Kansas.

"It just so happens that we're headed toward," the lead rider said, "that place, that Quindaro. We were out here mak-ing sure there ain't no raiders in these parts. Haven't found any, just you and the dar ... your slave girl there."

Junius was fairly certain they didn't even know where Quindaro was or what its significance was. It dawned on him that they weren't who they said they were. They certainly weren't Jayhawkers interested in getting Ruby or any slave to safety. The Underground Railroad wasn't something peo-ple talked about openly, and he regretted having mentioned Quindaro to them, but now it was too late.

"If you want, we can finish taking your slave girl to Quindaro and you can head on back to Cass County."

Ruby gasped, and he felt her heart pounding against his back.

Junius was stuck. He needed time to think of how to get out of the situation. "You'd ... make sure she gets there safely, right?"

He felt Ruby tense behind him and imagined her eyes opening wide. Fortunately, she didn't make a sound.

"Hell, yeah, boy, that's exactly what we would do. Guaranteed."

"I don't know. I promised my paw and hers that I would see her all the way to Quindaro. See her safely delivered. I think it best if I just continue on with her. Appreciate the offer to help, though," he said.

Junius turned in his saddle to face what, in fact, were Ruby's wide eyes. In the time it took him to face the front again, all three of them had drawn their pistols and were pointing them at him. A click assured him that the rider behind him had done the same.

"No, son," the leader of the group said, "we'll take care of her from here on. Now get her off your horse and be on your way."

Before he even had time to think about what to do, Junius spurred his horse forward through three of the riders, hoping the surprise and the sudden movement would confuse them enough that he and Ruby could escape. But the jolt made Ruby lose her grip on him, and she fell backward. He had to stop the horse before she slid completely off the animal.

The riders quickly caught up to him. As they did so, one rode ahead of him, two flanked him on either side, and the fourth one brought up the rear. After they surrounded him, the one on the right grabbed his arm, pulling him off the horse and onto the ground. Ruby looked down at him, shaking her head no, no, no ...

As he tried to stand up, she suddenly looked away, up and behind him. "Junius!" she screamed as he turned around quickly, but not quickly enough.

Then everything went dark.

Chapter 13

When Junius awoke hours later, he tried to sit up and get to his feet, but his head hurt terribly. Bit by bit, he remembered what had happened up to the point when the man had pistol-whipped him. What he remembered most of all was the ugly, gap-toothed smiles on the men's faces, their wild eyes, the lopsided grin on the one, and the expression on Ruby's face as she screamed his name.

Once he got his bearings, he spotted hoofprints, but he couldn't be sure that they were headed in what he thought was the direction of Quindaro. It looked like the men had ridden back the way they had come, going further into Kansas. Maybe he was confused by the pain he still felt in his head. The crude map he had drawn with Jim's help before leaving Harrisonville wouldn't do him any good since he had only planned to ride north to Quindaro and then back to Harrisonville. He would have to follow their tracks if he had any hope of finding Ruby. Still woozy from his beating, he mounted his horse and started off. "Ruby, Ruby, I am so sorry," he repeated over and over through tears that he couldn't stop.

Then he felt it. Anger. At first, it was anger toward the men who had taken Ruby. But then his anger turned inward. He was angry at himself. Not just for what he had allowed to happen to Ruby, but for thinking that he could have protected her along the way to Quindaro in the first place. Who was he to take on such a perilous mission with only a rifle and hunting knife to protect them from whatever threats would emerge on their journey? What a fool he had been. And then with what happened between them, what he had felt, what he knew she had felt when they had made love.

How could he have been so naïve? About so many things. He should have known what would have happened between them. And why had he consented to bring along his fife and, worse, play it at all? What a foolish thing to have done. And now, how would he ever find her? And what shape would she be in if and when he did?

He took the instrument case out of the saddlebag and opened it. As he held the fife in his hand, tears flowed. If he hadn't taken it out to play a couple of notes for Ruby, nothing would have happened to them, and they would be safely on their way to the Underground Railroad. Without thinking, he flung the fife as far as he could and rode away.

After a short while, he came across a stream, and the tracks stopped. The men must have ridden the horses up the stream, but how far would he have to ride until they left the stream and he could start tracking them again? He dismounted to see if he could find any more tracks and dipped his hat into the water for a drink.

With that, he quickly realized how hopeless it would be trying to find them again. He didn't know what would become of Ruby and hoped that somehow she could still make it to Quindaro. Maybe they really were Jayhawkers and didn't trust him to get her there. Even as he thought it, he knew that wasn't the case. Maybe he should ride to Quindaro anyway and find someone to explain what had happened. Who would believe him? And what good would it do? There had to be a way, but his head wasn't clear enough to think things through. The only thing he could do was ... what? He couldn't remember the last time he cried, but now he was bawling as he said her name repeatedly. "I am so sorry, Ruby. I didn't mean for this to happen. I don't know how I will or when, but I'll find you and bring you home. I promise."

He mounted his horse and started riding again, retracing

his steps back to where he had thrown the fife away. Once he got there, he searched for half an hour in the brush before he found it. After he had brushed the dirt off, he inspected it thoroughly and found a scratch near the embouchure hole. It didn't look like the wood had been damaged, but he would have to be careful with it just in case there was a tear in the wood that would cause it to splinter. He wanted to yell at it or apologize to it but couldn't decide what to say.

Ultimately, he decided simply to forgive the fife for exposing them to the Jayhawkers. After several minutes, he simply picked it up, replaced it in its case, and put it back into the saddlebag.

Then he rode as fast as he could to the north, toward Kansas City. He vaguely remembered seeing a ramshackle collection of houses that could have been Quindaro slightly to the west of Kansas City when their steamboat had finally docked after the near-disastrous voyage five years earlier. As he entered Kansas City from the south, it was obvious it had grown considerably in the intervening years. The river was just ahead, so Quindaro couldn't be that far away. He studied the map that his father had given him before he and Ruby left Harrisonville and thought that it confirmed his suspicions.

Junius's head had cleared, and all he could think about was the tenderness he and Ruby had shared. She was too good a person to just leave behind to an unknown fate, and now they were permanently linked to each other. The faces of the men who had taken her kept reappearing in his mind. He made sure to remember each and every facet of what they looked like, what they wore, the horses they rode, everything he could. If, by some miracle, they really did take her to Quindaro after they were through with her, he knew what he would have to do to them if and when he found them. No matter the cost.

His head was pounding, and every so often, he had to stop. After resting a bit, he would resume the ride to Quindaro with renewed determination and a growing rage inside him.

Once he reached Kansas City, he asked for directions to Quindaro. The first couple of people looked at him oddly, shook their heads, and turned away without answering. They probably weren't accustomed to seeing a White man asking for directions to Quindaro, he told himself. He was about to give up when, finally, a White man down the road riding out of town stared at him for a moment when he asked for directions, then turned and pointed north toward the river.

"Quindaro is that way?"

The man looked away from Junius. "Yes, and you'll find your kind just before you get there, perched up on a hill they use as a lookout."

"What do you mean, my kind? Lookout?" *How did he know so much about Quindaro?*

"I have business that takes me up to the river, near where the steamboats dock. Have to pass by where everybody suspects the slaves hide out, waiting for that Underground Railroad of theirs to take them elsewhere. Occasionally, I see them sneaking off down a path here and there. Never say anything to anybody, though. Not yet, anyway. I've had a mind to, but I don't see how it benefits me to help someone else catch a runaway. You must be new to this line of work. Of course, you don't expect a slave-catcher to just waltz into a bunch of Africans and expect them to cough up a fellow slave, do ya?"

"No, I guess not." The man thought he was a slave-catcher? What would possess him to think that?

"You guess not? You have a lot to learn about your business, I guess. How many you looking for?" the man said.

"What?"

"How many slaves? I hear it's a good business to get into. Been thinking of doing it myself."

So, it must be true. There were groups of slaves that somehow made it to the Underground Railroad in Quindaro.

"Oh, just one."

"Good strong buck, was he? Owner wants him back bad?"

"No, a female, a young one." Junius invented the story quickly, hoping to convince the man he was a slave-catcher. "I think he wants her back to have her bred."

"I'll bet he does. Probably to breed her himself no doubt!" The man looked off into the distance.

After a moment he said, "Had a right purty one come through here day or so ago. If I remember correctly, four catchers were with her. Looked like she had had a rough time of it, if you know what I mean. Don't know why they took the time to bring her here, though. One of them said that her owner didn't want her no more, so they were supposed to get rid of her, but they must have felt sorry for her, so they brought her up here."

Four catchers. A pretty slave girl. Junius's stomach knotted. Poor Ruby. And yet, maybe he'd be able to find her if he could just coax a little more information out of the man. Junius asked, "What did she look like?"

"Hard to tell. She wouldn't look at anyone and didn't speak at all. Seemed real scared," the man said.

It had to be Ruby. Junius could feel it.

"Where would I find these other catchers?" he asked.

"Oh, they're probably gone by now. They didn't look like the normal slave-catchers, something different about the way they talked and acted. Can't put my finger on it."

"So, you don't know anything else about what might have happened to the girl?" Junius asked.

The man had already turned away from Junius but eventually said, "I couldn't tell you that. If she made it to Quindaro, maybe those railroad folks took her up north somehow, but by the looks of her, I'm not sure she would have made it much further."

Junius felt as though he was about to get sick to his stomach, and it was all he could do to keep from vomiting. He decided to ride on ahead to Quindaro despite the long odds against finding Ruby, or finding anyone who would talk to him about her. He couldn't accept that it was an impossible mission. He rode in the direction that the would-be slave-catcher had pointed out. He went slowly, imagining seeing shadows in the woods off of the road and looking ahead for any encampment that the slave-catchers might have established. Every time he heard a rustling in the woods, he wasn't sure if it was an animal or a runaway slave. This time, however, he kept his rifle by his side just in case he needed it.

Finally, a collection of rough-hewn houses appeared before him. There weren't too many people out and about, and when he occasionally saw a black figure, the person would rapidly disappear inside a building. A man ran into another building that seemed to be more of a permanent structure than any of the other ramshackle huts he had seen so far. He wasn't going to get anywhere with these people. They would obviously conclude he was a slave-catcher. Why else would a White man be roaming the streets of Quindaro? Riding back down the muddy street he had just traversed, he turned around just in time to see a hand reaching out of a building, pointing in his direction.

Just as he passed by a church, the doors opened, and a White woman came out and stood on the steps staring at him.

"May I help you with something, young man?" she said, looking him over suspiciously.

"Yes, ma'am. I am looking for a young African woman," Junius said.

"I'm sorry, I don't know of any young African women here," the woman said, quickly turning away from him.

She probably thinks I'm a slave-catcher. "I was told back in Kansas City that I might find her here."

The woman stopped, turned, and said, "What do you want?"

"Ma'am, I'm not a slave-catcher. I promise you." He began to dismount but thought better of it and stayed on his horse. He took off his hat, thinking that if she saw how young he was, that might convince her that he was being honest with her.

The woman examined him up and down carefully. He figured she must have had this kind of conversation before and had learned not to trust any other White man who entered Quindaro. But he had ridden into town in the middle of the day and didn't try to hide the fact of his arrival. Surely, that would count for something.

Finally, the woman seemed to make up her mind. "No? If you aren't a slave-catcher, then what is your interest in this young woman?"

"I was charged with seeing her to freedom, but we ran into some trouble along the way here, and some Jayhawkers took her from me. We weren't too far from here. It's where I told her father I would bring her."

"I see. So, her father knew what you were doing and approved it?"

"Yes, ma'am, he did."

"These men you claim were Jayhawkers, they took her from you? Is that how you got that cut on your face and how your shirt got torn like that?"

He touched the spot on his cheek she must have been referring to and noticed the tear in his shirt for the first time. "Yes, ma'am, it is."

"What makes you think they brought her here, these Jayhawkers?" she asked. "Jayhawkers aren't normally the type of men who kidnap and abuse slave girls."

"I don't know, ma'am. I don't rightly know. But I need to find her, or find out what happened to her." He felt his eyes starting to water but forced the tears back. The woman had already noticed, however.

The woman leaned forward and reached for her handkerchief. She started toward him but caught herself. "This young woman. She means something to you?"

"I guess you could say that, ma'am. I grew up with her.

First in Alabama then in Harrisonville, down south of Kansas City, on the Missouri side."

"I see. Well, if some Jayhawkers relieved you of her care, why are you concerned? Seems like they would have made sure she is taken care of."

Junius didn't know what to say. How could he explain what had happened between them and then what the Jayhawkers had done to him, and then likely to her?

"There's more to this story, isn't there?" the woman said.

"Yes, ma'am, there is," he said.

She nodded. "All right. We'll discuss that later. It looks like you have been riding hard. Why don't you get off your horse, get him some water, and come inside and tell me the rest of the story? By the way, my name is Clarinda Nichols, and I know most of the people here. And what I don't know, I can find out fairly easily. In the meantime, don't you go asking anyone any questions, do you understand? None of the folks here would trust you for an instant even if I told them that they could. And you stay away from Happy Hollow, you hear?" she said.

"Happy Hollow?" he asked.

"Yes, the hollow where the escapees hide out until we can get them situated," she said.

"Where is that?" he asked.

"Never you mind, young man. At least now I know you're telling me the truth. Any catcher would know about Happy Hollow," she said, "even if they don't know exactly where it is."

Chapter 14

After Junius told Clarinda the whole story, except for the part about his and Ruby's intimacy, she sat silent for several minutes.

"I'll see what I can find out. It may be difficult. If the girl is here, or if she has been here, the people involved in the Underground Railroad may have trouble believing your story. Why would a young White man from Missouri be so interested in finding this young woman when he had delivered her to Jayhawkers?"

"I understand."

He thought carefully about what to say next.

"Ma'am, there's more," he said. "The girl, Ruby, I think she means something to me."

"I figured that might be the case. You say you have known Ruby since you were both children? It stands to reason that you would have developed an affection. That won't make my task any easier though. Not too many African folk who take kindly to the idea of one of their own mating with a White boy such as yourself. Most of them have White men in their blood lines, and not by choice."

Junius thought that through and realized the same would have applied to Ruby. Ruby's mother must have had White blood coursing through her veins for Ruby to have turned out so fair.

"All right, I will try to find out what I can about your precious Ruby. In the meantime, you need to get cleaned up, have a decent meal, and get a good night's sleep," Clarinda said.

The sky was darkening, and off in the distance there was a flash of lightning, then another. They didn't hear any thunder for several seconds, and then only faintly. But the storm was coming closer.

"Yes, ma'am. I'll roll out my bedroll outside of town and sleep with my horse."

"You'll be drenched when the rain comes, and it will. And you can't just find a place to sleep on your own here. You would be viewed with suspicion by both White and Black. Second, given what you have been through, indeed what you are still going through, you need rest. I know the folks who run a decent boarding house here in Quindaro. They won't rent to you, but with my word they will take you in, at least for one night."

Junius allowed himself to be convinced she was right.

Indeed, it did rain all night long, and the streets in Quindaro turned into mud. Clarinda's news the following morning wasn't good either. No one had seen hide nor hair of anyone fitting Ruby's description. Or no one was willing to admit that they had. Someone had seen four men ride into town two days before with one of the men having a bundle tied to the back of his horse, but no one knew what was in the bundle. Three of the men had ridden out of town the next day, but the fourth one tarried a few hours, and rather than going in the direction the others had, he had ridden to the overlook, where the slave-catchers congregated after a few hours. If the bundle had been in his possession, he must have left it behind somewhere.

Junius thought it odd that no one had any information to provide at all, and he wondered if Clarinda perhaps wasn't telling him the whole truth.

Regardless, he decided he had to try one more time before giving up. He couldn't just leave it the way it was. But that meant he had to ask Clarinda for her advice.

"Ma'am, if you were to hazard a guess, where do you think Ruby might be?" he asked her as soon as he saw her the next morning. As she looked around, he held his gaze on her steadily. Without flinching.

She paused long enough to make sure no one could hear her answer him.

"There are several ways she could have gone north, depending on who would have taken her," she said. "It's possible she could have gone straight north, but I suspect whoever is acting as her agent has decided to follow the track called the Lane Trail, as it is the safest way of all of them. Her agent would have taken her west toward Lawrence through several depots where they could hide, if need be, and then on to Topeka, where they would meet a conductor who would be responsible for getting her to the Promised Land, Canada."

Topeka. How far away was that? he wondered.

As if reading his mind, Clarinda said, "Junius, Topeka is over sixty miles from here, and you have no way of knowing if she even went that route, let alone where the station masters' houses that might be serving as her hiding places are."

He considered what she said carefully before answering her. "Ma'am, I can't just give up on finding her. It's my fault this all happened. I can't even live with myself right now, thinking about all she has endured," he said.

"I see. Well, you have to do what you will, I suppose," she said. "Wait right here," she said as she went back inside her house.

When she returned a few minutes later, she was carrying something wrapped in paper and tied with a string around it.

"Can't let you starve. This won't last long, but at least it'll get you started until whatever happens to you," she said as she handed him the small package of food.

"Thank you. When I find her, I'll make sure to come back this way to let you know," he said.

"No, don't you even think about that. That wouldn't be safe for either one of you. You just head to wherever home is as quickly as you can, whether you find her or not," Clarinda said. "Just write me if you do find her once you have her safe and sound at home."

"I'll find her, and when I do, we'll be sure to let you know. Somehow," Junius said.

As he saddled his horse, he thought of one more thing.

It was essential to know more about the place where the slave-catchers positioned themselves, but he had to do it carefully. He asked Clarinda if she knew how he could manage it.

"If, for some reason, I don't find her, someone will have to pay. Where could I intercept the people who took her without giving away where I am?"

He couldn't tell what her look conveyed as she started to answer him.

"There is a spot in the road, near where their lookout is, where you can see them but they can't see you," Clarinda said. "You would have to stay hidden among the trees until one of them rides out, and if he fits the description of one of your four Jayhawkers, you could approach him if you have a mind to. No telling how long you would have to wait though."

Time didn't matter to Junius. Only Ruby's whereabouts and condition were important. He had to find her or find out what happened to her before he could head back to Harrisonville and face Radolfus and Jim. Plus, he had a score to settle with the Jayhawkers. If one of them was involved with the slave-catchers, he needed to understand why.

"I'm so grateful to you, ma'am," Junius said after he mounted his horse.

"You're a good man, Junius. Don't let what happened poison you; that would only be your ruin."

Instead of calming him, her words brought his anger back to the surface. He struggled to control himself as he tipped his hat, pulled on the reins, and began to ride out of Quindaro.

West. To Lawrence and then on to Topeka. The horse seemed to know that they weren't going home. It wasn't walking as fast as it normally did, and Junius thought it was trying to tell him that their search was pointless.

After a couple of hours of unrelenting wind and rain, Junius realized that Clarinda might have been right.

And then it started hailing. Some of the hailstones were as large as his thumb. When the horse started to buck, he finally understood. To continue was senseless. He would never find Ruby. Not without having a clue as to where she had gone. Which direction. He didn't even know if she had made it to Lawrence. And he couldn't continue in this weather.

The rain mixed with his tears as he faced the choice he had to make. There was no choice but to return to Harrisonville and make the best of the situation.

As soon as he turned the horse around, it sensed that they were heading home and picked up its gait. *It knew that the search for Ruby was hopeless,* he thought.

After about two hours, fighting back his doubts and his tears and having skirted around Quindaro, he found the spot that Clarinda must have meant. He did as she suggested and hid amongst the trees. If nothing else, it would keep him from getting any wetter. The rain had gotten into the package of food that Clarinda had wrapped up, and its contents were practically inedible.

After only a few minutes, several riders approached a rise in the distance, and several others rushed down a nearby slope and headed south. Although he couldn't make them out clearly, they were dressed differently than the men who had attacked him and seized Ruby. He rode his horse into the woods on the opposite side of the washed-out road and tried to find a spot where he could watch the riders come and go up and down the slope.

Eventually, a lone rider left the encampment at the top of the rise and started riding slowly toward the south. The slippery conditions were slow going, and the man's horse didn't appear to like walking through all the mud.

He slowly drew closer until Junius could get a good look at his face. *It's him*, Junius thought, and his heart raced. The scar gave the man away.

Leaving the thicket of woods where he had been hiding, Junius rode back into the road, pulled out his rifle but kept it at his side, pointed it downward so the rider wouldn't see it, and approached the man from the rear.

Once he was within twenty yards of the man, Junius called out. "Hey fella, hold up there."

The man pulled his horse up and swiveled in the saddle to cast a bleary glance at Junius. "Who are you?" he asked, his voice thick.

He's hungover, Junius thought. No wonder he was riding so slowly. *And he has no idea who I am.* Junius wondered if the stranger even remembered what he and his friends had done.

Well, it was time to remind him. "Where's the slave girl? The one you took from me," Junius said.

"The one we took from you?" the man said, scratching at the scar on his cheek. "Oh yeah, that young thing," he said, smiling in a way that emphasized his scar even more and reaching down into his saddlebag.

The man smiled awkwardly. Shaking his head, he peered at Junius. "That cute little filly was something. Don't worry; we delivered her to a man who will take care of her the rest of the way."

The bundle. What had they done to her? "Take care of her how?" Junius clenched his jaw and gripped the reins so hard that his knuckles whitened.

"You know, get her north or sell her to the highest bidder. If anyone wants to bid on her," he said. He continued to fumble in his saddlebag. *He really is hungover.*

A sudden noise spooked Junius's horse a bit, which turned in the road just enough to expose the rifle Junius had been hiding until then. The man reached for his pistol. Junius was ready for him. He aimed and fired once. The bullet caught the man in the leg. He cursed Junius as he fell from his horse and, by reflex, fired his pistol in the air. As he fell, the horse bolted and dragged the man along with one foot caught in the stirrup for a couple hundred yards.

Junius approached the man, who was now unconscious, only to find that his foot was twisted and mangled. There was no point in searching the man. His horse had run off, so Junius should just leave the man where he had fallen. If he died, the vultures would pick his bones clean anyway, and that would be what he deserved.

Where would the man's horse have gone? It might return to the slave-catchers' encampment, and if it did, the others would come looking for man lying wounded before him.

He had to leave, and fast.

As Junius galloped away from the man he had shot, he realized his only choice was to return to Harrisonville as quickly as he could. Whatever had happened to Ruby, he couldn't go back to Quindaro. If the slave-catchers found him, there was no telling what they would do to him. And they were bound to be looking for their friend soon, whether they had heard the gunshots or not.

As he put distance between himself and Quindaro, the full horror of what had happened weighed on Junius like a terrible storm that was about to destroy the year's crops. *How will I tell Jim?* he thought. *He trusted me with his daughter's life, and look what I have done.* He couldn't tell either Jim or Paw the truth. He would have to lie. He would say that they had made it safely but that he had returned very quickly so had only said a quick goodbye. On the way home, he had fallen off the horse when it had been spooked by shots in the distance, which accounted for the scratch on his face and the bump on his head.

It would be all right because he'd find her eventually. He had to. And he wouldn't play the fife again until he did.

Chapter 15

As Junius rode back to Harrisonville, he was confident that he could explain things satisfactorily to Radolfus and Jim, even if he himself knew whatever he would say would be a bald-faced lie. His story was certainly believable, and after all, he had actually been to Quindaro and had seen how the escaped slaves comported themselves while awaiting their journey to Canada. Of course, he could explain the bump on his head and the scratches on his face and his torn shirt.

The only problem he could think of would be the scratch on the fife. If Radolfus were to see that, he would wonder how it could have been damaged. As he dwelt on that possibility, his confidence in being able to pull off convincing his father and Jim of his story slowly evaporated. The closer he got to home, the more anxious he became. He had really caused a tragedy to occur, and it was all his fault. No one else's. Just his alone.

When he returned home, Junius explained that their trip had been relatively uneventful and that he had safely deposited Ruby with folks from the Underground Railroad in Quindaro. The more he talked, the more each lie built upon the previous one, but he found it easy to continue. The alternative was to be discovered as a total failure, so the lies just mushroomed. He had to remind himself to smile in between the successive lies; otherwise, his whole story would fall apart. In order to continue with the fairy tale he had created, he couldn't look at his father or Jim because they would see right through him.

He described the trip and how they slept during the day and traveled by night, what they did for food, and how they stayed warm, omitting the obviously intimate parts. He explained that as they got closer and closer to Quindaro, Ruby grew more and more excited but at the same time would start crying at what she had to give up. While she had seemed nervous at first, she gradually grew calmer and occasionally would even comment on the different trees and flowers that they passed, saying, "Junius, look there!"

"I never knew the girl could talk so much!" Junius said, forcing a smile.

Jim, somewhat recovered from his back injury, paid close attention to every word Junius said.

Radolfus said, "Well done, son!" and went back inside to retrieve his pipe.

Sarah Anne stayed behind to listen to the rest of what Junius had to say.

"How did you get that scratch on your cheek?" she asked as she ran her fingers over the scratch and examined him for any other wounds.

"Oh, that. The horse stumbled due to all the rain, and I was so tired I fell off and hit a rock."

Sarah Anne shook her head and said, "Must have been a mighty big rock."

Jim had lots of questions about Quindaro. Junius tried to describe to him as well as he could what the settlement looked like and how the people acted and reacted to him. Each time he volunteered additional information, Jim asked additional questions. And each question he asked forced Junius to develop bigger lies. His stomach knotted more and more with each lie, and he was perspiring, but everyone seemed to accept what he said as the truth.

He mentioned that Quindaro wasn't that far from the spot where the steamboat they had been on five years earlier had almost been swamped. Junius said that he had even met a number of other contrabands there. He swore that he had seen Ruby being welcomed by a group heading for Canada soon thereafter. That would surely convince them that he had succeeded in getting Ruby to safety. How could they doubt him when he told them that?

Knowing that that was anything but the truth and that Ruby's fate was very much in doubt made him sick to his stomach.

At that moment, Jim asked, "The other contrabands talked to you?"

There was nothing to do but continue to lie. "Not at first. But when they saw I was leaving Ruby with them, they smiled at me and wished me well on my journey home," he said.

When he was through telling them about the return trip and how uneventful it had been except for falling off his horse, Jim didn't say anything for a few seconds. Junius had pulled it off. They believed him.

"Did she give you anything to give to me?" Jim asked.

"Something to give you?" Junius said, and then remembered Ruby telling him about the letter Jim would be expecting just before answering no.

"Oh, the letter," he said, blurting out the words.

Jim smiled thinly. "Yes, the letter."

Junius made as if to search through his pockets looking for the letter. "It must have fallen out when I fell off the horse."

Jim looked hard at Junius but didn't say anything.

Radolfus returned, pipe in hand, and asked to see the fife. Junius handed it to him and watched intently as his father opened the case and smiled down at the instrument. "I'm glad to see that no harm came to Opa's fife," he said as he closed the instrument case without examining the instrument any further.

Junius tried to avoid Jim's gaze as best he could, but could feel the tension mounting. He'd had no choice but to lie about what happened. If he hadn't, they would've thought he had betrayed their trust. Besides, there was no way they would ever find out what had really happened to Ruby. As soon as he could, he would figure out how to get back to Quindaro, or Canada, or wherever she was, and bring her back safely. He had to.

Radolfus smiled at his son. "Well, that is a disappointment, but at least you got her there safe and sound. And now she's probably on her way to Canada."

Junius avoided looking at Jim and Sarah Anne as his father congratulated him. "If you'll excuse me, I'd like to go lie down for just a bit and then maybe take out my fife for a while," he said, looking down at the ground.

Chapter 16

April 1861

Word arrived via the telegraph late that Friday afternoon, April 12, 1861, that Confederate forces had fired on Fort Sumter. Junius stayed late at the *Gazette*, printing out the special one-page edition of the paper per Mr. Fogle's instructions. Mr. Boggess barked instructions at everyone in the offices to hurry up and get the paper printed. He smiled as he walked around the office, proclaiming, "Finally, it's begun."

Junius couldn't stop thinking about Ruby and what might have become of her, especially now that war had broken out. Then Fort Sumter fell, and the two sides were bracing for what everyone in Harrisonville was sure would be a short affair culminating in the Confederacy being victorious. Most of the residents of Cass County believed that preserving the Union wasn't as important as preserving a way of life predicated on maintaining the institution of slavery, which was what God intended.

Junius couldn't really imagine what it would be like to live in a country that wasn't the United States, but at the same time, what the Jayhawkers had done with Ruby made him wonder if it wasn't the best idea to simply allow the states to go their separate ways.

On top of worrying about how he would ever find Ruby, now that the war was making things more difficult, Junius lived in dread that the Jayhawkers who had kidnapped Ruby would hunt him down. They were sure to find out what he had done to their comrade. Did they remember that he had said he was from Cass County? Had he mentioned Harrisonville to them? Every time he saw a stranger in town, he would conjure up the kidnappers' faces. Only when he was satisfied that they weren't staring back at him did he lower his guard. Even then, however, whenever he heard gunfire, he flinched. It didn't matter whether someone was shooting rabbits or deer; he was half-convinced that someone was aiming his rifle at him.

It was true that the Jayhawkers had betrayed his trust, and if that was what it was like to be on their side in the conflict, Junius didn't want any part of dealing with them as allies. Not after what they had done to Ruby. Nevertheless, he would have to contend with going to war sooner or later. The question was which side offered the greater opportunity to find Ruby and would take him closer to Quindaro. And, from there, where she had gone and how they could resume their much-delayed trip to California.

As anxious as he was to learn as much as he could about what was happening in South Carolina, Junius was also desperate to return home and tell his father the news. His father would be distraught that his adopted country had, in fact, not only splintered but was warring against itself over an issue that shouldn't even exist. Slavery, not just the slave trade, should have been banned and the whole system dismantled years ago. Junius could only imagine what Jim would think, especially if Missouri were to actually secede and the future he had imagined for himself and Ruby in California thoroughly destroyed. He couldn't even imagine how Sarah Anne would react to the news, given her feelings about leaving her home in Alabama, now at war with the rest of the country.

One of the two other printer's apprentices who worked with Junius on the presses was babbling away about how it was about time the Southern states were standing up for themselves. Finally, one of them simply removed his smock and rushed out of the building, saying he was off to join up.

"I'll ride my horse to South Carolina if I need to, but I'm gonna get me some Yankees!"

Several bystanders had entered the offices to find out the latest once the initial news arrived. Other men stood outside the building, craning their necks to see inside the offices as if they would be able to absorb the news in that manner.

The other apprentice, who had just started at the paper the week before, was much quieter. Junius accepted a tray of type from him, but as he grasped it, a droplet of water landed on one of the lines of type. Junius looked up from the tray and realized the apprentice was weeping.

Mr. Boggess approached the young man. "What is it, boy? Those aren't sad tears, are they?"

The apprentice kept his head down and didn't answer.

"You'd best be glad of this, or you might as well head on out of here now!" Mr. Boggess bellowed.

Junius watched as the boy tore off his smock and ran out of the building to catcalls from the assembled multitude. Paw was right. *Can't let on what your true sympathies are. Not in this neck of the woods.*

Junius arrived home just before sunset, later than usual, to see Radolfus waiting for him on the front porch. Sarah Anne was just inside the front door, peering out. Jim walked from across the road toward the Hart household.

"Is it true, son?" Radolfus asked.

"Yes, sir, I'm afraid it is. The fort has been surrendered, and it appears that war is the likely outcome."

Upon hearing the news, Jim shook his head and headed back toward his cabin.

Making sure he was out of earshot of Sarah Anne, Radolfus took his son aside and whispered, "The folks at the paper, they don't know what our politics are, do they, son?"

"No, sir. Not a chance. You should have seen what

Mr. Boggess did to the new boy as soon as he realized that his family are Lincolnites," Junius said.

The following month was agony for all of them. As anxious as they were to hear the latest news, they kept to themselves as much as possible. Junius would report back on what little new information came in to the newspaper offices daily, but there wasn't much to report.

Then, on May 10, news came that Union Brigadier General Nathaniel Lyon and his six thousand federal troops had marched on Camp Jackson in St. Louis, where Governor Jackson had assembled nine hundred men of the Volunteer Militia, most of whom were new recruits. Once Lyon's men attacked, only about one-third of Jackson's men were able to escape. Lyon had the captured militia recruits march through the streets of the city, which made violence erupt, and in the ensuing melee, over one hundred civilians were killed and wounded, along with two federal soldiers and three members of the volunteer guard.

News of the Camp Jackson Affair spread by telegraph throughout the state quickly, as the Yankees hadn't yet cut the telegraph lines. Junius heard the news the following morning and immediately left for home to let Radolfus know. Four days later, the General Assembly authorized the governor to disband the militia and recreate it as the Missouri State Guard.

"So, what's it going to be, Junius?" Mr. Boggess asked before he left work the next day. "You gonna join up? The militia will become the State Guard pretty soon."

Junius wasn't sure how to respond and even more unsure whether he even wanted to.

"I don't know, Mr. Boggess. Seems like it might be a tricky affair. A short one maybe, but tricky anyways," he said.

"I doubt there is going to be anything tricky about it. I have it on good authority that the State Guard is going to stay put right here in Missouri. The governor wants the Guard to protect communities like ours from any more raids by those Jayhawkers. The most the Guard might do is venture into Kansas to keep people like that abolitionist John Brown from freeing any more of our property and kidnapping our farmers and ranchers. Devil's spawn that he was," he said as he spat some tobacco on the floor.

"The Guard would deal with any Jayhawkers?" Junius asked.

"That's what my sources tell me, that's for sure," Mr. Boggess said.

Fire came into Junius's eyes.

Mr. Boggess nodded and smiled. Junius took off his apron, gathered up his few personal belongings, and left the building, walking home briskly.

He made up his mind on the way home. The outcome of the war, or the first part of it, wasn't anywhere near as important as finding Ruby, regardless of what that entailed. And it was because of the war that he probably had a chance to find her. Without it, he would be hard-pressed to find a reason to leave Harrisonville again. The best way to get revenge for what happened to Ruby, he believed, was to join the State Guard. Mr. Boggess was probably right. The State Guard would surely be staying in Missouri and might even head to Kansas to retrieve runaway slaves.

That meant there was a chance he could find Ruby if, in fact, she hadn't made it as far as the Lane Trail. A slim chance, but a chance, nonetheless.

"Where's Paw?" he asked his stepmother as soon as he got home, breathless. She pointed with her head out to the field where Radolfus was tending to the tobacco.

"Why?" Sarah Anne asked.

"I'm leaving. I'm joining the militia. As soon as I pack, I'll tell Paw."

Sarah Anne's mouth fell open. "Well, I'll be. It seems you

have some sense in you after all. And here I thought your father had messed with your mind so much that you had lost all reason."

Junius raced past his younger brother and sisters and to his bedroom, and grabbed his knapsack, his other pair of boots, three shirts, two pairs of trousers, stockings, and his knife. Then he picked up his fife and carried it in his free hand. Saying goodbye to everyone, and lastly to Sarah Anne, he walked outside just as Radolfus was returning from the tobacco field.

Radolfus put down his hoe and his bag.

"Junius, what are you doing?" he asked.

After Junius loaded his belongings on his horse, he turned to Radolfus.

"Got to go, Paw."

Radolfus sagged and shook his head. "I guess I know you do. I just didn't think it would be so soon. The U.S. Army hasn't even started accepting volunteers or conscripting in these parts yet. You be careful. Remember what your grandfather told me. Don't trust the officers," Radolfus said.

"Paw ..."

"And don't you forget who you are, son! You make us proud of you but don't do anything stupid. I see you've got your fife. Don't you forget what that instrument means to this family. You take care of it and make sure you stay out of the way of any fighting. When this thing is over in a few months, you come back home. Don't be heading off to anyplace else, like St. Louis or Cincinnati."

Radolfus wiped at his eyes. "You be careful until you find them soldier boys. There's the State Guard and lots of other secesh hereabouts, and they won't take kindly to you riding off to join the Yankees."

He thinks I'm going to fight for the Yanks! Junius couldn't face his father as he almost choked on what he knew he had to say next.

"I'm not joining the Yankees, Paw. I'm joining the Volunteer Militia," he said.

"You're what?" Radolfus grabbed his son's shoulder with a shaking hand. As Junius tried to break free, his father reached out to him with his other hand as well and wouldn't let go. "You can't mean it."

"I do. I can't explain it to you. It's something I have to do, and when it's all over, you'll understand."

With that, he mounted his horse and rode off toward Jefferson City. He didn't look back.

Chapter 17

It took Junius four days to ride the 130 miles to Jefferson City, where the Guard units were being formed. Along the way, he met a number of other men of all ages who were also headed there to join up.

One man riding a horse that looked like it was just this side of dying, however, was riding in the opposite direction. He stopped and looked at the men marching toward Jefferson City and wiped a tear from his eye. Then Junius noticed that his other eye had a black patch over it, and he was missing his left hand.

"You make sure you give them Yanks hell, boys! I wish I could be with you, but they say I can't fight. Not sure why that's the case, just cuz I lost my eye and a hand in a tussle some years ago. Hell, I can still see outta my good eye and load my pistol with my teeth," he said to general laughter.

One of the men next to Junius said, "You better get yourself on home, old man, and make sure you can protect your family from any Yanks we send running away from Missouri!"

"I'll do that, I reckon, but I'm gonna miss being with you boys. Where you fellas from, anyway?" he said, looking directly at Junius.

"Harrisonville, over in Cass County near Kansas," Junius answered.

"I suspect you're in luck then. You'll probably be under General Price's command. Old Pap is a fine man and a good soldier, too, going all the way back to the Mexican War. I don't care what anyone says about him; he'll take care of his boys," the old man said.

He explained that he understood that the Guard was to be organized geographically, based on Missouri's existing congressional districts. As Harrisonville was the county seat for Cass County, Junius subsequently discovered he would be assigned to the Third Regiment of the Eighth Division, the division commanded by Brigadier General James S. Rains under the overall command of General Price.

As a member of the Guard, he would be in the infantry and wouldn't need his horse. Instead, once his horse had been rested, it would be loaned to one of the officers and returned to him at the cessation of hostilities. He wanted to protest because it seemed grossly unfair, but was told that doing so would be an act of insubordination. Paw would be furious if anything happened to the horse, but there wasn't anything he could do about it, at least not right away. Maybe he could find a way to make sure the horse was looked after if he could somehow befriend the officer to whom he was assigned. He'd have to scour the hills for apples, and maybe he could squirrel away a sugar cube now and then for him, too.

"Don't worry, we'll take good care of the animal," said the young man who would get his horse. Junius wondered why that man was destined to be an officer. He looked to be no older than Junius but had a nicer uniform, a brand-new rifle, and a saber that looked expensive.

"You will?" asked Junius.

"Course I will," the young man responded. "My paw has a whole bunch of horses back home. Good ones, too. Some we even race against others. I know what I'm doing when it comes to taking care of these animals. Trust me."

Is that how he became an officer? Junius wondered. His paw was a rich man?

"What's your name?" Junius asked.

"Michael, Michael Burns. I'm from Rolla. How about you?"

"Junius Hart. Harrisonville."

"Nice to make your acquaintance, Junius. I'm sure we'll meet up again in the coming days. And you can visit your horse whenever you want to," Michael said. "When you look for me, just look for Lieutenant Burns. That's what Paw said I'd be."

Soon-to-be Lieutenant Burns looked to be a nice enough young man, but Junius quickly realized that it would be the rich ones who would become the officers. Why couldn't Michael Burns have brought his own horse to this affair? His paw had several, so what would it bother him to have one for his son, for whom he had probably just purchased a commission? Well, things would be different when everything was all organized, Junius was sure.

Some of the men expressed their surprise when told they wouldn't need to sign any paperwork. That would come later when things were more organized.

"I guess this really is a volunteer outfit!" Junius heard one of the men say. "Hell, back in the Mexican war, we all had to sign up to make sure we got paid."

One of the sterner-looking men who was assigning different new arrivals to their units said, "As this is a volunteer organization, pay is something that has yet to be worked out. It may take a while. In the meantime, you'll be fed whatever is available, and we'll make sure you have plenty of water to drink."

After they dispersed, a group of men from the same town up north groused, "Gonna be tough to stay afloat with enough Apple Lady without any money to buy any." Junius laughed when he heard them talking about the hard cider his classmates would sneak occasionally after school. "Guess we'll have to rely on the kindness of the folks we're protecting to be good to us! Lord knows these folks must drink liquor, too!"

"Man can't fight without Apple Lady!" one man protested, to a rousing cheer.

After the cheering died down, general disappointment

was obvious. A few of the men were no longer in the camp the next morning, apparently having slunk off during the night back to their farms.

When Junius announced it was his intention to become a member of the Guard's band after reveille, some of the older recruits laughed derisively.

"You gonna be a drummer boy?" one grizzled old soldier asked.

"No, fifer."

"What in tarnation is a fife? Couldn't you learn how to play a real instrument? One of them horns or something?" the grizzled man asked as the other soldiers laughed.

Just then, Lieutenant-to-be Michael Burns reappeared on another mount. The men weren't sure whether they should salute him yet since they weren't technically in the Guard yet, and he wasn't really an officer yet. They more or less just looked at him questioningly.

"Come on, man, you must know what a fife is. Or are you just joshing my friend Junius Hart here? A fife goes with a drum sure as shooting, and I suspect we'll all find that out real soon," Lieutenant Burns said.

The grizzled soldier said, "I suppose you're right, there. Here's hoping you know how to play that thing good, Junius."

Most of the men were bearded and looked like they had lived most of their lives outdoors. Junius had spent his fair share of time outdoors as well, and his neck was burnt from the sun at times, but not like these men. Nevertheless, he was quickly mustered in and welcomed by his company, which consisted of another fifer and a drummer.

Around the campfire at night, a few of the men whom he met along the way showed him what they called daguerre-otypes, which supposedly illustrated what their wives and mothers looked like. It was hard to believe that some sort of infernal machine could capture their image, and none of them looked all that appealing. But the men who had them treasured them. He wondered what a daguerreotype of Ruby would look like. He shuddered when he imagined one of Sarah Anne.

He quickly found out from the music teacher who had volunteered to be the bandmaster that the fife was the only wind instrument that the larger regimental band would have and that there were only a couple of other fifers. There was one bugler, but he was kept in reserve at regimental HQ. There were numerous other drummers of various ability and talent. Some of them thought they could play the drums, but it was more like guys just beating sticks without any rhythm. Junius thought back to the times he had heard the slaves play whenever Jim took him places and longed for musicians of that caliber. There were numerous horns in evidence, too, but once he heard them play, Junius wasn't sure that many of the fellows with the horns had ever had lessons on the instruments. He even spied a fiddle and a banjo when he was introduced to the rest of the members of the band and was at a loss as to how they would be able to blend their music into that of the rest of the band. Time would tell.

The bandmaster decided it would be a good idea if the band members bivouacked together, but the members of the fledgling band flocked back to sleep with their comrades from their hometowns or counties every chance they had. Junius didn't mind either way because he didn't really know anyone from Harrisonville in his regiment. Most of the members of the regiment were from other towns in Cass County and were farmers with little to no formal schooling. All of a sudden, Junius felt good about how Paw had insisted he stay in school as long as he had. Not only could he read music, but he could read and write without having to sound out or spell out each and every word that was written on the orders posted around camp. He didn't advertise this ability, often declining to offer to read letters from home for other soldiers, however, especially since, even though no one knew he was Jewish, that alone would make him stand out from most of the others in the Guard.

The members of the band had to scamper back to their assigned area as soon as reveille sounded at 4:30 every morning. Before that time, as much as he could, Junius tried to use the latrine when he figured no one else would be around. That meant getting up before reveille most mornings and waiting until twilight at night. He was pretty sure he had been able to keep the other members unaware of the fact that he had been circumcised.

"We got us a drunk for a commanding officer," one of the men from Sarcoxie who knew of Rains said around the campfire the first night Junius was with his unit.

"How do you know?" one of the other men asked.

Spitting out a wad of tobacco toward the fire, the first man said, "Hell, we all know what he's like down in Newton County. Every time someone goes to see him to ask him for a favor, he reeks of alcohol. All you need to do is bring a bottle of Kentucky bourbon with you, and you'll have your request granted. No Tennessee Whiskey, though; that's a sure no."

Despite Junius's newfound misgivings about his decision to join up, he thought that he had done the right thing, if for no other reason than he might have an opportunity to find Ruby. In addition, he had never been amongst a bunch of men before who all seemed united in their purpose. Nor had he ever really been able to play his fife accompanied by other musicians with a wide assortment of instruments.

He already knew most of the tunes that the bandmaster wanted the band to play, and it was surprisingly easy to incorporate the fife music into the band's repertoire, even if it was only a minor contribution. Unlike the other band members, he didn't have to put his fife in his tent once the band was finished playing, as the battle began. Instead, he could simply stick it into its case and slide it under his belt. One of the tunes, however, that he was unfamiliar with but was popular with the men was one called "Maryland, My Maryland." It was a rousing tune full of the fighting spirit he felt imbued the Guard units he saw marching and drilling, but he didn't understand why it was so popular. Maryland hadn't joined the Confederacy, had it?

"No, Maryland hasn't yet seceded from the Union, but it certainly will soon enough," Sergeant Barnard said.

"It will? You're sure of that?" Junius asked.

Ignoring his questions, Sergeant Barnard continued, "And when it does, Lincoln and all the rest of those Black Republicans in Washington will be surrounded by the patriotic sons of Virginia and Maryland, and it will just be a question of time before this war is over and we can all go home. Might be too soon for me, really. I need to dip my hands in Yankee blood a little more."

Junius studied Sergeant Barnard for a long minute before asking again, wanting to make sure he answered him this time. "When do you think Maryland will secede, Sarge?"

"Any day now, any day."

As time went on, it became obvious just how different being in the band was than what Junius had imagined. Band members certainly weren't afforded any special treatment, and, in fact, they were looked down upon by many of the regular soldiers since they also performed other menial duties that didn't involve soldiering. Digging latrines was the one Junius hated the most.

The bandmaster was a man from St. Louis by the name of Stevens. He was thin and wiry, but Junius sensed nerves of steel in him. He wore the rank of a brevet captain, and Junius thought that eventually, the brevet would be removed and he would be made a captain permanently.

"You men have an important role to perform whenever we meet the enemy. And that is to prepare the men for battle. Some of them will be wounded, possibly even die. And even though you will be the ones who they will follow into battle and off the battlefield, it will be up to you to tend to them if and as they fall when they're fighting," Brevet Captain Stevens said when he was finally able to assemble the entire band together days later.

"You will see men whom you know and become friends with fall, and there won't be anything you can do about it, no matter how quickly you get them off the field. You will have to simply go back to work to get the next man off the field when he falls. And you will see other men lose their limbs in ways that you can't even begin to imagine. And those images will haunt you if you let them, so don't. Then, when it is all over, you'll have to get your instrument, your drum or your horn or whatever, and make sure the men stay together. They will be counting on you. We all will be," Brevet Captain Stevens concluded.

Junius decided to talk to the young drummer, who he had learned was also from Cass County, about being his fellow stretcher-bearer. He looked like a strong young man who wouldn't panic when the fighting began and chaos ensued. All he knew about him was that his name was Timothy.

In July, the Eighth Division had its first taste of battle in Carthage. The band, such as it was, offered its rousing introduction. Before they were even finished, Junius heard gunshots. Not from the Confederate side toward the Yankees, but the reverse.

Junius tucked his fife into his belt and joined the other members of the band as they hastened to claim the stretchers they would need as they assumed their battlefield duties. Although it had been explained to him and to the rest of the band what they were expected to do, he had a hard time imagining what would happen.

"We probably won't be that busy," one of the younger

drummers said.

"No?" Junius asked.

"Naw, them Yanks are gonna run the other way as soon as they see us coming their way. You watch and see. We'll be playing them a lullaby as they head out of town after we whip 'em good."

"There's twenty of us in the band. And we're paired up with ten stretchers. Somebody must think we're gonna be needed," Junius said.

"Yeah, but not for no Rebs. Mainly for the Yanks we're gonna be killing! We'll drag 'em off the field after the battle and find out what's in their pockets. Maybe get enough greenbacks for a poker stake," the drummer said to rousing laughter.

Before he could say anything else, chaos erupted around him. Officers rode horses back and forth, darting into the commander's tent and just as quickly rushing away. One of them was shot off his horse as soon as he left the camp and was dragged along for several yards before the stirrup finally broke. Two soldiers raced to pick him up and carry him back to camp, risking their lives in the process. Junius wasn't sure the man was still alive, and then he saw the doctor shake his head and the soldiers remove his body from the operating slab and take it to where a pile of bodies was beginning to grow.

As the battle progressed, Junius and Timothy carried several soldiers off the field for what must have been an hour before they stopped to drink some water. Junius tried to stay focused and not think about the men's wounds, but couldn't help glancing at their faces. Some moaned in agony, others wailed, a few cried, and several stared blankly at the sky.

Eventually, seeing their wounds was simply unavoidable. Sometimes, putting a man on a stretcher meant coming in contact with the wound, and that meant the blood and whatever else was associated with it. Then he had to turn his head away as quickly as possible before he felt his stomach turn and heaved his breakfast onto the ground or, worse, onto the wounded man on the stretcher. Whatever the other stretcher-bearer said to him, he either couldn't hear or didn't remember. It was as if he couldn't hear anything, not even the gunfire or the barked orders from presumed officers or the cannons firing in all directions. Only if a soldier was hit near him and crumpled to the ground beside him did he hear the man's fall.

Bullets flew in every direction, but, amazingly, none came close to him or to Timothy as they worked the battlefield. All he wanted to do was hear the battle end and enjoy a smoke together and maybe a bit of Apple Lady. He had recently discovered that a smoke now and then helped calm his nerves.

He no sooner thought this than Timothy's head was lying beside the wounded man on the stretcher. They looked angelic, lying together, but only the wounded man was smiling, at least until he saw the head next to him and either fainted or died himself; Junius was too numb to care. He dropped the stretcher, put Timothy's head next to his body as carefully as he could, and then, with the help of a retreating soldier, dragged the stretcher back to camp and dropped the wounded man at the surgical tent. The surgeon simply glanced in his direction and shook his head before the orderlies whisked the body away to a pile of other bodies.

Looking back toward the battlefield, all he could see for a time was smoke of different colors: gray, black, and white. He wondered what kind of armament produced each color but snapped back into the present when he heard a scream. One of the men he had just brought off the field was biting into a filthy cloth as one of the doctors held a scalpel with a Catlin knife lying next to him.

"Watch what happens now," one of the soldiers from his unit, a fellow named Clem, said as he walked up beside Junius.

"Why?" Junius asked.

"You'll see. And hear!" Clem said, looking intently toward the action. "Now, old sawbones is gonna go to work."

The doctor picked up a scalpel and cut through the skin of the man's arm, then reached for a double-bladed surgical knife and cut through the muscle. The muscle twitched. He picked up a saw. Junius tried to look away but sat transfixed on his haunches as he watched the surgeon go to work. The soldier screamed, and once again, Junius's ears simply closed up. He couldn't hear anything, although the sounds of the surgeon separating limb from body were all too obvious to everyone else.

The doctor sawed and sawed until another soldier's arms dropped by his side. One of the medics tried to catch it before it hit the ground, but it was all too quick. The doctor told him to pick it up, wash it off, and stick it in a bucket. The medic did so as the bucket rapidly filled with numerous limbs. Junius swore some of them were still moving. Then he got sick.

Suddenly, he and the other members of the band were called into formation. They were to prepare to play the soldiers off the field. The bandmaster hadn't thought to instruct them how to do that. Did they think they would never have to retreat? What was the appropriate song to play at such a time? One of the buglers in the band stepped forward and started playing taps.

The men started to fall back. Junius kept playing as more and more men emerged from the battlefield, some using their rifles like walking sticks, others helping those more seriously wounded. Junius started to go forward to assist when the bugler stopped playing. Junius wondered why the man had dropped his bugle. Junius bent down to pick it up just as the bugler pitched forward onto the ground beside him. He must have tripped on something; that was Junius's first thought until he saw the bugler's mouth had disappeared.

He tried to get his fife out to sound retreat, but it wouldn't carry far enough for the soldiers to hear it. With that, the band members broke ranks and joined in a generally disorganized retreat. Confederate soldiers were running every which way out of camp, hiding behind trees and boulders when possible and occasionally taking potshots at the Yankees who ventured ahead of their lines to hunt them down. Slowly, they began to emerge from their hiding places and cautiously retrace their steps back to what was left of their camp. Junius lay motionless in a shallow hole covered with leaves until it was quiet.

At dusk, the firing stopped. The Yankees had evidently given up chasing the Confederates for the day. Junius didn't understand anything about what had happened. Who had won, and who had lost? Had either side won anything?

The Rebs were still bivouacked where they had started the day, although there were fewer of them around the campfire. And there was moaning coming from inside the surgeon's tents, punctuated now and then by a scream and then sudden silence briefly before the screaming started again.

Occasionally, an officer would ride slowly by and try to mutter something encouraging to the men, but Junius could tell it was a half-hearted effort at best. There was no standard rally-around-the-flag impromptu speech given, and there were no huzzahs by the men. They were too exhausted, and there weren't enough of them to make enough noise.

They must have lost. Half the men who had been there the night before laughing and swearing at the Yanks were simply not there. This probably would be a short affair after all, only not the way that they had envisioned it.

"Did you see what happened when that Yankee colonel attacked? I heard the major say his name was Sigel. Hell, it looked like they were gonna wear us down. Then, all of a sudden, those recruits of ours started marching in. Sigel must have thought they were his own reinforcements. Then he realized they were butternuts just like us and decided to fight them. But they didn't even have guns!" Corporal Brown said when they were all able to lie down and rest.

"Yeah, but when the Yanks retreated back into town, how come we couldn't finish them off?" a private named Grover asked.

"Not really sure what happened there. But it shows us that the people of Missouri are behind our cause; that's for sure!" the first soldier said.

Junius wondered how accurate that statement was. Governor Jackson called the battle a victory for the Guard, but at what cost?

Just as it had happened at Carthage when Sigel had out-smarted Union Brigadier General Lyon and Governor Jackson, Junius found the after-battle routine to be frighteningly similar. When the fighting finally ended for the evening, the men would lick their wounds, try to wash a little of the blood and muck off their hands and faces, and get in line for chow, if there was any to be had. There usually was, but you could never take that for granted, the men would say. Even when they had food, the complaints about how wretched it was would start even before they had their share ladled out into their mess kits.

"I saw one boy who lost half his face," one soldier said.

"One of us or a Yankee?" another one laughed.

"I think he was one of us, but I looked away so quickly I don't know whether he was wearing blue or gray," the first soldier said.

"I saw one who was wounded pretty bad, but I thought he had a chance, so I started to pull him by the legs to put him on the stretcher, but his leg came off in my hand. Never heard a man scream so loud," another chimed in.

"What did you do with him?" another asked.

"Left him there. Screaming. But I got his boots off first. Mighty nice ones, too."

"Must have been a Yankee then," another said to general laughter.

Junius didn't contribute to these conversations. He tried to put the images he saw out of his head as much and as quickly as he could. One wounded Reb soldier stuck in his mind, though. As Junius had bent down to place a soldier lying next to him, the soldier had stared back at him. His eyes had never wavered as Junius went about his work.

"I'll be right back for you!" he had said as he and the other stretcher-bearer carted off the first soldier. The other soldier carrying the stretcher had stared at Junius.

Once they dropped the first soldier off, Junius had said, "Let's go get the other one out there."

"Hart, there's no point in going back for the other one."

"Why not? He looked hurt pretty bad."

"Hart, his head wasn't attached to his body. He wasn't staring at us. His eyes were open because he was dead."

Trying to put the image out of his mind, Junius forced himself to concentrate on his duties despite the sounds of the cannons and the officers barking orders and the men yelling in pain as they were mowed down. He found himself thinking about anything but the battle they had just experienced, and that usually meant thinking about Ruby.

Rather than talk about what they had seen and experienced that day, the conversations around the campfires at night inevitably turned toward loved ones left behind. Mothers, wives, lovers, girlfriends. The same daguerreotypes were produced over and over. Some had stories about more than one; others had only one. Whenever a daguerreotype was produced, it was passed around. A soldier would hold it in front of the soldier who had a fiddle, and if he approved, he would add a little flourish to the next notes that he played. When he didn't approve or found the daguerreotype lacking, he'd play softer and the men would laugh.

Junius had no daguerreotypes or stories about women he could share. He hardly remembered his mother and didn't want to talk about his stepmother. And Ruby wasn't his girlfriend, or was she? Lover? Yes, but he couldn't admit to that. Could he? Some of the men, the older ones, took pride in regaling the younger soldiers with their tales of how they had conquered this or that slave girl when they had worked as foremen on different plantations, but you could never tell whether their stories were true.

At first, Junius had been proud of his role in the ensemble leading the troops into battle while at the same time being able to stay above the fray. But then he realized that every time the band played a note, countless of his comrades would be dead or wounded within hours, or sometimes even minutes. From the time the band quit playing, he would soon be picking up pieces of men he had eaten with and drunk with the night before. After a battle ended, when he was able to return to the encampment, he usually got sick, often violently. Initially, the other band members mocked and laughed at him, but slowly, surely, they, too, became just as afflicted. Once in a while, as they sat around the campfire, someone would realize that one of their company was missing. Unable to search for the missing member until the next morning, they would raise a silent toast to the missing and presumed dead member.

A month after what was supposedly a victory at Carthage, the Eighth was about to enter into battle again fifty miles east of Carthage at Dug Spring. Seeing the more experienced Guard commander retreating as the federal cavalry broke through the lines, Colonel Rains ordered an all-out retreat, and the Eighth was at least spared the ignominy of participating in the disastrous battle.

"Why did we retreat? We had them outnumbered!" several

of the soldiers grumbled once they bivouacked for the night. Corporal Brown merely said, "Rains got scared." The men took to calling the battle of Dug Spring "Rains' Scare" after that, and his command of his troops started to erode.

Sensing an opportunity to get more directly involved with a commander with more experience and ability than Rains, several of the men simply left their bivouac and joined the ranks of the 1st Missouri State Guard Infantry. The disorganization of the State Guard's Eighth Division in the wake of Rains' Scare meant that no one noticed the men were no longer with their unit, and if they did, they were simply presumed dead or missing. As a result, they were able to participate in the Confederate victory at Wilson's Creek a week later.

Junius, amongst others, decided to remain with General Price's troops, who broke away from the Eighth and went north, Junius hoping that the general's thrust would take him closer to Ruby's potential whereabouts. On their way, Junius realized that they were passing not too far from Harrisonville, which lay only a few miles to the west. For a moment, he was tempted to just pack up his things and head home. As he considered his options, though, he decided that doing so would only create too much commotion for Paw and the rest of the family. How could he explain to them why he had run off the way he had and then why he had decided to give up so quickly? So, he stayed with his adopted unit and tried to integrate himself into a new band with about the same measure of success he previously had.

In mid-September, Price's men approached Lexington, Missouri, where they again defeated Union troops.

Junius was even more thrilled that the unit he had attached himself to was moving north, toward Kansas City and closer to Quindaro. Maybe it was true, after all, that he could revisit Quindaro.

His hopes were soon dashed, however, once General Price decided not to continue marching any further north after the battle at Lexington. Instead, they were headed farther south again, away from Harrisonville and nowhere near the Kansas border. Junius wasn't going to be able to find Ruby this way. The whole idea of joining up had been a colossal mistake, but there was no way to change that except through desertion, and the consequences of being caught were too severe. The penalty could be death, but manpower was so limited that that remedy was rarely utilized. Instead, those caught deserting were usually branded or tattooed in ways that made it obvious what they had tried to do. He couldn't live the rest of his life like that.

Finding Ruby would have to wait.

Like the others who had done so, he ultimately decided it would be best to return to his unit. Dejected, he trekked south again and rejoined the Eighth Division.

Chapter 18

Junius marched back south, ruing the day he had joined the militia. Nothing good had come of it, and now he was even further away from finding Ruby than he had been before he decided to enlist. There was no way he could hope to find her unless he deserted and tried to join the Union Army. In order to do that, he'd have to slip away and either head to St. Louis or back to Harrisonville and then into Kansas. The chances of being successful in either course of action were minimal at best and probably would result in his capture or death. The only solution was to stick it out until the war was over in a few months and then search for Ruby. Everyone was still confident the Yankees would get tired of the war before too long and they'd all be able to go home soon as victors.

As Junius returned to camp, he noted that several other members of his group had already returned before him. There was no way out for any of them. He would simply have to resign himself to returning to the fold for now.

Grover and Clem, and a couple of other soldiers Junius knew, were standing in front of a sergeant he recognized sitting behind a desk. To the sergeant's left was a tent with another desk inside it and a man sitting there studying several blocks of wood. Two soldiers were escorting one of the men from his group into the tent with their arms clasped around him while his hands were tied behind his back.

After a few minutes, the men in front of him handed something to the sergeant and then walked briskly away from his desk.

The sergeant looked at Junius as he approached the desk. "Name?"

"Hart. Junius Hart." Junius recognized the sergeant from his pronounced accent. It was Sergeant O'Rourke.

"Where have you been?" Sergeant O'Rourke asked.

"I went north after what happened at Dug Spring and Wilson's Creek," Junius said.

"Another deserter, I see. Just like the rest of 'em," said Sergeant O'Rourke.

"Deserter?" Junius asked.

"Yes, you're guilty of desertion of your post. You just admitted it," Sergeant O'Rourke said.

Two other soldiers standing a few feet away from the sergeant prepared to move forward, but Sergeant O'Rourke waved his arm, and they stopped.

"But I didn't desert. I stayed with the Guard unit. Went all the way to Lexington with Price," Junius said. Surely, the sergeant wasn't serious. Junius had seen action and hadn't actually left the Guard altogether. He had stayed with a unit, even if it wasn't the one he was assigned to. It didn't really matter who was in command or assigned to which unit anyway, did it?

"Don't matter, young man. You weren't with your unit where you belonged. Where are your enlistment papers?" asked the sergeant.

Junius heard what he thought were muffled cries of pain coming from inside the tent the other soldier had entered a few minutes earlier.

"Ignore that, soldier. He'll be all right. Just getting a tattoo on his forearm. Not one he'll want to show anyone, of course, and not really a work of art either," said the sergeant.

So, it was true, Junius thought; they branded deserters.

"I don't have any enlistment papers. The sergeant in Jefferson City said we didn't need any," Junius said, unable to look away from the tent.

"I see. So, you've been accompanying a fighting unit of first the Volunteer Militia and now the State Guard without ever actually joining?" the sergeant asked.

"No. Not at all; I joined up as soon as I could."

"Even though you're not formally a member of any unit as far as I can tell, I could probably have you brought up on charges, and I guarantee you things would not go well for you," said the sergeant.

"But I didn't desert," Junius insisted yet again. Now, he was beginning to sweat. This couldn't be happening to him.

"You weren't here when you were supposed to be, and that's all that matters," the sergeant said.

Junius couldn't believe what the sergeant was telling him. All this because he thought he might have a chance to find Ruby somehow, and now he was looking at a possible firing squad for doing something that he hadn't done.

"What is that thing you're carrying by your side?" Sergeant O'Rourke asked.

"My fife."

"Your fife? You mean you ain't even actually a real soldier?" the sergeant scoffed.

Junius hadn't yet managed to control the anxiety he had felt when the sergeant started questioning him and now felt like he was cornered.

"I suppose there might be one way to resolve this issue satisfactorily, Private ... Hart."

"Resolve it how?" Junius asked.

"Missouri is just a backwater to where the real war is already being fought. The Confederacy needs men. I guess you qualify as one even if you are just a musician."

It was all Junius could do to keep from answering.

"What we could do, and I am empowered to do this, is enlist you in the Confederate States Army as of, say, four months ago, and then the matter would be solved."

"Why four months ago?" Junius asked, puzzled.

"That would take us back to approximately May 12, which, if I'm not mistaken, is several days before you men met in Jefferson City to form the Missouri State Guard," the sergeant said.

"Yes, it is."

"Good, then I could enlist you in ... Captain Grant's Company H of the 5th Regiment of the Missouri Infantry, Confederate States Army. And I could attest to the fact that you enlisted in Cumberland Gap, Tennessee."

Junius listened without comprehending what he was hearing.

"As part of the terms of your enlistment, you would be obligated to serve in the C.S.A. for the duration of the war, or, in other words, until we drive the Northern aggressors out of our sacred homeland, which should only take a few more months. There would have to still be a record of your service in the Missouri State Guard, of course, such as it was, but no details of this unfortunate incident would need to be recorded."

Junius looked around as if seeking someone to give him advice as to what he should do and realized he had no one to ask and no other option if he wanted to avoid going into the tent. He could break and run, but he wouldn't get far and would probably be shot within seconds. He could plead his case again, but to no avail. There really was no choice.

"All right then. Sign me up," Junius said.

Sergeant O'Rourke smiled at him and winked at the two soldiers standing beside him now. "Good. That will be twenty dollars," the sergeant said

"What?" Junius asked. Twenty dollars for what? He hardly had earned any money at all since enlisting and didn't have but a few greenbacks left.

"Twenty dollars. Everything in this man's army comes with a price, Private."

"Where would I get twenty Confederate dollars? What

little pay I have received from the Guard is in U.S. dollars, and precious little of that."

"Hell, I don't want no graybacks anyway. They're pretty useless. I'll take the greenbacks," the sergeant said.

Junius felt trapped. He doubted that Sergeant O'Rourke was telling the truth and figured that he was taking what he considered his commission, and Junius was in no position to argue or even negotiate. Well, perhaps. He reached into what was left of his worn wallet and saw the ten-dollar bill and two single dollars. Taking out the ten, he hastily put the wallet back in his pants pocket.

"I only have ten dollars," he said.

"Ten?"

The sergeant eyed him closely for a long minute, but Junius didn't break his stare.

"All right, give me the ten. The C.S.A. needs men more than it does the money," the sergeant said.

Junius handed the bill to the sergeant, who snatched it from him and quickly tucked it in his shirt pocket, where Junius saw a lot of other greenbacks.

Chapter 19

"But I'm a musician. I play the fife," Junius protested once he arrived at his new unit.

"Private, first, we need to make a soldier of you. Then we'll see what kind of musician you may be," he was told by Sergeant Miller, the drill sergeant of the 5th Missouri Infantry. The sergeant looked like he could have been Sergeant O'Rourke's twin. The same reddish hair and barrel chest.

Junius had no mind for being in the infantry again. He'd already seen what happened to infantrymen in battle.

"Soldier! You don't know how to play a banjo, do ya?" asked Sergeant Miller.

"No, Sergeant."

"That's a shame," said Sergeant Miller. "Might have come in handy around the campfire at night. Can't really play any jolly tunes with that there fife."

Despite his plea to join the regiment's band, he was fully integrated into the C.S.A. as an infantryman. Mistrustful of anyone and everyone in his new unit, he kept his fife in its case tucked inside his jacket so that it wouldn't be seen. It would have been a violation of uniform protocol had he been found out carrying it, and the last thing he needed was to land in trouble after his recent experience in the Guard.

Things seemed to be in a state of flux for a while, with unit designations changing fairly rapidly and men being shifted between units depending on some vague reasoning that didn't make any sense. No one seemed to really understand what the purpose of all the changes was, and even the officers seemed befuddled.

Finally, after a few days, life started to settle down when the high command decided to organize the troops according to their place of birth or last known residence. Since Missouri still hadn't seceded from the Union despite all the assurances that it would one day soon, Junius was reassigned to a unit representing his hometown, La Grange, Alabama, a unit that had just been formed in Courtland, Alabama, not too far from La Grange and Tuscumbia. He was assigned to Company F of the 16th Alabama Regiment under a Brigadier General Zollicoffer in September 1861.

Zollicoffer promptly marched the men six hundred miles from southern Missouri to the Cumberland Gap in Tennessee using the railroads, which were at least temporarily in Confederate hands. The weather throughout the fall and into the winter was brutal much of the way, and many of the men got sick. The incessant rain weakened the men's resistance, and with the addition of bad food and limited rations at best, dysentery ripped through the ranks. Their ranks thinned along the way due to the disease and accompanying death. Junius thanked God he managed to escape infection.

The unit saw action at Fishing Creek, Kentucky, in January of 1862, a battle in which Zollicoffer wound up confronting a Union colonel who thought that troops wearing blue were his men. Zollicoffer attempted to explain that many of his men also wore blue uniforms since the Confederacy didn't have enough gray ones to go around. In the fog and rain and resulting confusion over whose men were whose, the colonel shot Zollicoffer, who died instantly. Another four hundred men were wounded or missing after the battle, including a number of Junius's fellow band members who saw double duty as stretcher-bearers.

"The general has been killed! Move out, men!" Sergeant

Miller yelled as soon as he heard the news.

As they began to retreat, Clem remarked, "None too soon for me. We're out of ammo, hardly have enough to eat, and we're all soaking wet."

"What the hell did General Crittenden have us come up here for anyway? And now we've lost Zollie on top of that! We should have stayed in Tennessee. Got no business being in Kentucky. Was the general even thinking when he was drinking?" Private Jones said.

"Private Hart, can you actually play that thing you hide under your jacket?" Sergeant Miller asked him after the battle.

"Yeah, Sarge, I can." Junius grinned for the first time in what seemed like months.

"All right, take it out of its case, and let me hear you play it."

Junius obliged willingly. After listening for a few minutes, the sergeant said, "That's enough, Hart; you're now in the regimental band."

Junius's tenure in the band was quickly interrupted only two months later when Lieutenant Colonel John Harris, commanding the 16th Regiment, needed a new aide-de-camp. The only thing Junius really knew about the colonel was that he came from a place not too far from Tuscumbia.

Harris wanted someone who could read and write, wasn't essential in the infantry, and, as it turns out, was a native Alabamian. The four months Junius spent as Lieutenant Colonel Harris's aide-de-camp taught him a great deal about the Army and how the war was going from his superiors' perspective. None of it was good, especially when he considered what had happened at a church called Shiloh near Pittsburg Landing in early April.

Victory seemed to be in the Confederates' grasp until Grant's Union forces were reinforced overnight. One of the officers in the 16th, a Major Graham from La Grange, was particularly annoyed at General Beauregard's ineptness, and he spoke out in his tent, blasting the general.

"That man couldn't fight his way out of a schoolyard full of imbeciles if he had to," Major Graham would say. "Hell, Private, you could probably do a better job of commanding these men and giving orders than he can." Junius was the only one who heard his profanities directed at the general, and the major made sure to tell him to not repeat anything he heard.

Soon after the battle at Pittsburg Landing, as Junius's unit continued marching through Tennessee, Junius heard Colonel Harris erupt in his tent. Junius had already learned that it was unlike him to express any emotion whatsoever. Junius would have liked to get to know the colonel better, but he didn't have time for small talk or personal chats, given how busy he was. "New Orleans! My God, they're choking us now. How will we get the cotton out to England when we can't even control the Mississippi?" he yelled to no one in particular. Junius crept into the tent with more orders for the colonel to review and sign.

"Private, do you know what this war is all about? Do you?" Lieutenant Colonel Harris asked.

Reluctant to say what he really felt, Junius chose to remain silent.

"It's not about states' rights. It's not about slavery and the cornerstone of our society. It's about death. Who can kill more of the others more quickly. Death is what brings the two sides together and then forces us apart again until we meet again to mete out more death. What a tragedy this has become."

This was the first time Junius had heard an officer express this sentiment since he had joined the Guard.

Junius's respect for Lieutenant Colonel Harris was tempered by only one thing. He seemed to put his trust in subordinate officers who didn't command the men's respect. Once such instance was his adjutant, Major Graham from La Grange, a small man, and small not just in a physical sense. Short of stature with delicate features, he could pass for years younger than he was, even though he objected to that fact. What impressed Junius was just how tiny his hands were. His fingers resembled little toes rather than fingers, and his thumbs were just nubs of digits.

And yet he smiled constantly, an unnerving smile with what Junius knew was unbridled malice lurking just beneath his shallow gray countenance. Junius wondered what manner of brutality had been inflicted upon him and, in turn, what manner of malice he could inflict on others whom he deemed had crossed his path wrongly. But he was in Junius's chain of command, and he and the others in the battalion had no choice but to obey, and occasionally pander, to his every whim if they wanted to avoid hazardous or simply unpleasant duty. So, pander they did. Just as the major himself did whenever a superior officer was present.

"I swear, Private, I'm tempted to resign my commission and go home to see how the rest of this farce unfolds. At least I'd be around my loved ones instead of men whom I barely know and then send to their deaths," Lieutenant Colonel Harris said to Junius the next time the two of them were alone in the colonel's tent.

"I have half a mind to write to President Davis just as Generals Wood and Cleburne will do, if they haven't already, explaining Bragg's ineptness. This simply can't continue," Harris said.

Junius was sure everyone else in camp felt the same way but let a few moments of silence pass before speaking up. "Sir, those orders need to be signed."

"I know, Private. Please excuse me. Do you have family

that you long to see, Private?"

Junius thought first of Ruby and then his family. And Jim. "Yes, sir, I do."

"Do you know where they are?"

"I believe they are still in Missouri, sir. Most of them anyhow." Who knew where Jim and Ruby were?

"Wouldn't it be nice to be able to see them? To break bread with them? To worship with them again?"

"Yes, sir. It would."

"Are you a religious man, Private? Do you hold Christ near and dear in your heart?"

Before he could answer, Major Graham burst into the tent. "Colonel, I have bad news."

"What is it, Major?"

"It's for your ears only, Colonel."

"I see. Private, if you'll excuse us."

Junius departed from the tent, and once he was outside, he heard the major whispering rapidly to the colonel. It sounded like they were making plans to withdraw from Tennessee completely, but Junius wasn't sure.

What he did hear clearly, though, was Major Graham say something about Tuscumbia and suits of clothes, which struck him as odd. Why would he bring up anything about clothes when they were discussing plans to withdraw the troops? And why would he whisper so rapidly?

In early August, the colonel successfully applied for leave to go back to his home in Florence, Alabama, near Tuscumbia, to recuperate from the lingering effects of wounds incurred when he fell off his horse during the muddy, chaotic retreat from Shiloh. The colonel had fallen from his horse and been dragged a fair distance. Some of the troops had laughed when they heard about the colonel's accident, saying that no officer worth his salt would have let that happen. Some had even wondered if he hadn't faked the incident so as to avoid having to return to battle once the tide had turned against the Rebs.

"I'll be gone for no more than a week," he said to Junius. "I'll only have a short time to spend at home with my family, but at least I'll be able to see my children briefly. Who knows what's to become of us if this war lasts too much longer? Each day could be our last."

As a result of the colonel's leave, Junius was finally released from his aide-de-camp duties and returned to his unit.

"You missed a bit of action, Hart," Sergeant Miller said. "Did you learn anything?"

"Yes, Sarge, an awful lot." None of it was good, though.

The one thing positive about his experience was the fact that he had received an additional seven dollars and fifty cents per month while acting as the colonel's aide-de-camp.

In August, Junius got a letter from his father for the first time in several months. The envelope was smudged, and he couldn't see when it had been postmarked. It looked like it had been opened at least once or twice. He wasn't even sure if the entire letter was inside the envelope at first, and there were some odd black marks on the margins.

My dear son,

It has been so long since I have had any word from you that I fear for the worst at times. Despite my misgivings, I hope that you are surviving this conflict with only a minimum of discomfort. I suspect that isn't true, but please know that is what I wish for you, of course. You haven't been wounded, have you? I wish I could look into your eyes to see if you are telling me the truth.

We don't receive much in the way of news here, and I don't know for sure what has happened to you since you joined the State Guard, but I hear tell that your unit was absorbed into the Confederate Army. I can't begin to understand what led you to such a fateful decision, which I know goes against everything you believe, and I hope we both live long enough

*for you to make sense of it for me. Perhaps after all this commotion is over
and we can resume our normal life in Harrisonville or get to California,
you can make me understand.*

*I'm afraid I also have some rather sad news too. It's about Mayor
Younger. He was murdered while on a business trip to Kansas City. They
haven't caught anyone yet, but everyone suspects it was a Yankee. The
odd thing is that the mayor had been carrying one thousand dollars, and
the money was still on his body when he was discovered. The mayor had
asked me to accompany him, and Sarah Anne wanted me to go, saying
Jim could take care of things at home, but I had so many clients waiting
on clothes I knew I couldn't go.*

*The thing about the mayor's murder is that it caused your friend
Cole to leave Harrisonville. No one knows where he went, but rumors
persist that he joined up with Quantrill's raiders and is out terrorizing
Yankees since he thinks they killed his paw. At least you're in a real army,
even if that one, and not riding around the countryside attacking and
stealing from honest working folk.*

*I was so proud of you that day when you returned from deliver-
ing Ruby to Quindaro. Jim was so relieved that you had saved her, too. I
convinced Sarah Anne that what you had done was a good thing even
though she wasn't so sure about any of it.*

*I wish I could send you some coffee, which seems to be the one thing
you miss the most, but that isn't possible.*

*And greenbacks! If only there were some. Enough to go around, but
all the greenbacks have disappeared, and we barter with neighbors and
friends instead of relying on the worthless graybacks the Confederates
leave behind.*

*Is Opa's fife keeping you good company? Do you have the chance to
play it occasionally?*

*What are the men in your army like? Are they all from Missouri?
What about the officers? Are they good men? Opa always said never
trust an officer because they are only after their own selfish interest, not
that of their men. I hope that isn't true, but I suspect it is.*

*There is a rumor that the Yankee general by the name of Grant has
a thing about Jews and is trying to get them thrown out of the states*

that have seceded. It also seems like he may start to get rid of anyone in these here counties near Kansas City who has any kind of secession-ist tendencies. I hope everything settles down and we don't have to up and leave here because I have no idea where we would all go and how we would get our things there. Trust in our God that if we do have to leave Harrisonville, and Missouri for that matter, I will do whatever I can to make sure you know where we are headed. That I promise you.

I long for the day I can see you again, my boy, and I hope you stay healthy until that day, no matter how far off it is.

Your loving father

R.H. Hart

Junius was glad to hear from his father despite the disquieting news about Cole and whatever it was that General Grant had in mind for his family. Thankfully, Radolfus hadn't mentioned anything about them being Jews. There wasn't much Junius could say in response to his questions about how the war was going and how he felt about the officers. Obviously, his letter would also be opened by censors, and who knew if it would ever reach Paw and, if it did, what would still be intact? He couldn't even comment on what he had heard other officers say about their commanders for fear of being reprimanded.

Junius took pen in hand and decided to catch his father up on what he could share. He explained that aside from a couple of minor wounds, he was fine and that Opa's fife was in good shape, too. He promised to explain his decision to join the Guard when he could but wrote that now wasn't the time for that.

It was also at Pittsburg Landing that he had encountered an old friend for the first time since leaving Harrisonville, but he decided not to mention anything about what happened in his letter to his father. Nevertheless, he recalled the events as if they were yesterday.

"Buck, is that you?" he had said as the scrawny soldier

wandered across his path.

The soldier had turned around and looked at him, but it couldn't be Buck. The soldier had been gaunt, his arm had shook, and his face had twitched something awful.

"Sorry, I thought you were a friend of mine from back home," Junius had said and started back to his tent.

"Junius?"

He had turned around, the hair on his arms suddenly prickly.

"It's me."

"Buck? How are ... what has happened to you?" Junius had asked. What could have changed him so?

"I never imagined that I would see what I have seen in this war. Do what I have done. Had to do."

Buck's uniform, or what had been left of it, had been even more worn and tattered than most of the others Junius had seen. And he had smelled. Like something was rotting inside his uniform. Buck had tried to smile, but there had only been gums inside his mouth.

"I'm a corporal now, Junius."

"Congratulations, Buck," Junius had said, not sure how to respond.

"How's Ruby?" Buck had asked.

"Ruby? She ... I think she's fine, Buck. Why do you want to know?" Why was Buck asking about Ruby?

"I got to tell you something about her."

"About Ruby?"

"Yeah, well, really, it's more about what me and Cole used to do. When we knew she was home alone, we used to sneak up behind the cabin she shared with that darkie Jim and pretend we were varmints just to see how scared she would get."

So, it hadn't been Ruby's imagination. He should never have doubted her. None of them should have. And to think it was his two best friends who had been frightening her. He had been tempted to kick Buck all the way back to Harrisonville, but that would have accomplished nothing but getting him into trouble, so he had clenched his fists and walked away quickly without saying anything else.

He tucked that episode away to revisit after the war.

One day, Junius got caught up in some shenanigans some of the other band members were planning that would no doubt have antagonized the major. He didn't catch wind of what exactly they had in mind to do, but the major obviously had discovered something was going on based on his reaction, which was swift and immediate.

"I will not tolerate any disrespect to either this flag or to our country, the Confederate States of America. You men may think you are engaging in some mindless fun, but I assure you that orders are made to be carried out without question. For conduct unbecoming, I am sentencing each of the three of you to three days in the stockade with bread and water as your rations."

With that, he looked at the three men, who were newer recruits. Junius wondered what they could have done so egregiously wrong so quickly after arriving in camp but was in no mind to question the episode any further. They were probably secretly relieved that they wouldn't have to eat anything but bread for the next three days anyway, given how poor the cook's efforts had been of late.

Graham also had his spies. Junius knew of one instance in which the major called a corporal into his office along with a big, burly captain who was dumb enough to follow the major's orders without the slightest hesitation.

Once the captain accompanied the corporal into Major Graham's office, it was obvious to all who were within earshot that the major was levying incredibly personal attacks on the corporal simply to provoke him.

To do what?

The corporal couldn't respond verbally other than to repeat "Yes, sir!" or "No, sir!" as loudly as he could. And the captain would be the sole witness to whatever else might result from the major's tirade. The corporal wouldn't dare strike an officer, but that was exactly what the major seemed intent on provoking. Finally, after raging at the corporal for half an hour, the major booted him out of his tent. Normally, the men close by would have snickered and laughed under their breath, but this episode was even too cruel for them to respond that way. The corporal went whimpering back to his tent and refused to speak with anyone.

Once Junius returned to his normal duties, while the unit was still in southwestern Tennessee, a Union patrol was spotted in the distance, and one of the soldiers picked up his rifle and ran in the patrol's direction. For what purpose, no one knew. Running wildly, he managed to hold the rifle above his head and started to yell something at the patrol. From their remove, Junius and his comrades saw two of the patrol dismount and stand ready for whatever the corporal was going to do. Just then, a loud crack sounded from behind Junius and his comrades, and they saw the corporal blown forward by the force of the volley as the rifle flew from his hands and something else flew in the opposite direction. Major Graham then ordered a detachment of cavalry to pursue the patrol, which hurriedly rode off.

Riding out to see what had become of the corporal, the soldiers from the battalion found him with most of his face missing. Major Graham smiled awkwardly as he dismounted and picked up what the corporal had been carrying with him. It was a letter. The major read the first few lines and then tore it to pieces, laughing as he did so.

Junius was summoned to lead the burial detail off the

field and noticed that something about the soldier's uniform seemed familiar. Then he saw one of the shreds of the letter the corporal had written to his girl. It started out, "My Dearest Ruby ..." He looked closer at the body and then at the face. It was Buck.

"My Dearest Ruby ..." Junius flashed back to the day Buck had asked him if he had "tasted that" yet. He stared at him and wanted to kick his lifeless body, and only barely managed to stop himself. Major Graham barked another command. "Private ... I said move that body. Now."

He didn't want to pick Buck's body up but would have no way of explaining what was going through his mind. Tears streaming down his face, he forced himself to lift Buck's body and throw it across his back as best he could. With Buck's arms and legs akimbo, Junius staggered a bit as he tried to walk forward a few paces. Buck's deadweight was too heavy for him, and he really felt crushed by far more than that, so as soon as Major Graham was out of sight, he dropped Buck's lifeless body unceremoniously without another thought.

The other soldiers who had heard the major's order tried to convince him to pick the body up again, but after spitting on the ground near Buck's body, Junius simply walked away, wiping away angry tears.

Chapter 20

The more he marched and picked up broken bodies off battle-fields, the less he thought about Ruby. But then, when it came time to play the fife when the band was called upon, his mind returned to Ruby and how she had loved to hear him play.

That is when he felt it. The hole in his heart that could never be filled. No matter how he tried to forget her and what had happened on the way to Quindaro, his fife served as the object that haunted him endlessly and mercilessly. There were times when he simply wanted to rid himself of it, but that would only have made matters worse. *Soldier on, Private*, he would say to himself.

A year after Shiloh, in the summer of 1863, things looked even worse for the Confederacy. The Army had marched all the way to Chattanooga, Tennessee, where the Yankees were expected to try to take the town, along with its railroad termi-nus, and cut off Atlanta. As soon as the 16th Alabama arrived, however, General Bragg ordered Junius's unit, amongst others, to march quickly north to Knoxville. Even the 16th's com-manders didn't understand what Bragg was doing.

As they marched northeast toward Knoxville through the unattended fields and the resulting muck, Junius noticed that fewer and fewer men showed up at reveille each morning. While some of them were no doubt laid low by dysentery and other probable maladies, Junius was sure that homesickness and war-weariness had simply gotten the better of the ones who had run off during the night. Others simply played off for a spell, hoping to stay in camp rather than soldier or work.

Whether the sentries tried to stop any of them from deserting, or if they did, how hard they tried, was debatable. Junius even heard tell that a couple of the sentries had joined a group who had recently deserted. Even the provost marshall saw its share of desertions as they rounded up stragglers or would-be deserters.

It became more and more difficult on a daily basis to imagine his regiment being an effective fighting force, and the dispirited mood amongst the men was contagious.

Junius knew several soldiers who had deserted over the course of his enlistment, and he assumed that his regiment had at least as many deserters as any regiment in the entire army. Some of the drummers and one bugler had disappeared on the way north to Knoxville.

No doubt, some of the men had been killed in battle, but their bodies were nowhere to be found. The only ones he was certain had died were the ones he had seen carried off the battlefield. Who knew how many of the men lying on the field after a battle were truly injured or dying, and which ones were faking their injuries only to slip away after nightfall just to be taken prisoner by the Yanks and executed, or taken prisoner, or escape?

He had to admit that the thought had crossed his mind to do the same, but it would be more difficult for him, especially given his notoriety after serving as Colonel Harris's aide-de-camp just before the battle at that strange little church near Shiloh.

After the band had heralded the beginning of yet another battle near a place called Stone's River, outside of Murfreesboro, Junius had, as usual, become a stretcher-bearer to clear the field of the wounded, or at least of the wounded that he thought had a chance of surviving. Here, even more than on previous battlefields, he encountered more Yanks. Almost as many as his fellow Johnny Rebs.

As he often did, he wondered if the Yanks even wondered what it was they were dying for as they fell. Had all of them been convinced, just as his fellow Rebs had, that they needed to defend their way of life against evil? By this time, he thought that they were both evil for continuing the senseless slaughter that he had only agreed to participate in for a purely selfish reason. He wished he had been able to explain to Radolfus in his letter what had led him to his fateful decision, but he couldn't bring himself to do so just yet.

While trying to give some water to one wounded Reb and trying to determine whether it was worthwhile to carry him off the field, he noticed a movement to his left. A Yank, whom he had thought was already dead, was lifting his pistol to fire at him. Junius had no choice but to hide behind the soldier he was trying to help, who then took the bullet in his neck. Blood spurted from the soldier, and there was no chance he would make it off the battlefield alive.

Junius jumped over the dying soldier and landed on the Yank before he could aim again. Junius had no weapons, and the Yank, though weakened by his wounds, was on his knees, still struggling and trying to take aim again at short range. The gun kept slipping out of his hand due to all the blood he was losing. Junius reached down, felt his fife, and lifted the case from his belt. As he raised the instrument case over the Yank's head, the Yank reached out and grabbed him by the leg and pulled him down in the grass next to him. Now on his back, he saw the Yank about to reach for his neck to strangle him. With a savage blow, Junius cracked the Yank's head open with his instrument case and then watched the man fall on top of him. The cracking sound was louder than he had thought it would be. And what was left of the Yank's head was a disgusting sight. He had seen men die on the battlefield before and plenty of corpses, but he had never seen one die at his hands. And on top of him.

Gasping for air, he rolled the Yank's body off and saw the instrument case had splintered, and inside were two pieces of what had been his fife surrounded by a lot of red.

Opa's fife. Destroyed.

He stared at it, unbelieving. Then, remembering where he was, he rapidly returned the two splintered pieces to the case that he tucked in his belt and then scurried back to the Confederate lines.

Junius felt nothing about the man he had just killed. How many times had he tried to save other Yanks' lives and felt horrible when they died of their wounds anyway? What had it come to when he could kill a man—no matter who the man had been—and feel not a thing? The soldiers must have felt the same way.

After the battle, once he was back in camp, Junius sat down long enough to examine the instrument case and fife. How would he ever explain to Radolfus what had happened? Surely, he would have to understand, given the circumstances, if he indeed ever saw Paw again, and that was by no means certain.

Then he walked by the tent where wounded Yanks were being tended by medics and stopped short. One of the wounded was a young man who didn't sound like a Yank. A medic called over one of the doctors, and the two consulted in hushed tones while the young man grimaced. The medic and the doctor rushed off to another moaning Yank, leaving the wounded Yank unattended.

Finally, Junius's curiosity got the best of him. Once he was sure no one else could hear him, he asked, "Hey, Yank, where you from?"

The soldier looked up from his wounds, startled. "Nickajack," he answered. He gritted his teeth as he spat the word out.

"Nickajack? Where's that? Not any place I've heard of before."

"It ain't up north, and I guess it ain't rightly a state no more. But it's just a little east of here, I reckon," the Yank said.

"East? All that lies east of here are other states of the Confederacy. None of them is named Nickajack," Junius responded, suppressing a smile.

"You probably know it by other names. Maybe Alabama or Tennessee."

"I'm from Alabama. Like I said, never hear of Nicka ..."

"Jack. Nickajack. People round there ain't got no cause to join your Confederacy. So, we decided to secede from the states that seceded from the Union."

Junius looked at the soldier like he must be suffering from wounds to the head.

"What part of Alabama?" Junius asked.

"Mainly Winston County and the counties north of there."

Junius knew that La Grange and Lawrence County lay north of Winston County, which meant ...

"How ... when ... did this occur?"

"Independence Day last year. July fourth. I had to hide out for a while before I hooked up with the Yanks. Ain't been home for a year now, so I don't really know how things are going, but I'm sure we'll succeed, just like they did up in Virginia."

"Virginia? What happened up there?"

"The folks in the western part of Virginia didn't want to be part of the rebel states either, so they are breaking away from the rest of the state. Going to form their own state and join the Union."

Could it be true? Part of Virginia leave the Confederacy? Richmond, the capital of the Confederacy and where Jeff Davis ran the government, was in Virginia.

"Anyone from Tuscumbia, Florence, La Grange?"

"I don't rightly know, but I do know there are lots of folks in Tennessee, east of here, I guess, that make up some of the fighting units for the Union. Tuscumbia, maybe, too. Never heard of La Grange, though."

I wonder if Paw knows about Nickajack, Junius thought. He wondered if he should mention it in his next letter or if it was best not to say anything about it.

Just then, more rebel wounded arrived, and Junius was summoned back to the battlefield as night was about to fall to scour the ground for other wounded and dying. In the meantime, Lieutenant Colonel Harris had taken over a house, one where a family still lived, as a makeshift hospital. Junius heard the order being given to prepare the barn behind the house for the anticipated additional casualties and perhaps as a morgue to deal with the growing number of deceased soldiers as well. The colonel dispatched a lieutenant to enlist the members of the household and any slaves to assist in arranging the cots and tables to be used as operating platforms where Junius knew arms and legs would soon be amputated.

And buckets. Lots of buckets.

Soon, he saw several young ladies walking to the barn accompanied by the lieutenant and a handful of soldiers. Only one slave girl was in their midst, so the others must have been the lady of the house and her daughters.

The slave girl reminded him of Ruby for some reason, and he thought of their last few moments together after they had made love. She had asked him to play the fife, which now was just a shattered relic. He didn't regret killing the Yank, not any longer, but instead was angry that Opa's fife had been ruined. Paw would be upset regardless of the reason it had been broken. Of course, he would have to save the broken pieces to see if there was any way it could be repaired, knowing full well and good that was impossible.

The ladies and their slave spent a good hour in the barn while Junius went back and forth from the camp to the battlefield several times carrying several wounded, most of whom he thought were going to die. He returned just as darkness was falling.

Near the tents where the wounded and dying were being tended to, all he could hear were groans and pitiful confessions men were making to mothers, wives, and sweethearts. At least, that's what Junius thought. But there was another sound not coming from the tents but from the direction of the barn. A cry of some urgency, a woman's cry.

Without thinking, Junius sprinted toward the barn. He heard muffled sounds and squeezed through the door, which was ajar just enough to allow him through. He saw the back of a soldier grunting with his hand over a girl's mouth. A slave girl. Her eyes were wide open, and once again, he remembered Ruby's eyes just before he had lost consciousness. A lantern sat on a bale of hay next to them. Junius started to yell at the soldier to stop but caught himself. The girl, clawing desperately at the soldier, looked to the side and saw Junius and looked even more terrified.

She thinks I'm going to do the same thing he is doing.

The soldier half-turned to face Junius with a savage grin on his face. He was grunting the entire time. "You'll just have to wait, soldier. I should be finished here in a few minutes. Why don't you go round up some of the others, and they can all take their turns, too?"

Then he saw clearly what he had tried to avoid ever since that day in Kansas. This was only one man. Ruby had had to endure this from how many men? Was it four or five? He felt his heart was about to explode.

Instinctively, he reached into his waistband where he had put the jagged pieces of his fife. Silently, he approached the man from behind while the girl stared at him. Junius put his hand up in front of his mouth and motioned her to be quiet. She made a deep noise in her throat, which made the soldier look over his shoulder. Junius gripped one piece of his fife and plunged its jagged edge into the back of the soldier's neck once, then again, and then a third time.

The soldier gurgled, then swayed, flailing to pull the fife

from his neck. The slave girl covered her mouth to muffle a scream as the soldier tried to reach for his sword. Instead, his body sagged, and he fell against the bale of hay where he had placed the lantern. As the lantern fell on its side, the soldier's eyes glowed a brilliant red just as the flame from the lantern began to spread to the other bales and engulf the barn. Grabbing the slave girl, Junius rushed from the barn and back toward the house.

"Go inside! Quickly! Don't tell anyone about this!" he told her. Then, racing back to the camp, he yelled, "Fire!"

Soldiers came running, but there was nothing they could do as all the available buckets had already been placed inside the barn. All that was left was to watch as the building burned to the ground.

In the morning, the soldiers from Junius's unit entered the scarred remains of the barn. Lying there were the charred remains of the soldier with a smoldering black stake sticking out of his neck. Their lieutenant, only recently arrived from Richmond, examined the remains of the body and noted the stake. He stood over it for a minute and looked up to where the roof had been. After a minute of examining the dead soldier's neck and the stake still protruding from it, he faced the men who had accompanied him until his eyes landed on Junius.

"You're the one who yelled fire?" the lieutenant asked.

"Yes, sir."

"Aren't you in the regimental band?"

"Yes, sir."

"What instrument do you play?" the lieutenant asked.

"The fife, sir."

The lieutenant continued staring at Junius as he spoke, then back at the remains of the soldier, and walked past the men with a sidelong look at Junius, but he said nothing.

Later that day, as the unit prepared to break camp, Junius wandered over to the shell of the burnt-out barn. The reality of what had happened still hadn't sunk in completely. He had killed two men within a matter of hours. One a Yank, and one a fellow Reb. As he was about to leave the site, he glanced toward the house. The lady of the house stood with the slave girl Junius had saved. She looked closely at Junius and, after a moment, called out to him.

"Young man, would you come here, please?"

"Yes, ma'am. Is everything all right?" he asked.

"Yes, it is. Aren't you the young man who was in the barn last night?" the mistress asked.

Junius glanced over at the young woman whose face was firmly etched in his mind. She smiled at him, and he thought she blushed. "Yes, ma'am, I am. She told you what happened?" he asked.

She looked at the slave girl before continuing to address Junius. Taking the girl's hand and willing her to step forward, the woman continued. "Never you mind what she told me. But I'd like to thank you for what you did."

Junius didn't know how to respond. "Ma'am, if I may, what is your slave's name?" he asked.

"My slave? Oh, Margaret? She isn't a slave," she said.

"I thought ..." Junius started but didn't know what to say.

"Margaret is my late husband's daughter. His bastard child. I promised him I would look after her when he told me about an affair he had while on a business trip to New Orleans. It was the least I could do for the man who saved me from ruin after my first husband died, leaving me with my daughters," she said.

"How old is Margaret, Mrs. ..." Junius asked.

"Worthington. Elizabeth Worthington. Margaret, why, I reckon Margaret must be thirteen by now; wouldn't that be about right, dear?"

Margaret shrugged her shoulders. "I guess so, ma'am."

Margaret forcefully reminded Junius of Ruby. The same skin color. The same innocence. The same look in her eyes.

She came to him in the middle of the night. At first, he didn't believe it was her. Then he realized that she was wearing the same dress that she wore that day on the way to Quindaro, the only dress she had taken with her. Her hair was tousled some, and the dress was torn at the bottom. Other than that, she looked normal. There was a pale light surrounding her, but otherwise, it was dark. He thought she looked confused by her surroundings, unsure of where she was.

"Junius," she said.

"Ruby, is it really you?"

"Yes, Junius, it is. That was good what you did today."

"Ruby, I ..." he said as he tried to reach out to her. She moved ever so slightly away from him, floating backward. He looked at her carefully just to make sure it was her and not the girl named Margaret, in case she was trying to fool him.

"Shhhh ... no one must know I'm here."

"Ruby, where are you?" Junius asked.

She looked around the space and didn't seem to quite know how to answer. "You mean when I'm not here? Watching you?"

"You watch me?" he asked.

"Of course I do, Junius. Always."

"But where are you, Ruby?"

She put her hands around her arms and looked up and down and then side to side. "It's cold here, Junius, very cold."

With that, she blew him a kiss and started to dissolve.

Junius woke up with a start. Two of the soldiers to his left sat up, and one said, "Quit your muttering, Hart. What's done is done. Whatever you did. Who were you talking to? She sounds kind of sweet. Was she a darkie?"

A darkie. That's all Ruby or Margaret would ever be to men like these, his fellow soldiers. As long as there was a chance the Confederacy would be victorious, there would never be a chance for Ruby or Margaret or any other female like them to have any dignity or command any respect. Or even be safe when doing the simplest thing in their own homes. They would never be safe from men who valued them for only one thing.

And what he had done was betray them when he joined the Guard. Not intentionally, but out of misplaced emotions that only brought him to the lowest level he had ever felt about anyone or anything. He couldn't take it back; it was far too late for that. Saving Margaret from her obvious fate at the hands of the brute of a soldier served as partial atonement for what he had caused to happen to Ruby, but only that. And he would never be able to fully atone for that. Not until and unless he found her again.

"Hart, the major wants to talk to you. On the double," the lieutenant from Richmond said the next morning as the men gathered their equipment for another march.

Two soldiers walked over to Major Graham's tent, with two soldiers on either side of Junius, who followed Lieutenant Gephardt.

"Here's Private Hart, Major. You wanted to see him about the events of last night."

"Yes, quite. Private, I hear you were the one who first realized the barn was on fire. Is that right?" He returned to reading over papers on his desk and quickly signing his name to several of them.

"Yes, sir, it is."

"I see. Where are you from, Private?" he asked.

"Most recently, Missouri, sir."

"Missouri? How did you end up with the 16th Alabama,

then?" Major Graham asked. "Never mind," he said after a moment.

The major was silent for a long time, staring at Junius. "Private, what is your role in this man's army?"

"When I'm not assigned to other duties, I'm in the regimental band, sir."

"The band? I see. What instrument do you play in the band?"

"The fife, sir."

Major Graham stopped what he was doing and looked everywhere but directly at Junius. "Fife? And where is your fife, Private?"

The hair on the back of Junius's neck rose, and he started to sweat suddenly. "I ... it broke, sir. I had to kill a Yank with it."

"Do you still have it, Private?"

"Not exactly, sir."

The lieutenant looked down at Junius's side and asked, "What's that, Private?"

"That's the half that I still have, sir."

"Where is the other half, Private?" Major Graham asked.

Junius wanted to disappear into the woods and run fast, far away from the battlefield. But he was trapped. "I must have lost it in the heat of the moment, sir."

"Of course. Well, we'll have to see about getting you a new one, won't we?"

"Yes, sir."

"Private, what do you think about what happened in the barn?"

"I don't know, sir."

"Well, regardless, the trooper who died in the fire, however he died, deserves a proper burial, doesn't he?"

"Yes, sir. Of course, sir."

"A proper Christian burial. Private, would you do us the favor of arranging an appropriate ceremony before we break camp?"

"Yes, sir." Did the major suspect that something unusual had occurred to cause the soldier's death? No one else knew what had happened except for the slave girl, and she surely wouldn't have told anyone. No one could have guessed what had happened inside the barn, could they? Had another soldier been waiting outside the barn to take his turn with the girl?

Regardless, he had to learn what would be expected in a proper Christian burial. And he had to be careful who he asked and how he phrased his questions. The last thing he needed right now was anyone making comments about him being a Jew.

Chapter 21

Junius had trouble sleeping after the incident, so much so that he wandered around aimlessly near camp that night and the next. He was careful to be silent so as not to arouse the suspicions of the sentries who watched him wordlessly. He made sure to stay away from the tents that housed the wounded and the sick to avoid the wailing and the groans that continued to bother him regardless of their cause. He considered himself fortunate to have avoided coming down with typhoid or cholera the way so many other troops had, and he accepted the occasional bout of dysentery as a minor inconvenience no matter how much it pained him.

After Junius consulted with the other band members, he gained an understanding of what constituted a proper Christian burial, and the corporal he had killed was buried accordingly. Two days later, however, Junius discovered the vagaries of military justice.

"Private Hart!" Major Graham said as he approached the men while they finished their breakfast. He was accompanied by four soldiers who wore sabers and held their firearms by their sides.

Junius stood at attention as all the men looked toward Major Graham and his retinue.

"Sir?"

"You're under arrest for the murder of Corporal Jackson. Men, cuff him and take him to the stockade."

"Murder, sir?" What was he talking about? Surely not the corporal who had been raping the African girl. They probably had him confused with someone else who must have done something to a soldier who had become angry after an argument over his unit's bravery or some personal affront, which was becoming all too frequent. It would straighten itself out in no time, and there was no reason to worry.

"Yes, Private, murder. You didn't lose half of your fife on the battlefield. You stuck it in Corporal Jackson's neck and killed him for no reason."

He took a deep breath and made eye contact with the major for the first time. "Sir, that isn't true. The corporal was attempting to rape that girl. I had no choice but to—"

"No choice but to what? Everyone saw you talking to that slave girl afterward. Some of the men even confided that they suspect you're soft on a slave girl you had back home in Missouri. Seems like you have a fondness for African women. And when that one showed her preference for Corporal Jackson, as no doubt most women would, you lost control of yourself and killed him with your broken fife. Seems like an open and shut case, Hart."

Open and shut. The verdict that would be rendered would be obvious. Junius recalled the time after Shiloh when one of the troopers was accused of a crime he didn't even recall and was summarily executed by a firing squad. The major leading that squad had seemed unusually excited about the verdict. Then, it occurred to Junius that that major bore an uncanny resemblance to Major Graham.

"The court-martial will decide the truth, Private Hart. You do know the penalty for murder is death?" the major asked.

Junius couldn't think straight and swallowed hard. He couldn't stand still, and his eyes darted left and right.

"Your trial is to be tomorrow."

No one said anything in his defense. It was eerily quiet. The only person who would be able to speak for him was a young woman whom they wouldn't even consider listening to, and he couldn't have reached her even if they would.

The soldiers marched Junius to the stockade with both his hands and feet in chains, there to await the convening of his court-martial the following morning. Again, he searched the faces of the other soldiers and his fellow band members, but no one would meet his gaze. He couldn't believe what had happened. There would be no one to defend him.

Junius spent a sleepless night in an improvised stockade guarded by several soldiers. From a distance, he could hear his fellow bandmates acting no differently than they normally did, singing and playing instruments until, one by one, the men all fell asleep. It had now been several nights since he had actually slept, and his mind raced all over. Memories of Ruby crowded out images of the corporal he had killed, and he saw Jim and his father looking at him accusingly. They wouldn't even listen to him when he tried to speak, and instead, their images simply vanished. Ruby's image remained, and she looked like she was crying. Sarah Anne appeared in the background, shaking her head and wagging a finger at him. Finally, shortly before dawn, he fell into a dreamless sleep and awoke to the sounds of birds singing a plaintive song what felt like only minutes later. Did the birds know what was about to unfold?

The door to his cell in the improvised stockade burst open, and four soldiers surrounded his makeshift cell. Two of them grabbed him by his arms and practically threw him out. He caught himself just before stumbling over the chains that bound his feet.

The soldiers marched him as he stumbled along to the improvised outdoor courtroom. Major Graham had apparently appointed several junior officers to be the jury, a captain and three lieutenants, one of whom looked like he was barely eighteen years old and appeared just as terrified as Junius felt. Major Graham himself was acting as the prosecutor and studied several documents laid out on a desk as Junius was left standing alone in front of him.

No one said a word. All Junius could hear was his own breathing.

Twelve soldiers stood off to the side, all of whom looked very serious and carried their rifles as if they were preparing to use them.

After a painful interval, Major Graham stopped shuffling through the documents and raised his head, and his bloodshot eyes bored into Junius's head. The birds had stopped their plaintive song, and even the slight breeze had died down. Junius felt he was in a graveyard and everyone around him was dead until the major cleared his throat, but he still didn't speak.

Finally, Junius couldn't stand the suspense and the silence any longer.

"Sir, pardon me, sir. Will I have anyone to defend me?" he asked.

Major Graham merely looked down at his hands and simply shook his head. Was he smirking as he did so?

"Sir, will I be allowed to talk? To defend my actions?" Junius asked.

This time, Major Graham stood up straight and nodded toward the other officers on the jury. There would be no defense, and there would be no arguments. *He's already made up his mind. I haven't a prayer.* His thoughts raced ahead of him, each one propelling itself forward into his jumbled mind even before he finished the previous one. Ruby, Paw, Jim, and the rest of his family, even Sarah Anne, came forward again. This time, Buck and Cole were there too. He would never see any of them again. Would they even know how he died? That he was innocent?

Paw, I am so sorry that this has to happen. I was wrong to go off the way I did, but I didn't murder the man. Ruby, I am sorry I had to let you go like that. I wish I could have had time to find you and make it up to you.

"Private Hart, the facts speak for themselves. You killed Corporal Jackson in a fit of jealousy. Lord knows why. You will be pronounced guilty in accordance with the laws of war," Major Graham said.

No birds squawked; no men coughed; no leaves rustled. The silence rang in his ears.

"I'm sorry to say that we don't have one of your clergy here, if that is what you call them, to commend you to your heaven, but if you would like, we can substitute one of our own chaplains to perform the required service. I think one must be available somewhere here," he said. "If not, it probably won't matter anyway where you're headed."

How did Major Graham know he was a Jew? He was from La Grange. Could he have known Paw?

Two of the soldiers guarding him proceeded to bind Junius's feet together more tightly so he couldn't even stumble away if he decided to try to escape. Some of the twelve men carrying the rifles watched him try to wrestle free from his handcuffs. Two of the men looked down toward the ground when he looked in their direction. The drummer boy, who had beaten out a steady drumbeat the entire time, looked like he was about to cry.

This can't be happening.

Then Junius felt something warm running down his legs, followed by another sensation in his bowels. He had soiled himself.

"Happens all the time," one of his guards said.

So, this is how it would all end. He would die without ever knowing what had become of Ruby, and all because he tried to atone for his grievous mistake in taking her to Quindaro.

As the guards started to turn Junius around, the blood rushing in Junius's head covered the clop of horses' hooves.

The horses must be approaching the site of the court-martial. Who would be arriving in the camp at this time? What did it matter? He had been sentenced to death for a crime he didn't commit, and he would never understand how this had all come to pass.

"Major, cease and desist!"

Junius recognized the voice. Lieutenant Colonel Harris! A moment later, he marched into the makeshift courtroom.

"Sir, we are in the midst of a court-martial of this soldier who murdered one of our own. I must ask you to allow me to conclude our business here," Major Graham said.

"Have you spoken with the widow Worthington, Major?" asked the colonel.

"No, sir. There was no reason to. It was evident what happened."

"Did you check with the witness?" the colonel pressed.

"Sir, there were no witnesses."

"Yes, there was. The girl herself," the colonel said.

"The slave girl? You can't really think that she would be a reliable witness, Colonel." Major Graham smirked as he answered the colonel.

"She isn't a slave girl, Major. She's Mrs. Worthington's adopted daughter," Colonel Harris said. "She's the daughter of the man who owned this plantation. And her word is good. Now, release this soldier immediately. The court-martial is over."

"But, sir—"

"No buts, Major."

Two of the soldiers guarding Junius instantly removed his cuffs and unbound his feet. Junius didn't move at first. He couldn't. When he finally had command of his body again, he turned away from the group and rushed toward the latrine, but after only a few steps, he puked and puked until there was nothing left inside him. He found what he hoped was a pail of clean water outside one of the medical tents nearby, poured it over his head, and then drank what was left, spitting it out when he feared getting sick again.

"Private Hart. I am sorry this happened to you. I am sorry for what else could have happened to you," Colonel Harris said when Junius had cleaned himself off and returned to the group.

The men with the rifles all still kept a watchful eye on him. Some of the members of his company smiled when they saw him. Others turned their backs to him.

Junius didn't say anything. His mind was a blur. Major Graham had almost had him shot. What kind of a world was he living in? What kind of army was this? How fortunate that the colonel had returned when he had.

"Thank you, sir. It's fortunate you returned from leave when you did, sir."

"Quite so, Private. I have had the pleasure of knowing Mrs. Worthington for quite some time now," the colonel continued. "The widow had one of her men, at great risk to himself, ride out to find me and have me hasten here once she understood what Major Graham intended. A fine woman indeed. I suggest you go to the house and thank her for what she did for you. After you clean yourself off first."

"Sir?"

"You can't go into her home with your pants soiled like that, Private. Orderly!"

"Sir!"

"The private needs a new uniform."

"Sir, we only have—"

"A new uniform, now."

The orderly dashed off without another word.

"Go ahead, Private, you have my permission to visit the widow. And her daughters."

Still reeling from what had transpired over the last—how long had it been? Ten minutes? Fifteen? "Yes, sir. Thank you.

"Oh, and by the way, you'll no longer be under the command of Major Graham. I'll have you reassigned—for obvious reasons."

"Yes, sir."

Junius started to walk toward the main house, but Colonel Harris stopped him.

"Private, we never had the chance to talk while you were my aide-de-camp, did we?"

"No, sir."

"All I really know about you is that you were originally from Alabama, is that right?"

"Yes, sir."

"Where in Alabama, Hart?"

"Originally La Grange, sir. Then Paw moved his store to Tuscumbia."

"Your paw had a store in Tuscumbia?

"Yes, sir."

"Hart. Hart." The colonel hesitated. "Tell me, Private, was your father R.H. Hart, the tailor in Tuscumbia?"

"Yes, sir."

The colonel was quiet for a moment. Then he looked back to where the major still stood conversing with the soldiers who were to have been Junius's firing squad.

"Your father was a fine tailor, Private. I knew a man there in La Grange. A Colonel Cochrane. Classmate of mine at West Point. Good man. We lost him last year. Tragic. A born leader. He was proud of your father's handiwork."

"Sir?"

"Is he still alive, Private?" the colonel asked.

"Paw? Far as I know, sir."

The colonel kept glancing in the major's direction as he spoke to Junius.

"What happened to California, Private?"

"Sir?"

"I thought R.H. was going to California back in '57,

according to Colonel Cochrane."

Junius was surprised at what the colonel knew, and it showed. "Yes, sir, we were, but there was an accident on the river, and we had to stop in Missouri."

"I see. If I remember correctly, Colonel Cochrane said your father claimed you liked to play the fife, correct?"

"Yes, sir."

"And that is what you used to ..."

"Yes, sir."

"Now I understand," the colonel said. "Private, I'll make sure you get a new fife."

"Thank you, sir. I sure would appreciate that."

"Do you have any money?"

"Yes, sir. Why?"

"Never mind. How much do you have?"

"I reckon about five dollars. From a poker game the other night."

"Give me the five dollars. Here is five dollars from me. I am going to use it to settle an old debt."

Not comprehending, Junius nevertheless fished out his five dollars to hand over to the colonel.

"They're graybacks, sir. It's gotten hard to get any greenbacks."

"That's all right, Private. Go on and see the widow now."

"Yes, sir." As Junius walked away, he turned his head and watched as the colonel approached Major Graham, said something to him, handed him the ten dollars, and turned away quickly. Junius sensed something more was going on than simply repaying a debt. And then he studied Major Graham again more closely.

It dawned on him. Major Graham had been a client of Paw's before the Hart family left Tuscumbia for California. And not a pleasant one either.

The major turned and stared at Junius for a long time.

Chapter 22

Junius walked across what must have at one time been a well-cared-for lawn. The closer he got to the plantation house, the more damage he saw to the house itself. How would the South ever recover from the devastation that had been visited upon it, once the fighting was over?

No, how would it recover from the devastation its leaders, if you could call them that, had unleashed upon their own people? For what? For a dream?

No, a dream, a nightmare. That was what slavery was. And what it would always be. He had known it before the war, even before he saw all its horrors, and now that he had seen them, at least some of them anyway, it was so much worse than he had ever imagined.

So, he had been right in getting Ruby to Quindaro if, in fact, she had gotten from there to Canada safely after enduring whatever the Jayhawkers had put her through.

Junius approached the front porch of the plantation house gingerly.

Only a few feet from the steps leading up to the porch and still unsure what to do, Junius stopped at the sound of piano music coming from inside. Either the composition itself being played was that much more beautiful than any other he had heard, or the pianist was far more talented than any other he had heard. Or both.

He quickened his pace up the few steps, now eager to see who was playing the tune, and barely had time to decide how to announce his presence since the door stood wide open.

"Come in, young man," the widow said, stepping out from where she had been standing just inside the door.

"Thank you, ma'am," Junius said, taking in the main parlor eagerly.

"I don't know anything about the ranks of the military, but I suspect you're not very highly placed, are you?"

"No, ma'am. That's for sure. Private Hart, ma'am."

"I understand from the colonel that it took a lot for you to stand up to that dreadful person and do what you did. I am, and we are, eternally grateful to you."

"Yes, ma'am. Thank you. I'd like to think that anyone else would have done the same thing."

"Well, thank you again. I don't want to keep you from your duties. The colonel said you wouldn't have long to chat with me."

"No, ma'am. I don't. Before I go, though, I was wondering, could you tell me who was playing the piano just now?"

"Why, that was Margaret. The girl you saved."

Junius started to take his leave, but the widow interrupted him before he could say anything.

"Private, would you like to hear Margaret play a little more?"

"Yes, ma'am, I would."

"Follow me then. I am sure the colonel won't mind a few more minutes of your time here." She took Junius by the hand and led him into a room where Margaret sat at the piano with her back against the far wall.

"Margaret ..." The widow waited until the girl looked up to face them. When she did, she immediately stood up.

"Margaret, this is—"

"I know who he is, ma'am. I remember well."

With that, she started to play. Junius recognized some of the tunes but had never heard them played with such finesse. Margaret's playing was effortless as her hands glided over the keys. She briefly mentioned the names of the tunes she was playing for him, and he tried to commit each to memory but quickly surrendered himself to simply enjoying them. Rousing himself from his seat by the window after what must have been half an hour, he bowed his way out of the house and down the front steps of the porch with his ears still full of Margaret's playing, which had ignited his imagination in ways he hadn't anticipated.

As he returned to camp, he marveled at what a day it had been. Some of the men who would have formed his firing squad sat around the officers' tents, and he wondered if they were relieved or disappointed. Only a couple of them whose faces he recognized even acknowledged him with a wave and a smile. The others spat out a wad of tobacco as he walked by. He would have to watch his step from now on, that was for sure. Some of these men must have known the corporal he had killed and would want revenge.

The fear of what had almost happened at his court-martial returned briefly, but he resolved to banish it from his mind and concentrate instead on what he had just heard. That there was such beauty in the world in the midst of such devastation was a testament to the future.

Chapter 23

April 1865

Nothing changed over the next year and a half in any way that the men could say was positive. Bragg managed to completely undo the Confederate victory at Chickamauga by losing to Grant two months later at Chattanooga and being pushed back into Georgia. Grant was everywhere, and where were the Confederate generals to be found? The competent ones, anyway.

By March 1865, even Lee was just biding time in Virginia. The only positive change was that President Davis finally recalled General Bragg, but then he worsened the situation by making Bragg his chief military advisor. The men joked that it was as if Davis was scheming to lose the war.

Junius had received yet another flesh wound at Resaca as the Confederates were pushed back to Atlanta by Sherman, even though General Johnston had replaced Bragg. It was Junius's third such wound, but none of his compatriots remarked on it since they thought he was simply lucky enough to have survived as long as he had.

As he thought back, he remembered the wound that he had received from the Yankee soldier at Shiloh, but he couldn't recall the circumstances of the second wound, which had been to his leg. He felt his ankle but didn't find the scar that had been there, and then he realized he was looking at the wrong foot. There were other wounds that had left little scars, but he couldn't recall where he had received them. He also had a scar from the sword that had fallen from the dying soldier's hand as Junius had tried to lift him onto the stretcher. *Where was that?*

Once Sherman conquered Atlanta and finished his march to the sea, it was just a question of time before the entire useless ordeal would be over and they could go home. To what? What was home now? And what was home without Ruby there? The hole in his heart would only grow larger, and his sense that he had betrayed everyone's trust would only worsen.

Ever since his aborted court-martial, Junius had but one goal.

To survive the war. Nothing else mattered. Not that it ever had.

There was no point in thinking about victory, even if he wanted the Confederacy to win the war simply so he wouldn't be executed for being a traitor or sent to a prisoner of war camp. It simply wasn't going to happen. What would become of him and his fellow graybacks was already written. And they were all focused on the same thing he was. Survival.

Junius's unit headed north. The battle for Richmond was about to begin, they were told. If they could save the capital, then Lee's forces could regroup and counterattack to drive the Yankees out of Virginia. Saving the capital of the Confederacy was vital to the war's continuation.

Then something unexpected happened. Just as they were about to break camp, the mail arrived. Lots of it. Junius couldn't imagine how the bags of mail had reached them, but somehow, the mail had even as the army fled the fighting and the Yankees.

Junius figured that there wouldn't be anything for him as the sergeant who had replaced Sergeant Miller proceeded to empty the contents of the bag, calling out the names of soldiers, many of whom were dead or gone. What words were contained in those many unopened letters from loved ones hoping to receive news that their sons and brothers and husbands and lovers were still alive? And what had become of Sergeant Miller, who had mysteriously vanished?

As the sergeant was finishing his job, Junius heard him call his name.

"Private Hart, Junius, right?"

"Yes, Sarge," Junius said, noting that the new sergeant's name was LaFarge.

"One for you. Looks like it barely made it here in one piece. Must have had quite a journey to get here," Sergeant LaFarge said.

Junius took the letter, which did indeed look like it had barely survived the ordeal of reaching him. Part of the envelope and some of the letter from the upper-hand corner was torn off, and for a moment, Junius thought that the letter had been opened by someone along the way. Even some of the ink on the envelope was smudged, but at least his name was still legible. He waited until he was alone and sat underneath a shade tree while he carefully sliced the rest of the envelope with his jackknife.

My dear son,

I hope this finds you well. We get nothing but bad news about the progress of the Confederacy these days. Needless to say, I think there never should have been a Confederacy and can't understand so many things, but at least I hope you are still in one piece. I wish I could see you and talk with you about what has happened. It is my sincerest hope that I will be able to look upon with you my very own eyes one day soon.

There is much to tell you, Junius, and I don't know where to begin.

First, you should know that General Grant did decide to depopulate Harrisonville and all of Cass County of anyone whom the Yankees suspected of sympathizing with the Confederates. Much of Harrisonville was destroyed by the Yankees for some reason. I don't understand why it was necessary to do that, and it made me wonder just which side was the right one in this dumb war. Since townsfolk knew of your decision to join the Guard, we were, of course, amongst the first to be forced by the Yankees to leave. They made us go to Fort Scott in Kansas, where we had to decide what to do. Sarah Anne prevailed upon me to return to Tuscumbia, so that is where we are headed. I have no idea how we will get there yet, given the state of the railroads, but at least Sarah Anne isn't expecting this time around.

In the meantime, Jim accompanied us to Fort Scott, where he was given an opportunity to join what they called the Colored Troops, Union forces composed of former slaves. I don't know if you have run across any of them where you are. Of course, Jim's status was different from most of the others, but he went willingly, and I suspect he has done well with the army. The last thing he told me before we parted was that he would try to return to New Orleans after the war is over if the good Lord allows it.

Jim also got a letter from Ruby. Not the first letter that you lost when your horse threw you on the way back from Quindaro of course, but the second one that Jim wrote for her. The one she was to send when she got to Canada. Apparently, she made it there, but she was very vague on the specifics of how and where she is now. Even though he was relieved by her news, it seemed like something in the letter—which he didn't share with us—troubled him.

I doubt that you have thought too much about your mission to Quindaro with Ruby or what has happened to her since then, but I mention it only to show you that you did a good thing. I am still very proud of you.

The rest of us are fine although I fret about your sister Lizzie. Sometimes, I just don't know what has gotten into that girl. It's all I can do to keep her and Sarah Anne apart sometimes.

I promise to write you again when I know where we are going or where we have arrived. In the meantime, I remain hopeful that you are alive and well.

Your Loving Father,

R.H. Hart

Ruby was alive. She had made it to Canada. Junius's hands shook as he reread the letter a second and then a third and a fourth time. His tears stained the letter and made some of the words indistinguishable.

Where in Canada Ruby was didn't matter for now. Life made sense again. There was hope. He could atone for his mistakes and his cowardice if only he could survive the end of the disastrous war.

They reached the border between North Carolina and Virginia in early April. The problem was that no one seemed to know what to do next. It was difficult to get any information from General Lee's HQ, as there were no telegraph lines uncut and the trains no longer functioned. Officers conferred with each other endlessly and would make decisions, issue orders, and just as quickly have those orders countermanded by another officer. Ultimately, they started to march north toward Petersburg, hoping to connect with General Lee's troops, even though they weren't sure where Yankee forces were deployed.

While the debate over what to do and where to go continued, no one expected things to end so suddenly.

"Lee gave up the fight!" Private Grover yelled when he heard the news from the colonel.

The men in Junius's unit looked at each other. Some were trying to hide their tears, while others looked at each other blankly, trying to absorb the news that had been inevitable for months. A few stood up and held their rifles at the ready, refusing to accept what they were hearing.

"That ain't true. Lee would never give up. Must be some mistake!" a corporal from another unit yelled.

"Oh, it's true, all right. It's over," Clem yelled back.

One minute, they had been on their way to Petersburg, Virginia, to try to help save Richmond from falling into Yankee hands, and the next, they were scrambling to escape southward into North Carolina to avoid being captured by the Yankees who had forced Lee to surrender at Appomattox. How could it have happened so suddenly? But should he wonder? Junius asked this of himself. The war had been prosecuted so poorly that he was amazed it had lasted as long as it had. Ever since Shiloh, he and the others had known what a disaster their generals were. And they all knew that the only capable generals had grown tired of being overruled or overlooked for promotion, such that they had either given up in disgust or lost the will to fight.

"Maybe it's over for Lee. But not for the rest of us. As long as old Jeff Davis is president, we still have a fighting chance," the second soldier, the one from Mississippi, swore.

"Rumor has it old Jeff is headed to join up with General Johnston's army," another soldier, one from Texas, piped in.

"Johnston's over in Greensboro, ain't he?" the bugler, Clarence, now a corporal, said. Junius still boiled over the fact that Clarence had been promoted ahead of him after only two years despite the fact that Junius had been in the army for four years now. He was embarrassed that he remained a private even though it had been safer to not call attention to himself by being promoted. It wasn't Clarence's fault, of course, but still, being promoted just because he played the bugle instead of the fife didn't make sense.

"Maybe we should head that direction," the lanky soldier from Florida, whose name Junius didn't remember, said.

"Step lively, men. We need to get back south where we can regroup and continue the fight!" the sergeant would say at least several times a day during the first week after Lee surrendered.

"Where are we going, Sarge? Greensboro?" Clem asked.

"We'll know when we get there, soldier. Now file in," Sergeant Browne, answered.

"File in? File into what? There's barely enough of us to form a line," said Corporal Brown.

"How will we know when we get there, Sarge?" Junius asked.

"We'll know," Sergeant Miller growled.

Most of the men grumbled under their breath as Sergeant Miller spoke. Junius thought that he must actually believe what he was saying about continuing the war. Out of respect, no one said anything in response because he had been good to them. After all, it had been the sarge who saw battles unfold before the generals did and knew where to deploy the men smartly before the shooting started. As a result, they were still alive and had their limbs, while so many others had been left in far-off fields or had various body parts crudely amputated. Some of the men were unrecognizable even to their fellow soldiers, and Junius wondered how loved ones would react to seeing them come home with half their faces shot off.

Nevertheless, regardless of their own relatively healthy situations, if one could call them that, it was obvious that the men just wanted to figure out how to get home as quickly as possible. The problem was most of them were so far away from home that they had no idea where to start.

And, of course, there was another problem. Most of them had no idea what they would find when they got home or if their homes still existed. If their families had survived the war. If their families were still in their homes.

Men kept disappearing from the ranks as they trudged southward, sometimes singly and at other times in small groups. Junius guessed that the small groups who disappeared like ghosts were each from the same town, while the individuals who no longer had any surviving comrades to desert with did so alone as they tried to make their way to whatever it was that awaited them.

There wasn't even any pretense of marching any longer. Breakfasts were a thing of the past, and they were lucky if they could find any sort of varmint to shoot for what would pass as dinner. Junius was too tired and scared to even consider the fact that he stayed hungry most of the time. At least water was easily obtained, and now that the fighting had stopped, they didn't have to worry about how it tasted and what color it was. Remarkably, no one got ill after drinking the water from the nearest source, and the men had learned not to piss upstream of the water they intended to drink. Most of them, anyway.

Every day, there were fewer and fewer men answering reveille. Junius would have decamped, too, if he knew where to go.

Finally, even the bugler slipped off one night. The silence that morning was eerie until Junius broke out his new fife. That seemed to restore a sense of order briefly and lifted the men's spirits as well. The men responded to the sound they knew from early in the war as if it were an old friend who had returned home. How he wished it was Opa's fife, not the new one the army had paid five dollars for. Even though he only had half of Opa's fife, he couldn't let go of it, no matter how useless it was. He had to keep it to explain to Paw what had happened.

Junius had had enough. It was senseless to continue fighting or trying to rejoin units led by officers who refused to recognize that all was lost. Officers who had bought their rank or achieved it simply because of who they knew or how much money their families had, officers who cared more for their own personal glory rather than the safety of their men, had simply gone home. Men who had fought bravely and valiantly for four years but who were being sacrificed for nothing continued to believe in the cause to their own detriment.

Clearly, now was the best time to leave if he wasn't going to be captured. He waited until nightfall and then simply walked away from the camp, slowly at first and gradually picking up speed as he grew confident that no one was coming after him.

As he scampered through the woods, however, he heard rustling in the bushes and hid behind a tree. Had a bear lurking nearby picked up his scent? He craned his neck around the tree trunk to see what might be close to him and discovered a large group of men doing exactly what he was doing. He joined the group, who nodded to him and kept walking in a straight line noiselessly. There was more order in the process of deserting from the army than there had been in the chaotic retreats he had observed and participated in over the past three years.

At least heading southwest made sense to Junius. It was a start in the right direction if he ever wanted to get home to Harrisonville. Although he hadn't heard from Paw in well over a year, he hoped that things had been quiet out west and the family had survived intact. In his last letter, Paw had said something about having to leave Harrisonville. Radolfus wouldn't have been able to convince Sarah Anne to head for California. She would no doubt prevail, and they would return to Alabama. But if so, where? Moulton?

Now, Junius had to get away from anything that suggested he was a Confederate soldier if he was to survive. Who knew what would happen to him if he was captured? No one really believed that the Yankees would be merciful to anyone wearing the rebel gray regardless of what surrender terms had been negotiated.

It took two full days of what could only generously be called marching eight hours a day to reach Greensboro, where they discovered from others who had escaped Virginia before Lee surrendered at Appomattox that old Jeff Davis had already left Richmond. Shambling, perhaps, but what they were doing certainly didn't resemble marching in any sense. Evidently, Davis intended to cross the Mississippi and resume the war in the west. News of his flight, however, triggered an even greater exodus of men from what remained of the ranks of the now skeletal army.

The single greatest problem Junius had, however, was a huge one. Tuscumbia was over five hundred miles from

Greensboro. He had no money that was worth anything, only Confederate dollars, which even the rare shopkeeper they encountered sneered at as they refused to sell the soldiers anything. He had no food, only his tattered uniform to wear, and a canteen that had seen better days. The only thing of any value that he had was the fife that the army had purchased for him two years earlier, and that had suffered from neglect, too. He could still play a tune on it but had lost any desire to play it unless absolutely necessary. There certainly wasn't any joy in it anymore. And playing it when he had to simply reminded him of how Ruby would watch and listen when he played Opa's fife. Now more than ever.

As Junius and a group of soldiers from various parts of Alabama made their way west, they were overtaken by a Yankee patrol one night. Fearful of being made prisoners of war and even more afraid of being executed, they scattered into the forest. Junius found a hillock where he could see what transpired along with a couple of other soldiers. They remained silent while the others in front of them readied their rifles for whatever was about to come their way. The Union troops marched with precision down the lane just outside of the clumps of trees that lined the road. They were more disciplined than any unit Junius had served with since joining the Guard. Clem cocked his rifle as the lieutenant leading the Yanks approached their position.

Suddenly, he and the others who were lying prone were surprised by a squad from behind, well in front of where Junius lay on the side of the hillock, just out of sight from the impending action.

"Don't fire!" one of the Yanks yelled. Clem turned around to face the Yanks with his rifle pointed at the Yank, who fired his pistol and winged Clem in the arm.

"Drop your weapons!" the Yankee lieutenant barked, and

the Rebs all did so.

"Tend to that man," the lieutenant ordered, and imme-diately, a medic rushed to the wounded Reb just as Junius reached him, too.

"We're not here to harm you or take you prisoner. You're all free to go. General amnesty ordered by General Grant."

Grant? The same Grant that Paw had written about?

Junius and the others waited to see what happened next. The other Rebs slowly rose from their positions and stood their ground, uncertain what to do. Sergeant LaFarge was nowhere to be seen.

"Where are you boys from?" the lieutenant asked.

One of the Rebs said, "Tuscaloosa."

"That's a good distance from here, isn't it?"

"Yes, sir, that it is."

"You fellows are going to need some transportation to get there. You can't walk all that way now, not in your conditions."

"How else are we going to get there, Lieutenant?"

"I am authorized to grant you passes on the railroad to get you home, men. I'm not sure what the easiest way is to get to your homes, wherever they are, but you can use the railroad if you can find one that goes anywhere close."

Junius had a hard time believing what he was hearing. Passes to get home? On a train. Guaranteed safety by Yanks? At least this way, he would save time getting to ... where? He guessed he should start in Tuscumbia, just in case Radolfus had been able to convince Sarah Anne to return there, although he assumed that wouldn't be their ultimate destination.

"Didn't your superior officers explain to you the terms of surrender?" the lieutenant asked.

Junius and his compatriots were silent, and most of them simply looked down at the ground or at each other.

"No, sir. They didn't. Basically, they left us the way they led us," Junius answered.

The lieutenant stared at Junius for a long moment. "They

left you the way they led you, Private?"

"Yes, sir. That they did never made sense to me, or to us, what they decided to do or how they reached their decisions. Seemed like our actions, especially over the past couple of years, were made on the spur of the moment rather than with any particular objective in mind." A number of the men around Junius nodded.

"What made you decide that this was the case, Private? Were you in the infantry or artillery? I'm guessing you weren't cavalry."

Junius wondered how the lieutenant would react to what he said next. He sensed that much depended on his answer, not just for him but for the entire group accompanying him.

"I was in the band, sir."

"The band, you say? Then how did you reach this conclusion concerning your generals?"

"Sir, I was privy to lots of things that were going on when I was seconded to be the colonel's aide during the battle at Pittsburg Landing."

"Oh, you mean Shiloh?"

"That old church there. Yes, sir. I got to hear the colonel referring to some of the commanders' decisions and what he thought were damn fool orders being tossed around. Turns out he was right. Ever since then, I knew we were in trouble. I'd see what was being decided because I was often on the battlefield picking up pieces of men who had no business dying on the battlefield. Yours and ours."

The lieutenant didn't say anything, so Junius decided to continue. He was angry and decided that he had no reason to contain his anger anymore.

"These are good men, sir. They don't deserve to be treated the way they have been. The way we've all been treated. They deserve to live out their lives at home with their loved ones, unlike our fallen comrades, who will never be able to. We're probably walking over spots where our comrades fell for no reason."

"Well, the war's over now, and there's no changing what has happened. I wish you all well on your journeys home," the lieutenant said.

Junius made his way back to Tuscumbia weeks after the encounter with the Yankee patrol. By the time he arrived there, he was drawn and haggard, having lost thirty pounds from his already spare frame. He asked around for his family and eventually found the minister who had assisted him in saving Ruby years before.

"Yes, I remember you, young man. You saved that young slave girl that day."

"With your help, yes, sir. We did that."

"What became of that young woman, Mr. ..."

"Hart, Junius Hart. My father informed me that she is safe and sound somewhere in Canada."

"I see. I suppose that is a good thing, then. Well, you'll be happy to know I had the pleasure of seeing your family some time ago as they passed through here on their way to their new home. Your mother, or if I recall correctly, your step-mother, came into the church to give thanks for the family's safe passage from that town in Missouri. She was in good spirits despite all that the family had been through."

"Their new home?"

"I believe they set out for Gadsden. Your father was able to get in touch with merchants he had known before your departure for California, was it? A shame the family never made it there."

"Yes, sir. Truly a shame." He thought about how much pain would have been avoided had they managed to continue on to California and wondered again at how their fortunes in this war would have differed had they settled in San Francisco.

But most importantly, Ruby was alive. He didn't know where, but she was somewhere. And his family was alive and well and not too far away.

Chapter 24

It was more difficult than Junius had anticipated to get to Gadsden. It appeared that life was slowly returning to normal, something he saw evidence of when he peered out the window of the train. What lay beyond the tracks the train passed through was all too easy to imagine, however, and he tried not to think about the broken families who would never recover from a lost son or brother or husband or father.

He made sure to feign continuing agony from the wounds whenever the conductor would come by, and more often than not, that kept him from having to produce a pass that might or might not be examined closely. The rest of the time, he would pretend to be asleep, or if there was no way to avoid the conductor, he would walk in between two cars and scurry up the ladder to the roof of the wagon for a spell. Eventually, he got tired of all the uncertainty and did what many other ex-soldiers did; hop aboard freight trains whenever they passed through the towns that had passenger stations.

Sometimes, when he looked out the window, he would see Africans who must have been slaves only recently but who now were free. Had Jim made it to New Orleans if, indeed, he had survived the war? Maybe he could somehow find a way to reunite with Ruby if only he could find out where in Canada she was.

When Junius reached Gadsden, he threw his satchel over his shoulder and walked into town, taking in the sights and sounds of the city. Even though he had never seen the town before, it reminded him of Tuscumbia. The principal landmarks were all the same, centered on the train station and river landing. The town was laid out just as Tuscumbia had been, and he could easily figure out where Main Street was and where the main businesses would be located. Surely, Radolfus would have established himself as soon as possible, and it wouldn't be too hard to locate him if he had.

There were only a few streets that he had to negotiate before he found what he was looking for. There, in a small, hastily constructed wooden storefront, hung a sign.

R.H. Hart Emporium.

He thought about rushing into the store to see his father, but something held him back at the last moment. Would his father really be glad to see him, especially given how he had joined the Guard so unexpectedly? Yes, his letters indicated he missed him and would welcome him back, but after all this time and what they had all been through, had he really meant it?

He waited on a park bench for two hours until late that afternoon when he saw Radolfus emerge from the store, and Junius followed him home. Once he got there, Junius waited across the street and sat underneath the shade of a tall oak tree while Radolfus entered the house. If he was right, Radolfus would emerge with his pipe in a matter of minutes.

When Radolfus reached the porch, he started to light his pipe, but he caught sight of Junius, who was now standing next to the oak tree across the street. He squinted and dropped his hands to his sides, threw his pipe aside, and ran across the street. The man had aged a great deal since they had last seen each other five years ago, but of course, Junius had aged well beyond his twenty-three years as well.

"It's really you? You made it! You came back! I can't believe my eyes," Radolfus said as he embraced his son.

They stood there together for several long minutes, and Junius felt the tears running down his cheeks and mixing with those his father had shed. Neither of them spoke, simply holding each other as if the longer they embraced, the more the pain and the heartache of the past several years would be erased.

"Is it in your satchel?" Radolfus asked.

"What?"

"Opa's fife. Where is it?"

Junius leaned down to open his satchel and pulled out what remained of the half he had been able to save.

"It's a long story, Paw. And one I regret having to tell you, but Opa's fife saved my life." With that, he recounted the stories of what had happened. Radolfus watched him tell the story without interrupting him. When Junius finished, he simply patted him on the shoulder.

Finally, Radolfus motioned for his son to go inside the house. Junius thought he had prepared himself for the welcome he would receive, but he hadn't anticipated how strong the emotions would be.

Hearing a commotion, the other family members started to trickle downstairs and inside. Lizzie broke into a big smile and came rushing forward to hug him as soon as she saw him. The other children looked at him as if he were a stranger come to visit, which he was now, he thought. He recognized Lalea when he saw her blue eyes, and he guessed she must be eighteen now.

The other children gathered around their mother, and Junius thought he could figure out who was who for the most part. As he took in the whole scene, he studied Sarah Anne more closely.

"Unless I am mistaken, it looks like there will be another Hart running around here soon."

"Next year, Junius. Yes, another one. Your father ..." Sarah Anne said as she patted her belly.

Junius tried to smile but felt that Sarah Anne had much more to say than she was letting on. "My father, yes. And you take care of him and your brood all by yourself?"

"Well, yes, Junius. If only I had someone to help me. Like Ruby ..." Then she stopped.

"Like Ruby," Junius repeated.

Sarah Anne stopped watching the children, and Junius thought she was going to say something to him, but she didn't utter a word.

"At least we know she is safe," Sarah Anne said.

Rather than answer her, he simply took in all the children again and walked out of the house. It was just as easy to ignore her now as it had been before the war.

"Paw?" he finally said, trying to break the silence that seemed to engulf them.

"There's something I need to know, son."

It was the conversation Junius had known would have to take place, but he wasn't sure how to begin it. So, he waited.

"Why did you do it, son?" Radolfus asked him when the others were well inside the house.

"Paw?"

"Why did you go off to fight with the Rebs, Junius? I've never understood. It's always puzzled me what would have possessed you to do such a thing."

Junius tried to formulate an answer, but the words wouldn't come. How could he begin to explain?

"I don't know, Paw. The Underground Railroad ..." And there he stopped, not knowing how to continue.

"She never made it to the Underground Railroad, did she?" Radolfus asked.

Junius thought back to the last time he had seen Ruby, just before he lost consciousness. The look on her face as she called his name before the Jayhawker pistol-whipped him.

"I don't know, Paw. I lost her."

"Lost her?"

Junius explained what had happened, recalling everything he could leading up to that awful moment. Junius only told

Radolfus the parts that he could handle. There was no way he could tell Radolfus what had transpired between them before she was taken away. He would never have been able to understand how he and Ruby could have been together the way they were. For all his feelings about slavery, his opposition to the reprehensible institution, Paw couldn't possibly appreciate what it would be like being with a colored girl, no matter how light-skinned she was.

"So that's why you joined up with the Rebs then, isn't it? You were angry."

"Yes, that's true. I just didn't know what else to do. I thought if I joined up with them, they might head to Kansas City where I could somehow find her and bring her back. It was foolish on my part, but I was sick with grief."

"And you couldn't tell me? And you couldn't admit your failure to Jim, could you? You knew he would have blamed you, and me, for letting you take her up there on a fool's mission. A mission which was totally unnecessary."

Junius's head snapped back when Radolfus said that. "Unnecessary? What do you mean? We agreed she had to be saved. The slave-catcher. He was there. He was planning on kidnapping her. To sell her."

"She wasn't a slave, Junius. Nor was Jim."

All of a sudden, things made sense to Junius. Ruby and Jim weren't slaves. That's why Radolfus treated them so well. Unlike the other slaves that other families they had known had owned.

"Then why did you let me take her? Why did Jim agree to it?"

"Things were confusing then. I was worried that if Ruby stayed with us, something might have blossomed between you two. I could see it in your eyes. And I could see it in hers whenever she heard you playing the fife. Hard to keep that a secret."

"But to let us go on a trip like that? You didn't think that something might ..."

"I suppose I did. Yes, probably. But it was such a short time that I am sure you had her safety uppermost in your mind and that you wouldn't have allowed yourself to take advantage of the situation."

Junius didn't say anything. He looked out at the country-side. The memories were almost too much to bear.

"Am I right?"

Rather than answer his father, Junius said, "I'm still mighty tired. Is there somewhere I can lie down?"

Chapter 25

Soon, Junius went to work in Radolfus's store, stocking shelves, doing odd jobs, sweeping when needed, and occasionally waiting on customers. But his mind wasn't on his work. Something was missing.

At the same time, he was surprised that, of all the things that he recalled from their previous homes in La Grange and Tuscumbia and Harrisonville, it was Sarah Anne's piano-playing that brought back the fondest memories.

Although they had never been close and he at times thought he knew she resented him for even existing, their relationship developed after the war. It was as if she had come to respect him for surviving amidst all the carnage the war had produced. She never asked him anything about the war or his experiences, but it seemed to him that she actually felt concern for his well-being, something he had found lacking in their days in Tuscumbia and Harrisonville.

Whenever he came home from work, if she was sitting at the piano, as she tried to do at least a little bit each day, she would offer him a smile, and her playing would become a little lighter, as if there were more energy in it, even if only for a moment.

Coming home from work one day, he found her sitting at the piano, apparently lost in thought.

"What is it?" he asked.

"Oh, I wish I had a grand piano instead of this spinet. I know your paw got me this one, but I feel like I could do so much more with another one. I wish I could understand better how it wants to be played. How it needs to be played," she said.

"What do you think would help you play better?" he asked.

He was surprised when she answered him, saying, "Oh, Junius, there is so much the piano can teach you if you understand it. I suspect it is like your fife. Not just your grandfather's fife, but any fife. You have to learn to coax the instrument to speak to you in its own special way. If I had more sheet music, different kinds of music, instead of these few little pieces, I know I could play them. But I don't know how to go about collecting them."

He looked inside the spinet as she continued playing. It was obvious that some of the hammers were broken and several of the strings were corroded. It looked like the wood on the right side of the piano had swollen, which he suspected was due to the constant humidity. Those were the keys that sounded off to him whenever she struck them.

"I understand, Sarah Anne," he said as he stepped forward to embrace her, an act that surprised even him. But she had taught him something that he needed to learn. Something that opened his mind to possibilities he hadn't considered before.

She started to recoil, but he held her firmly by the shoulders, saying, "Thank you!"

"Whatever for, Junius?" she asked as she blushed.

Without answering, he went out to the front porch to digest what she had just revealed to him. There were other instruments that were important, especially the drums and the banjo, but everything rested on there being a piano at the core.

Junius recognized that this single instrument needed to be at the core of any song if that song were to truly impart the range of emotion that only music could generate. He was sure that there were folks who could make her spinet do things even Sarah Anne couldn't have imagined.

Sarah Anne had just unlocked the vault to his future. He couldn't imagine going back to Harrisonville or anywhere else to work at a newspaper or follow Paw's footsteps and become a tailor. Not now.

No, music was the one thing that kept the soldiers' spirits up during the war, before and after battles. There had to be a way to continue to involve himself in music, even if playing the fife no longer would be the source of that joy.

Chapter 26

Junius had decided what his future career would be, and now he had to set out to make it happen.

Despite the memories of the war, he missed, more and more, having music in his life. The fife that the army had purchased him didn't have the magic of Opa's fife, and toward the end of the war, there hadn't been much call for playing the instrument at all as the Confederate Army had retreated after each additional defeat.

The guilt about whatever had happened to Ruby continued to plague him at odd moments. Something would remind him of her look or her laughter, and he would be transported back to their fateful journey and time together.

For whatever reason, Sarah Anne no longer protested when Junius sat at the piano and tried to play a simple tune. Nor did she protest when he would prop open the lid and peer into its bowels. And this he did with increasing frequency and ever greater attention to the details of its intricate workings. Whenever he traveled to Mobile or Cincinnati, he would make sure to include a detour to the finest hotel and restaurant to listen to the piano being played in the lobby.

On one such excursion to Cincinnati, he approached the pianist in the lobby of his hotel, whom he had observed before when the man smiled at him. The man played the piano as if he had been born to do so, and Junius wondered how and where he had learned to play. The piano reminded him of the one that Margaret had played, but it was even grander.

"Excuse me, sir," Junius said cautiously. The man arched

his eyebrows as he continued to smile at Junius.

"I was wondering," Junius continued, "would you mind if I bent your ear with some questions concerning your piano?"

"By all means, ask me anything you would like," the pianist said.

"I want to learn more about the business of manufacturing pianos. I have in mind to learn how to play the instrument and then find a reputable manufacturer and sell them back home."

The pianist stopped playing and stroked his chin. "I see. Well, I suppose that would be quite interesting. And could be very profitable. Do you know of anyone who plays the piano?"

"My stepmother does," Junius answered.

"Well, that's a start, I suppose," the man said. "What you need to find is someone near where you live in ..."

"Alabama, Gadsden," Junius said.

"Gadsden?" the man said. "That would never work for what you need. You'll need to go to Atlanta probably, once that poor city recovers from the effects of the war."

Junius considered what the man said as he examined his piano more closely, seeing a nameplate that read *Steinway*.

"Louis Arnold. Folks just call me Lou."

"Junius Hart. Pleased to make your acquaintance. I would appreciate your advice, Louis."

"I would think about Atlanta one day soon. There are other manufacturers, but perhaps none quite like the man who made this beauty."

Looking at the piano in and of itself was intimidating. There were so many parts that didn't make any sense to him.

Louis noted what he was doing and started to chuckle. "You're wondering what all the mystery is, aren't you? You can't figure out how and why the whole thing comes together, can you?" he asked, his eyes dancing in amusement.

"No, I can't. I play the fife and have been able to learn the drums somewhat, too. But this beast is mystifying!" Junius said.

"I'd be happy to make it all make sense to you, but that would require some time. Would you be willing to dine with me tonight?"

Junius couldn't say no, even if it meant that he would be paying for both of their dinners.

Louis and Junius were seated at the table nearest the piano Louis had played earlier that evening. Louis explained that he had arranged that in advance in the event he needed to demonstrate anything to Junius. Over the course of a sumptuous meal that included two bottles of wine, Louis went over the architecture of his grand piano with exquisite detail.

"The keys are real ivory," Louis said.

"I see," Junius said, unsure what else to say.

Then Louis demonstrated the difference between hitting the hammer of a key hard and hitting it gently, and Junius began to understand why Sarah Anne had trouble refining her skill.

Before they finished the second bottle of wine, Louis turned his attention to the dampers, and Junius listened intently, trying his best to grasp what Louis was telling him.

At the end of the meal, he felt sufficiently informed to begin to hatch his plan. Somehow.

Junius returned to Gadsden full of ideas but without any clear notion of how to proceed. He found himself daydreaming more and more as he continued working in his father's store but was increasingly bored, and with that came frustration. He kept to himself more and more as he tried to figure out what he could do next.

Several weeks went by when something happened to change everything. As Junius was leaving Radolfus's dry goods store one afternoon, a man carrying a satchel brimming with what appeared to be books was making his way to a wagon he had parked just down the street from the store. When the man stopped alongside the wagon, he put the satchel down beside several others that were already loaded in the wagon. Seemingly trying to rearrange the books, the man pulled out one of the volumes and paged through it carelessly. Passing by the man and his wagon, Junius got close enough to see what the man was looking at. It was music! The man would trace a line with his index finger and then hum a tune. Junius wasn't sure where he had heard the song before, probably before or after a battle somewhere in Tennessee.

Unable to continue walking any further without finding out more, Junius asked, "How do you know that tune, good sir?"

"I had the distinction of serving in the Confederate States Army, my good man. I've probably marched across the states of that defunct entity more than any man you know," he said.

Junius doubted the man could have marched more miles than he had, given that his war had begun in Missouri and taken him across most of the states with the exception of Virginia, but he allowed the man the luxury of thinking that he had traversed more states than anyone else had. For now, anyway.

"What books are those?" Junius asked.

"Books? Not exactly books. I represent my employer, Root and Cady, out of Atlanta, publishers of songbooks. They are compilations of tunes that I and others like me heard while we tried to defend our sacred way of life. Not that we were able to accomplish all that much, as it turns out, nor was it all that sacred!" he said.

"May I see one?" Junius asked.

"Did you serve during the recent conflict?" the man asked Junius.

"I did."

"You must have seen and heard what I did then. Do you

have a musical background by any chance?" the man asked.

"That I do."

"Well then, here, have a look. See if you recognize any of these tunes."

Junius picked up the volume lying in the wagon closest to him. He thumbed through it and recognized most of the songs in the book. He started humming to the ones that his fellow soldiers had sung most often.

"I know all of these songs. We sang some of them in camp. Others I heard here and there as we marched," he said.

"Then there's 'Flight of Doodles' and 'Root Hog or Die.' I never understood how two songs could emerge from the same tune, one for the Yankees and one for us Rebs, but there you have it. And 'Tramp, Tramp, Tramp,' our version, not the Yankee one!" He smiled to himself, remembering the good time around the campfires in between battles, when the men could appreciate the fact they were still alive, telling tales of sweethearts left behind and what they would do when the war was over and they could all go home.

"And there's even a section for the Negro spirituals! I started hearing them more and more as the war dragged on. Why, there's 'Go Down Moses' and, of course, 'Slavery Chain Done Broke at Last'!" Junius said.

"Then you can imagine how much time it took to gather all these together and transcribe them," the salesman said. "We need to keep these songs alive for future generations, my good man. Even the ones the Negroes sing. Otherwise, just like everything else, our heritage will be lost. No telling what will happen now that all the slaves are freed. Who knows what will happen when we cede the reins of government to them? Something which will surely happen."

Junius ignored the man's observations and concentrated on the books.

"Do you sell many of these songbooks?" he asked.

"We are starting to, yes indeed. Unfortunately, we are

confined by necessity to the area near Atlanta, such as this part of Alabama. What Root and Cady really need is a way to penetrate the larger markets. Places like Nashville and, dare I say, it, New Orleans even."

"New Orleans?" Junius asked.

"Lots of music comes through New Orleans from the Caribbean. Places like Cuba. By the way, who do I have the pleasure of speaking with?"

"My name is Hart, Junius Hart."

"Aaah, that's why I find you here, not too far from your father's store, I suspect? I'm William Arnold."

"Your line of work sounds intriguing, Mr. Arnold."

"Does it? Well, I wish we could use someone like yourself here in Gadsden to promote our business, but that would make things difficult for me, of course," Arnold said.

Junius hardly heard the man as he continued speaking. His mind was already selling songbooks and pianos together.

New Orleans. That would be a place to establish such a business. Not only was the city returning to its pre-war eminence, or so it seemed from the accounts of customers to Radolfus's store, but the steamboats all needed pianos. And if the steamboats needed pianos, sooner or later, the bars and restaurants and hotels would too.

Chapter 27

After Junius had spent a year in Gadsden, Radolfus sent him out on buying trips more and more. Junius's repeated visits to Cincinnati convinced him that the city and its inhabitants were too wedded to the old Southern way of life even though it was in Ohio. It was just like being in Kentucky during the war, and that brought back memories he'd just as soon forget. Even the Africans who lived there acted more like the slaves he had encountered during the war rather than freedmen. Mobile, on the other hand, had some potential for what he was planning, but he wasn't sure it would be able to escape its past either. Plus, there were continuing outbreaks of yellow fever that scared him.

Yellow fever plagued New Orleans, too, but the city's future was bright, nonetheless. And people there not only had money but also knew how to enjoy life to the fullest. If it was anything like what Jim had told him long ago, Junius was confident it was the logical place to make his dreams come alive. He managed to convince Radolfus that he had to go to New Orleans yet again, and that he needed to do so at the soonest.

On his next trip to New Orleans, Junius went to Alciatore's restaurant on St. Louis Street, thinking he would get a bite to eat before continuing with his business. One of the patrons at an adjacent table asked him where he was from and why he was in New Orleans. Junius explained briefly what he had in mind to do, and the man seemed quite interested. As he left the restaurant, the man stopped to talk with Antoine Alciatore, the proprietor, on his way out, who then approached Junius's table.

"My friend told me that you have an interesting idea for a business," Alciatore said.

"Interesting, I suppose it might be, but I have yet to figure out how to get started with it," Junius said.

"You need to see Steinway," Alciatore said.

That was the maker of the grand piano in Cincinnati.

"Who is this Steinway?" Junius asked.

"German immigrant. I met him on my most recent visit to New York, when I ordered two pianos from him. He and his sons have been making pianos in New York for over a decade now. Knows what he's doing. Don't know if that is because he is Jewish or not, but the man builds a mean piano."

"Go to New York?" *Steinway might be Jewish? Or might not be? Isn't that what he had become, too - uncertain? Was he still Jewish? Had he ever really been a Jew?*

"Of course, New York. Everything that happens in this country happens because of New York," Alciatore said.

With his head full of ideas about going to New York, Junius returned to Gadsden. As soon as he and Radolfus were alone on the front porch after dinner, while Sarah Anne was putting the children to bed, Junius took a deep breath and just launched into it. "Paw, I'm going to New York."

"What? Why? We don't need to go to New York, Junius. We can get whatever we need here."

"No, Paw. Not for our store. I want to go into business for myself."

Radolfus paused before answering, looking at Junius blankly.

"Doing what? You want to compete with your own father?"

He thinks I want to be a tailor. Just like him and his father and his father too.

"No, of course not. I don't want to stay in Gadsden either. I saw too much during the war to be content here. Besides, a lot of things that happened to me during the war happened not too far from here. I've got to escape from those memories."

Radolfus took his pipe out of his pocket and started playing with it. "Yes, I suppose you do. I'm sorry; I forget that you didn't just play your fife during the war. The things you must have seen. What you had to have experienced. Even though you don't talk about it, I know it left scars on you. Some of them are very deep, aren't they?"

Junius didn't answer.

"So, what did you have in mind, Junius? For your business, that is?"

"Pianos. And sheet music." He held his breath, waiting for his father's reaction, which he was sure would be swift and probably negative.

"Tall order, son. Where would you set up your business? Atlanta?"

"No. New Orleans."

Radolfus looked away and didn't say anything.

"Paw?"

"New Orleans," Radolfus said, taking off his glasses and cleaning and drying them with the handkerchief he always carried in his vest pocket.

Neither one spoke for a few minutes, each instead just looking out across the lawn at the Coosa River as it wended its way south.

"Well, son, I suppose you should try it if that's what you want to do. Here, business has been very good of late, primarily due to your efforts. Do you have any money saved to finance such an adventure?"

"I have a little. At least enough to get me there and back."

He thought the conversation would end there and started to stand up.

"Why is New York important to this undertaking?" Radolfus asked.

"Henry Steinway lives there. That's where he does his business. I need to talk to him."

"What makes you think a man like Steinway would listen to anything you have to say?" Radolfus said.

"I haven't any idea whether he would even hear me out, Paw. I just know I have to try. Ever since that man in New Orleans suggested the idea to me, I haven't been able to think of anything else."

Junius continued, "Paw, it's not like I don't appreciate you giving me a job to do. It's just that I don't feel like I have the same calling as you. You love making clothes and seeing how they fit your customers. I can see it in your eyes when they look pleased. And now, with the dry goods store, your new customers like you too."

Radolfus sat still. Junius couldn't tell whether it was sadness, curiosity, or sudden interest in his father's eyes.

"I just don't belong here. But you do. You are one of the most respected businessmen in town," Junius said as he waited for his father to say something.

Why is he looking at me as if he has never seen me before? Junius thought.

"Paw, I want to find something to do that makes me happy the way your work and your store makes you happy. I know that it took you a long time to save enough money to open the store in La Grange, and then you took on a huge risk moving to Tuscumbia. We never made it to California because of ..." He couldn't help thinking of the trip up the river and Sarah Anne's demands that they go no further.

His father smiled at him and nodded.

"That's what I want to be, but I can't do it under you. I need to be on my own, chasing my own dream. And I learned what that dream is as I listened to all the music I heard during the war. Wherever I went, what I heard resonated in a way I never could have expected. I think when my fife broke, it may have been the best thing that happened to me."

"You're glad Opa's fife broke?" Radolfus said, incredulous.

"No, I don't mean that I don't miss the fife. I loved it. I loved that you entrusted me with it. It saved my life, too. What I mean is that for that brief period of time when I didn't have a fife, I realized just how much I missed making music. Without my fife, I could only listen to other instruments being played. It forced me to open my ears to other instruments more than I ever would have otherwise."

Radolfus stroked his chin, took off his glasses, and rubbed the back of his head.

That meant Paw was thinking. Whenever he rubbed the back of his head and cleaned his glasses on his shirt sleeve, he was formulating something in his mind.

"So, what do you propose to do exactly? How will you make a living?" Radolfus asked.

"I sincerely believe that I can sell pianos. It all started when I heard Sarah Anne play. Everyone is going to be playing the piano; I just know that. And people will need to buy the sheet music to learn to play the songs, their favorite tunes. And I need to find out if I can do it, whether I succeed or fail. Can you understand?"

"I understand. And I don't blame you. How can I help you realize your dream?"

Junius couldn't believe his ears. His father wanted to help him? Not for an instant would he have thought that would happen.

Radolfus continued, warming to the idea. "It will take you at least one week to get to New York and then another week to get home again. You'll need a train ticket there and back, at least three or four nights in a hotel, enough money for food, and enough to buy your stepmother something from New

York to make her think this trip is worthwhile. So, you should plan on being away for at least a month, perhaps a bit longer. In the meantime, you'll also need a new suit to meet this man, which I can make for you. Some shoes, too. You'll have to look your absolute best. He'll need to know that your family is behind you, too. After all, he is a German, too, correct?"

"Yes, sir."

Junius couldn't believe what his father was saying.

"When was the last time I made you a suit of clothes, Junius?"

"Before the war, Paw. Long before the war."

"I thought so. You've grown some since then, haven't you?" he chuckled.

Chapter 28

July 1868

Two weeks later, Junius sent a telegram to Mr. Steinway asking to seek a meeting to present a business proposition. It was several days before a response came, and when it did, it was short and to the point.

HART STOP COME IF YOU MUST STOP I WILL LISTEN TO YOU FOR FIFTEEN MINUTES STOP THOROUGH PRESENTATION EXPECTED STOP SEPTEMBER FIRST 9:00 A.M. STOP 375 PARK AVENUE STOP STEINWAY STOP

"Well, at least you will meet the man!" Radolfus said.

"A presentation? What kind of presentation can I make?" Junius asked.

"I guess you better think through a little more what you have decided to do," Radolfus said. "Here, I can help you with some ideas, and we have at least a week before you will have to catch a train to New York. This will give us plenty of time, and if, after that, you don't think you have a strong case, you can always cancel your trip and meeting with Herr Steinway."

Junius had no idea what to present or how to present it. All he could do was talk through his plan, as rudimentary as it was. Everyone needed pianos, and there was a dearth of piano makers in the South.

Radolfus did indeed help him, however, drawing upon his experiences from starting his own dry goods stores both before and after the war. By the time Junius was ready to begin his journey, he had a coherent plan to present to Herr Steinway.

Junius took the train to New York two weeks later. First, he had gone to Birmingham from Gadsden to get another train to Atlanta, passing near where some of the last battles he had participated in had been fought, including Resaca, where he had been sure he was going to die. At least the train didn't go anywhere near Chattanooga, where he felt the war had truly ended long before it actually did. From there, the train went through the Carolinas and into Virginia. Once he had reached Richmond, he had seen the devastation that both sides had inflicted on the former capital of the Confederacy and had again wondered why anyone had thought that the war would make sense.

From Richmond, he had continued via train through Washington, and northward. Once he had reached Baltimore, he traveled on the Baltimore and Ohio Railroad through New Jersey into New York City, arriving at the central station in lower Manhattan in the early morning hours, after numerous delays caused by unknown but apparently common problems. Passengers who had made the trip on previous occasions appeared to be reconciled to the delays and took them in good stride, even joking about them and placing wagers on how long the various delays would last.

Carriages were everywhere, and the stench of the manure was almost overwhelming. Hansom cabs were readily available, but he didn't know where to go, so he simply took his valise and marched across the street to the nearest rooming house that didn't look too expensive nor too run-down. Just crossing the street from the station to the rooming house, he heard several languages being spoken by people of every different hue he could imagine. As he did so, he tried to imagine what New York must have seemed like when Radolfus had first set foot in America thirty years earlier.

He had no problem securing a room for several days at a reasonable rate from the desk clerk, who was wide awake, even in the early morning hour, and as Junius climbed the stairs to his room, gentlemen were coming and going the entire way. Once he finally fell asleep, he found that the incessant hub-bub was something he could get used to, and he slept not only through the night but also well into the late morning and woke up mildly refreshed.

The next two days in the city, he tried to familiarize him-self with his surroundings and walked past buildings, wait-ing until he heard piano music emanating from one, and then would go in to get a closer look, acting as though he had an appointment, and sit in a corner trying to distinguish what kind of piano it was. Sometimes, he would simply stand on the sidewalk looking up at a building, listening intently to how accomplished the pianist was. At other times, he would walk into a restaurant or saloon and pretend he was waiting for a table or a barstool while listening to the pianist try to extract what the piano would offer him. If no one was playing the piano at the time, he would simply catalog its appearance in his mind.

After two days of getting acclimated to the city, it was time for his appointment with Mr. Steinway. He showed up at the address he had been given and discovered an ornate building that itself was intimidating. Or maybe it wasn't that which intimidated him but rather simply the enormity of what he was about to propose. Either way, he had come too far to go back now. Succeed or not, he had to try because he couldn't imagine returning yet again to Gadsden and living his life there. The war had changed him in ways that he was still discovering.

As he started up the steps to the building, he pulled out his handkerchief to mop his brow, as he was perspiring pro-fusely. His stomach started doing flip-flops, and he paused to settle his nerves before entering the building.

The building had four floors, and signs pointed to a con-cert hall behind the showrooms and offices. Gaslights illumi-nated the entire building even though it was a very sunny day, and all he could see was a sea of pianos. Impossibly, signs suggested that there were additional ones in the upstairs rooms as well. In addition to the numerous pianos, the divans and armchairs and side tables were made of the finest materials, and the woodwork was intricately hand-carved with scenes depicting all manner of things.

His eyes, however, kept returning to the pianos. Two of them, in particular, in the center of the showroom were like nothing he had ever seen before. They were grand not only in size but also in the quality of the workmanship and the beauty of the keys. He stood transfixed for several minutes, unable to decide whether to touch one of them or simply continue to admire it from a short distance.

After several minutes, a middle-aged woman with an accent that was vaguely familiar approached him and addressed him promptly. She wasn't unattractive, although rather severe in appearance.

"Mr. Hart? Junius Hart?"

"Yes."

"Very well. Please be seated. Mr. Steinway will see you shortly. Please be aware that Mr. Steinway is very hard of hearing. You'll have to speak up at times to make sure he hears you, and it may seem as though you are yelling."

Mr. Steinway is hard of hearing? How is that possible? he wondered.

"Thank you." He studied the room carefully as he seated himself on one of the luxurious divans. There were newspapers and magazines neatly arrayed on a mahogany coffee table. He counted at least five different newspapers, not just from New York but also from Boston and Washington. The headlines bemoaned the fact that Andrew Johnson was turning out to be a disastrous replacement for the assassinated Mr. Lincoln. Even though he had been acquitted by one vote in his impeachment trial three months earlier, most observers were anticipating a stinging defeat for the Democrats, who had dumped him in favor of Horatio Seymour in the upcoming presidential election. It was all but a foregone conclusion that former General Grant would be the next president of the reunited United States.

While he waited, Junius wondered again what had possessed him to undertake what loomed as an impossible mission. What skills did he possess to succeed at a business enterprise of the scope he was considering? Steinway would think him to be presumptuous for even considering his idea, let alone approaching him about it. All of a sudden, he began to feel ill. As he turned toward the desk to ask the woman who had greeted him for some water, the door to the inner sanctum opened, and an august, stern-looking man gazed out at the showroom. Junius stopped dead in his tracks as the man's piercing eyes alighted upon him.

"Hart?" he demanded more than asked.

"Yes."

Steinway seemed to consider him a moment longer. "Speak up, young man."

"Yes, Junius Hart."

"No accent?" Steinway observed.

"Excuse me? Oh, no, from Germany, no, sir. My father was from near Tubingen, came here over thirty years ago."

"Very well, come along then, I don't have all day."

Steinway listened as Junius explained his proposal. Junius thought he must have gone on for much longer than the allotted fifteen minutes but, glancing at the clock on the wall, realized he had only spoken for about seven minutes. Steinway seemed to be looking past him as he finished his presentation and remained silent for the longest minute in Junius's life. Finally, he stood up and walked toward the window with his hands clasped behind his back. Junius thought Steinway would have to say something with his next breath or Junius would have to bolt for the door and run from the building as fast as possible.

"Intriguing," Steinway said in what amounted to the loudest whisper Junius had ever heard.

"Intriguing?" Junius repeated.

"Yes, indeed, it is intriguing," Steinway said. "You make a very strong case for what you propose to do. Unfortunately, however, I am not in a position to consider a working arrangement with you," Steinway continued.

Junius was crestfallen but remained silent and forced himself to stay still. He hoped his facial expression didn't betray his emotions.

Steinway rose and walked around the room for a minute. Junius thought he was allowing him to collect himself before telling him the interview was over.

Instead, Steinway continued.

"I find myself in a peculiar position where my, or rather our, business is so lucrative that I am unable to consider new ventures. I have turned over operational control to my sons, given my advanced age, as they remind me, and what I also believe is their desire for my early demise. They now determine what new endeavors we shall be undertaking. Right now, they are contemplating a venture that would include selling our pianos in Paris. France, can you imagine? American-made pianos exported to Paris to sit in all the lounges of that great city." Steinway chuckled as he said this.

Junius thought how ridiculous his proposal must have sounded even though Steinway had said it was intriguing. Perhaps he was just humoring Junius after all.

"I suppose I should say they have taken control rather than that I gave them control, but such is life," Steinway said.

"I have a friend, however, a former colleague, who arrived from Germany at approximately the same time I did. He is also in the business. We were partners for a while until we decided our friendship couldn't survive our partnership, so we parted ways. Amicably."

"I see," said Junius, not really seeing but wanting to say something.

"His name is Heintzman. Theodor Heintzman. He is in the piano business in Canada. Toronto, in fact. Probably one of the few habitable cities in that god-forsaken wasteland of a country. How people survive in that cold, I have no idea, but survive they do. Theodor and I are good friends, and I can inquire whether he would be willing to arrange a visit with you to discuss what you have proposed to me. Unlike my situation, I suspect he will be more than eager to entertain your idea. Would it be permissible with you for me to contact him accordingly?"

Canada. Even though Junius hoped Ruby had made it there, he rarely thought of Canada as an actual place. It was more a state of mind that came to him when he dreamt of Ruby.

"That's a long way from here, isn't it?"

"Yes, but you came this far in pursuit of your dream, my good man; what is a little farther?"

Chapter 29

True to his word, Steinway made the arrangements with Heintzman. Junius was to travel to Toronto the following week. In the meantime, Steinway offered Junius the opportunity to see how pianos were built, how he acquired the requisite materials for their construction, and interviews with the craftsmen who melded the twelve thousand parts into the coherent whole that became the piano, as well as with the men who were responsible for the marketing and sale of the instruments. The most prized jobs were those that dealt with the wealthy clientele—clientele who commissioned a particular piano with an ornate case for a grand salon, hotel, or restaurant.

As he learned more and more about the entire process, Junius started doubting, yet again, the wisdom of what he had decided to undertake. How could he possibly succeed?

Then Steinway did something that bolstered Junius's self-confidence beyond measure. Steinway invited him to accompany the great man himself to a concert in Steinway Hall, where he was greeted like a king. The two marvelous pianos that Junius had admired at the center of the showroom were the ones used in the concert. He couldn't believe how wondrous the sounds emanating from the magnificent beasts were as they resonated throughout the room, which remained otherwise completely silent.

"New York is too big for you. And I'm too big for what you're planning," Steinway told him. "You need someone who will take you on as a true partner if you are to succeed."

He paused and surveyed his domain as if realizing that

what he had created had taken over his life completely.

"You're better off with Heintzman, Hart."

"Better off? Why is that?"

"Heintzman is of your faith, no matter what he professes to be for the sake of his business."

Junius was confused. Surely Steinway was a Jew. He had to be.

"He's Jewish?" Junius asked.

"Yes, of course. Did you think otherwise?"

"And, Mr. Steinway, you aren't?" Junius asked.

"Whatever would have given you that idea? Of course not. I had Jewish friends in Braunschweig, but no, I myself am not." Why did Steinway feel it necessary to tell him that Heintzman was Jewish? Was that the real reason behind his decision not to go into business with him?

Radolfus had responded to Junius's telegram informing his father of his plans with what Junius decided was jealousy. He read and reread his father's telegram several times, trying to decipher what his father was truly feeling. Radolfus had been so supportive of his initial plan to involve Steinway in his enterprise, but now seemed to be backing away from supporting him. Was he leery of Junius going to Canada, or was he concerned that perhaps he had bitten off more than he could chew in what at first had seemed like a good idea? Had he decided that, on second thought, it was too ambitious an undertaking for a twenty-five-year-old whose main claim to fame was an ability to play the fife? Radolfus should have known Junius had inherited his gumption from the man who had braved the Atlantic at the age of eighteen and forged his own life in America.

After another conversation with Steinway about pianos, Junius felt ready to embark on his trip to Canada. Once he boarded the train to Albany, he remained lost in thought even as he peered out at the Hudson River.

"Veteran?" the conductor asked him as he boarded the train from Albany to Montreal.

"Excuse me?"

"Are you a veteran of the recent conflict between the states?" the conductor continued.

"Yes. I am."

"Thought so. I can usually tell. At least you came home to tell your folks about it. I lost a son to those damn Rebs myself. Never understand why they thought they had to preserve that horrid institution. Not that the Negroes deserve to be full citizens or anything, but they didn't deserve to live and die the way they did for all those generations. Where did you do your fighting?"

Unsure how to answer and aware that the conductor assumed he'd fought for the Union, Junius took his time responding. "I was primarily down south. Not really involved in too much fighting. Played the fife and cared for the wounded."

"I see. My boy got it at Gettysburg. Nineteen years old. Shot half his face off. Good thing Meade bested that bastard Lee. Can't believe the folks down south want to make him a hero now. Traitor that he was."

Junius listened to the conductor go on about what it had been like to travel to Pennsylvania to retrieve what was left of his son to bring him home to bury him in the family plot. He wondered how many others on the train had suffered the same sadness as a result of the ill-fated conflict.

"Ever meet anyone who owned slaves down there?" the conductor asked.

"Yes, a few."

"Did you give 'em what-fer?"

Recalling his incident in the barn outside Franklin with the soldier he had killed, he said, "Yes, I did."

The conductor smiled and said, "Good for you," and continued checking other passengers' tickets.

Getting to Toronto from New York City was an adventure in itself. First, Junius had to take a train to Albany, then straight north through rural New York. As the train wound its way north through incredibly verdant fields of various crops, Junius mused how different the North was from the South. How could the secessionists have ever thought they could be a match for this country, which offered so much raw material and produce in the way of opportunity? Life would have been so different if Paw had landed in Cincinnati or possibly even St. Louis instead of Alabama thirty years earlier.

The train veered away from the river as Junius passed Lake Champlain, continuing on into Canada, eventually reaching Montreal, far north and east of his destination. From there, another train, one hugging the border with the U.S., would take him to Toronto.

He understood why Gadsden suited Radolfus, who had begun to show his age after all the travails of his life, including particularly the hasty departure from Harrisonville back to Gadsden during the war. At least his father could now enjoy some peace. But the disappointment of not getting to California still weighed heavily on both of them. Occasionally, Junius wondered what had happened to Jim, but for some inexplicable reason, Radolfus refused to consider searching for him.

When the train reached the Canadian border, he was surprised at the attitude of the Canadians toward the passengers from America. He couldn't call it unfriendly exactly, but it wasn't what he had anticipated. The Blacks he encountered were unlike the ones with whom he had interacted before the war in the South. They smiled. They joked with each other. Even with Whites.

And the women. The Black ones. There were more of them walking around the city than he could have anticipated. They seemed to belong there in ways that no Black woman would ever belong in a city in the South. They were truly free in every sense of the word. He found himself trying to see if any of them looked like what Ruby must look like now. He tried to force her out of his mind but couldn't do it, even though she couldn't possibly have made it this far. It was as if something told him she wasn't far away. Was that why she came to him in his dreams? To lead him here?

Best to be on his way to Toronto to discover what, if anything, Steinway's friend Heintzman would have to say in response to his proposal.

Chapter 30

Junius finally reached Toronto after three days of traveling along the border, which was, for the most part, unremarkable except for the enormous lake that lay just south of the border. He couldn't imagine a body of water that large and wondered what it would be like during the winter. And if this was just a lake, what must it have been like for Radolfus when he crossed the ocean, which had to be that much larger even?

Toronto was much smaller than New York City and seemed far more provincial. Whereas New York City seemed to thrive in myriad ways with a cacophony of voices and accents, Toronto was more insular and altogether more White. Junius also found it hard to imagine that one could compete with the likes of Steinway and others in the same industry with what must have been such a small clientele. But Steinway had insisted that Heintzman was the man he needed to see, so here he was.

Heintzman and Company was located at 105 King Street West, between York and Bay Streets, just about a mile north of the ferry terminals on Lake Ontario. The wind whipped off the lake, and Junius imagined the chill must last all year round.

The Heintzman building wasn't all that imposing, although Junius supposed it must have seemed so to the locals. Certainly, it was nothing like the offices Steinway had in New York City.

A tall man stood up from a piano stool and approached him. Everyone else stopped what they were doing as soon as he stood up.

"May I help you, sir?" Heintzman asked.

"Yes, I believe you have received a telegram from Herr Steinway concerning my proposal? My name is Junius Hart."

Heintzman smiled as he introduced himself with a firm handshake and asked Junius to take a seat near the center of the room as he continued to scan the room.

Junius watched as he approached prospective clients gallantly with a smile that exuded total confidence. After a brief introduction and perfunctory questions about what the customers were interested in and why, he would quickly direct them toward one of the several salesmen in the room. If he didn't command a salesman's attention immediately, he would snap his fingers to get his employee's attention. Then, he would return to what Junius assumed was his favorite piano, sweeping his coattails aside and carefully studying the piano before starting to play softly. It was as if he was performing in some arcane theater production as he approached prospective clients and dominated not only the conversation but also the surrounding area simply with his presence. Once he started to play as if he were conducting a rehearsal for royalty, the room grew silent and everyone stared at his hands as they massaged the ivory keys.

Junius watched as the salesmen skillfully steered the clients in the direction Heintzman had instructed, regardless of what they had thought they were interested in. When a salesman would seek his advice on behalf of the prospective client, they nodded at any suggestion Heintzman made until they finally bought the piano of his rather than their choice.

After this virtuoso performance, Heintzman walked energetically to where Junius was standing and, with what appeared to be a sincere smile, suggested they withdraw to his office where they could discuss things privately. As they walked toward his office, Heintzman gave Junius a summary of his business and his approach to sales and asked Junius what he knew about the business. The occasional questions he asked resulted in him knowing far more about Junius than the other way around after half an hour.

Heintzman ushered Junius into his office just off the showroom. Although it was more modest than Steinway's had been, it still smelled of wealth, old and new. He directed Junius to a seat in a comfortable chair while the two waited for a nameless assistant to bring in tea to be served.

Heintzman had guessed at Junius's background and soon confessed to him that he and his family were also Jewish.

"My family and I are also of the faith, young man. But it is hard to succeed here unless you conform to one of the Protestant denominations or perhaps even profess to be Catholic. I began attending the Lutheran Church because I sensed a prevailing sentiment against doing business with Jews," Heintzman explained.

Junius wondered if Radolfus had ever considered taking such a step instead of trying to keep his faith alive despite the prejudices and biases that Junius knew his father had fought against for his entire life.

"Canada is too small a market for me, young man," Heintzman told Junius after Junius explained his idea for starting his business, possibly in New Orleans. "Yes, I would be interested in considering business with you, but I must say it would have to be on a trial basis. Need to test your mettle, as it were," Heintzman suggested.

He wants to work with me! Junius resisted whooping for joy and wondered just how his mettle would have to be tested.

"I don't understand. If you see the merits and the logic in my proposal, and we would both make money off of the idea, what exactly would need to be tested?" Junius asked as he rubbed his hands together.

Heintzman paused briefly. "You're eager, aren't you? You want to get started immediately. I understand, but we have to do this step by step in order to make sure everything works just so," Heintzman said.

Junius crossed and uncrossed his legs as he contemplated what Heintzman said. It was true that he was eager, but did he need to rush into anything? No, he didn't, so why not follow along with what the man suggested?

"Why don't we arrange to ship one of our pianos to New Orleans, and thereupon you will take delivery of it and see what happens?" Heintzman said. "Understand that shipping an instrument that far is no small undertaking. I will give you one month after receipt of the piano via steamship down the Mississippi, which you will confirm by telegram, and if you are successful, we can consider additional deliveries. On a consignment basis. Would that be agreeable to you?"

That was a far cry from what Junius had hoped for, but at least it represented a start.

Heintzman was testing him, too, Junius realized. Did he have the fortitude to deal with a delay to his plan until all the potential issues were identified and resolved, or was he so eager that he would overlook simple problems that would be compounded if not addressed properly?

"Yes, sir, it would be," he said.

"All right then, it's settled. Steinway seemed to take a liking to you, and I suppose I should respect his opinion in such matters even though I disagree with many of his practices. Come, I need to know more about you. I want to understand what happened to you during the recent imbroglio down south and whether we need to be concerned that you Yanks will try to invade us yet again!" Junius wasn't sure whether he was joking or sincere but didn't have time to ask.

"If your little war down there accomplished nothing else, at least it brought England to its knees as far as we are concerned. Without a Yankee victory, Canada would still be even more firmly under the queen's thumb. Perish the thought."

Junius thought that odd. Why were the Canadians afraid of the U.S.? Before he could pursue that subject, however, Heintzman continued.

"Tell me about yourself, young man. Although I suspect you're not as young as your appearance suggests. There has been some difficulty in your life of late, no?"

Junius related his life story, sensing he would receive a warm response, leaving little to the imagination. Occasionally Heintzman would interject a comment or ask a question, but for the most part, he simply let Junius tell his story.

Junius then told Heintzman about how he had considered finding Ruby after the war but realized that it would be senseless.

Heintzman interrupted him after he finished his story. "What was this Ruby's family name? If indeed she had one?" he asked.

Junius wasn't sure whether she would have given the name Hart or the name that Jim went by.

He considered the question and decided that Jim's pride would have required him to refer to her as Ruby Fontaine. "Fontaine."

"And you believe that she took the Underground Railroad to reach Canada?"

"Yes, sir."

"That route that the little lady who Lincoln said started the war wrote about."

"I beg your pardon?"

"Harriet Beecher Stowe. *Uncle Tom's Cabin*."

"Oh yes, her," Junius said, as he recalled his newspaper editor back in Harrisonville, Mr. Bogguss, complaining about her effects on how people thought about slavery.

"You know she based her story on a real person, don't you?" Heintzman asked.

"No, I didn't know that."

"In fact, that man isn't too far away from here."

"Who? Where?" Junius asked.

"Reverend Josiah Henson. A place called Dawn. That he established for escaped slaves, being one himself. It's not too far from here, in fact, near the British-American Institute. It was a thriving concern prior to your war between the states and in its immediate aftermath. Unfortunately, I understand that Dawn is slowly but surely being abandoned by what were over five hundred residents, many of whom have returned to your country now that the war is over," Heintzman explained.

Junius considered what Heintzman said but was unconvinced that there was sufficient reason to prolong his trip simply to satisfy his curiosity.

Just as he was about to express his doubts, Heintzman said, "Reverend Henson may even have information about your slave girl."

Junius wrestled with this new information. Dawn. What did he have to lose?

"How do I get there?" he asked.

"You might have to plan to go back to Alabama via Detroit. Would that be worth your while?"

"If I could find out what happened to Ruby, by all means, it would."

Chapter 31

Junius advised Radolfus that he would need more time in Toronto to continue his discussion with Heintzman and that he would need additional money to finance the rest of his trip. Rather than explain his true intent, he simply said that he would be returning via Detroit. It would probably take him at least two more weeks, if not longer, to complete the trip, and he might even be able to travel by steamboat down the Mississippi to see just what would be involved in the transport of pianos by river.

It took several days to reach the first stop, the British-American Institute that Dawn was part of and which Reverend Henson had established near Dresden.

He could see that only a few families and individuals remained in Dawn, and most of the buildings looked as though they were unused and unoccupied. They were strictly functional, with no trappings of any kind. He stood at the entrance for several minutes, imagining how welcoming it must have been as former slaves completed their journeys on the Underground Railroad. Finally, a young man approached him and asked him who he was and why he had come.

"I'd like to meet Reverend Henson if he is available," Junius said without seeing a need to give him his name. The young man simply shrugged and motioned with a nod for Junius to follow him into the settlement. They walked past several buildings that all resembled each other.

"These are the dormitories," the young man said. "Or rather, they were dormitories when everyone lived here."

He explained which ones were reserved for couples, which ones were for singles of either sex, and which ones were reserved for orphans whose parents had succumbed to the elements on their treks north to their hoped-for freedom.

Finally, they reached a building that had a spire and looked like it must be a church. "That's where the reverend preaches and where we hold meetings. Well, where we used to hold meetings before all the folks left to go back to where they came from anyway," the young man explained.

A few people shuttled in and out of the building. The young man led Junius inside, where a preacher stood in front of three or four pews, talking to several individuals. When the preacher saw Junius, he excused himself and walked toward him. The young man who escorted him nodded and silently left the building.

"My name is Josiah Henson. You must be Junius Hart," the preacher said as he held out his hand.

"Yes, Reverend. So, Mr. Heintzman has made you aware of my quest," Junius said.

"He has indeed. And I am curious, why is it that you are so desperate to find this young woman of whom Mr. Heintzman said you spoke? Surely there is more to the story than what you told him," Reverend Henson said.

Junius's face reddened as he ran his fingers through his hair several times. "There is indeed, Reverend. I fell in love with the young woman, and I suspect she did with me, too," Junius said. "I know that's not the usual way of things."

When Junius didn't say anything else, the Reverend spread his hands apart and smiled at him.

"Have you ever noticed the different shades and colors of our skin? Look around you here in Dawn, and you'll see bodies of men and women whose forebears have been violated more than once by White men. And, truth be known, some even took on White men as their lovers voluntarily. Indeed, few of us are without White blood coursing through our veins to some extent. I don't say that to criticize you for falling in love with a slave girl, but to think that such a thing is the exception is to overlook reality."

Junius felt ashamed of himself. Not for what he and Ruby had shared, but for assuming that they were unique. Although the reverend was anything but critical, Junius again debated the wisdom of his decision to even try to find Ruby. If he did, by some miracle, find her, or at least find out what happened to her, what could he then offer her after all this time? He hadn't really considered that problem until now and realized that should have been part of his equation.

The best thing to do was simply apologize to Reverend Henson for wasting his time while saving himself further embarrassment. He could continue on to Detroit, return to Alabama, make plans to go to New Orleans to receive the anticipated piano from Mr. Heintzman, and, with any luck, start to build his business. What a fool he had been to even think that he had any chance of success of finding Ruby and that finding her would be considered a success.

"Reverend Henson, I'm sorry for wasting your time. I should have known my mission was an impossible one."

"On the contrary, my good man. Your mission has been more successful than you yet realize. How much more successful it becomes will be determined shortly. Please have a seat. I must tend to something for a few minutes. You can pray if you like or simply observe what takes place here. I'll be back directly."

Chapter 32

Junius took a deep breath of the cool air, and tried to take in as much of the settlement as he could before he spotted Reverend Henson talking with two others, including one woman, between the two men. Although he couldn't hear what was being said, the other men were gesturing with their hands as they looked in Junius's direction.

The woman remained still. Then she started to walk toward Junius without waiting for the others to finish their conversation. There was something vaguely familiar about her mannerisms. The way she looked up toward the sky was reminiscent of ... Ruby.

He stood stockstill as he took in her movements and her uplifted face, even though she was too far away to make out her features clearly. She was thinner than he remembered her being seven years earlier, but he recognized her gait. She limped slightly, favoring her left leg, which she hadn't done before, but there was no mistaking who she was. At first, she kept her head down, but as she approached where Junius stood, she glanced up from time to time as if to make sure he was still there.

Junius's legs were shaking, and he was perspiring despite the cold. She was barely ten feet away when she stopped. Reverend Henson nodded at Junius, who then approached until he could almost reach out and touch Ruby. She curtsied slightly, surprising him by doing so, and then she said, "Good afternoon, Master Hart."

"Ruby, is it really you?" he asked.

"Yes," she said.

Junius started forward and reached out to touch the back of her hand. "It's good to see you, Ruby."

"How in heaven's name did you find me, Junius? After all this time?" she asked. Their eyes locked, hers looking like those of a wounded animal.

"I wish I could tell you, Ruby, but even I don't quite comprehend how I have managed it," he answered.

Reverend Henson cleared his throat. "You two should discuss things," he said. "That is, if you have a mind to, Ruby."

She shrugged her shoulders before answering. "I don't see how I can't since Junius has come all this way."

The reverend smiled. "Very well. Junius, if you would allow it, my wife and I would be honored to have you as our guest this evening for supper along with Ruby, and perhaps others, and then we can arrange accommodations for you until you decide to leave. It may take a day or two for you both to catch up on everything that has happened since ..."

"Yes, since that awful day," Junius finished his sentence.

"You tried to find me?" Ruby asked. Junius thought she seemed surprised.

"I did. Clarinda tried to also."

At the mention of Clarinda's name, Ruby's eyes went wide, and then she smiled a little.

"I wish I could have met her. I heard so much about her, but there wasn't time. I had to leave quickly once they ..."

When her voice trailed off, Junius said, "I understand."

Ruby continued, "I'm sorry for what happened to you that day. I saw the man hit you with his gun and didn't know if he had killed you. But I couldn't ..."

"Ruby, it is I who should be apologizing to you!" Junius said, as he couldn't help imagining what she'd had to endure, and thinking about how he had failed her at the time.

The Henson home lay just outside the Dawn settlement. It

was a two-story structure with a parlor and a kitchen on the first floor and the bedrooms situated on the floor above. Junius and Ruby walked there from the main part of the settlement together, accompanied by another couple and a boy that Junius guessed to be about six years old. The boy was very quiet and watched Ruby closely as another adult led him and the other children to another table.

They ate a dinner that Junius found surprisingly tasty, considering they served vegetables called fiddleheads, which were new to him. While the others quietly exchanged only the briefest of comments about the meal, Junius asked Ruby how long she had been at Dawn and what her life there was like. She kept glancing toward the table where the boy sat with another child, and she occasionally nodded in their direction.

"Reverend Henson seems like a good man. Has living here at Dawn been a good experience, given everything else that has happened?" he asked her.

Without looking at him, she simply said, "Yes."

Junius toyed with his water glass while he thought about how to proceed. "I understand a lot of people who were here have returned to their homes recently. Did you know many of them?"

"Some," she answered.

He noticed that she was hardly eating now, even though her plate was still full. "Do you think you would like to stay here? Or would you like to go back home?" he dared ask finally.

Ruby put down her fork and knife and stared straight ahead. He thought he saw a tear in the corner of her eye but then decided he must have imagined it.

She put her napkin up to her mouth before she answered and barely spoke above a whisper as she stared at her plate.

"Home, Junius? Home? Where is home to me? Do you mean where I grew up? Or where we lived before the war? Or where Jim is? Wherever that might be," she said, and he realized she was struggling to keep from crying.

Rather than continue to upset her with more questions, he changed the subject and started to explain how big Radolfus and Sarah Anne's family had become and how the children she would remember had grown. Gradually, she allowed a small smile to brighten her face as he explained what Lizzie was up to and how the younger ones sometimes drove Radolfus to distraction.

"I know this isn't the time or the place for this, Ruby, but I would truly like to learn what happened after that fateful day. You don't have to tell me things you don't want me to know, but I need to understand how you managed to survive everything. I've thought about what must have been an ordeal, or maybe more than one, and need to understand what I caused you to go through," he said, making sure only she could hear him.

"We can take a walk by the river after supper," Ruby said.

The river was a short, pleasant walk away through the woods. At first, they walked in silence as Ruby kept her head down with her arms crossed over her chest.

"Ruby, are you warm enough?" Junius asked.

She nodded, but as she did so, she wrapped her arms even more tightly around her chest and pulled her jacket even closer.

The light began to fade as nightfall approached, and Junius stopped and faced her.

"Ruby, we probably ought not go too much further."

She looked back at the settlement and nodded.

"You are cold. Here, let me help you stay warm just a bit." He put his arms around her. She was coiled tight as if she would strike out at any moment. He touched her waist slowly and gently, and as he did, he could feel her tension subside. When he managed to get his arms around her all the way, she melted in his arms and lifted her face to his.

"Junius, please kiss me."

They kissed, and all his memories of that fateful day on the way to Quindaro flooded his mind again. It was as if something precious that he had buried long ago suddenly resurfaced with a vengeance. He stroked her cheek and buried his face into her hair as they held each other.

After a minute, she broke free from his embrace and lightly pushed him away from her.

"You know, I have relived that moment probably a thousand times. Each time I do, I tell myself to forget about it, but then, days later, the memory comes back even more strongly, and I can't fight it. Sometimes, I think I make it stronger by trying to rid myself of it."

"I have done the same more often than I care to remember," he said.

"I always wondered what kissing you again would be like. Now I know, and it's exactly what I would have imagined it would be," she said.

They continued talking as they headed back toward the settlement. Junius was astonished at how much she remembered of their trip as she recounted what she had seen both then and later on the way to Canada.

Although she didn't go into detail about what happened after she was kidnapped by the Jayhawkers that day, she said something that startled Junius before they parted.

"Do you remember the man with the gun? The one who hit you with it?" she asked.

"Yes."

"You know which one I mean, the one with the scar on his face near his mouth?" she asked.

Junius nodded.

"He's the only one who didn't want to have his way with me. He made sure that they didn't hurt me while they ..." But she couldn't finish her sentence.

So, his worst fears were true. And he was responsible for what had happened to her. How could she ever forgive him?

Junius thought back to the day that he had wounded the scarred man after leaving Quindaro and wondered if he had survived. Maybe he didn't deserve what Junius had done to him, but still, he had been part of the group that had taken her from him and ...

Just before the twilight ended, they reached the center of Dawn and were about to part, taking care not to appear to be more than long-lost friends, showing no intimacy to what were sure to be prying eyes.

"Junius, there is something else you should know," Ruby said before they parted.

What else could she possibly want to tell him that couldn't wait a while longer? Was it really important to prolong this discussion, so painful to both of them in so many ways?

"It can wait, Ruby. Whatever it is, it can wait," he said.

Just then, the woman who had sat at the table with the children while they ate their dinner walked up to them with the boy Junius had guessed was about six years old and quite light-skinned, lighter than Ruby, with reddish hair.

"I have to tend to the younger ones now, Ruby," the woman said as the little boy took Ruby's hand.

"I know you do, Constance, thank you," Ruby said, smiling at the little boy.

He was a gangly young man, even at that age, whose eyes seemed to take in everything around him. Ruby continued smiling at him and he blushed.

"Junius, this is my son, Abraham," she said.

"Your son?" *Her son by whom? Someone she met on the Underground Railroad? Or one of the men who ...* He had so many questions that he couldn't separate one from another as he tried to fathom what she had just said.

She nodded and put her arm around the little boy, who

immediately leaned against her and closed his eyes.

After regaining his composure, Junius said, "Is he ..." but Ruby shook her head and put a finger to her mouth.

"Let me put him to bed, and then we can talk some more if you would like. And I suspect you do," she said.

Junius nodded as the two of them walked away. His mind continued to race with thoughts and questions about the boy as Ruby and Abraham crossed the camp and entered the dormitory. As if to interrupt his thoughts and further confuse him, the little boy turned around and waved at Junius just before he and Ruby entered the dormitory.

Ruby returned to the same spot a half an hour later to find Junius still standing where they had left him. She stopped in front of him and waited.

"Ruby, Abraham, what a fine-looking young man," Junius said.

"He's a treasure," she said. She paused. "Junius, I know what you want to ask me. But I can't answer your question," she said. She shifted from one foot to the other and wrung her hands before continuing, "I can't because I don't know the answer for certain. It could be you or any one of those three men. The men on the way to Quindaro. I have hoped that I would be able to figure out who the father truly is, but I have no way of knowing. I only know that I wish he were yours and that there was some way to prove it, but there isn't, and I can't."

She waited for Junius to answer, but he couldn't bring himself to say anything. He struggled to make sense of everything that had happened. He started to speak but choked on his words and fought to keep from crying, unable to imagine what she had endured all these years.

"Sometimes I look at him, and I think I see you in his features, but I can't be sure," she said.

Then Junius came to a decision. It didn't matter who Abraham's father was - he could be the boy's father if Ruby wanted him to be. He could be just as good a father as Radolfus had been to him, no, even better. That he could do. He took hold of Ruby's hands and looked deep into her eyes.

"Ruby, I'll be his father if you'll let me."

"What? What do you mean?"

"I'll be his father. I want to be his father. That should count for something, shouldn't it? I can convince him that I am his father if you'll support me. We can make that happen; I know we can. But you would have to believe it too," he said. "We can make a home, Ruby, a home for the three of us. A happy home."

"Where?"

"In Gadsden. Or, even better, in New Orleans."

She didn't say anything. Then she asked, "Junius, are you sure?"

"Yes, I am sure as I can be. Not a day has gone by that I haven't wondered about what became of you. And every day of my life, I have missed you. Please let me take you home with me, and Abraham too. And we can make a new life for the three of us. Please, Ruby."

Without saying anything, she reached up and took his cheek in her hands and kissed him fully on the mouth.

"Yes, Junius. I would like that. I would like that very much." She smiled as she said that, and they kissed again.

Chapter 33

The three of them journeyed to Toronto, where Junius introduced Ruby and Abraham to Mr. Heintzman and thanked him for his help in reuniting them. Mr. Heintzman even offered to help defray the costs of their return trip to Gadsden via Detroit, which Junius gratefully accepted.

On the way to Detroit and then to Gadsden, Abraham asked questions about everything. Fellow passengers couldn't help but notice and comment on how cute he was and how intelligent he seemed. They tolerated the little boy with the big green eyes and smiled as they endured his endless barrage of questions—questions about who they were and where they were going and why this and that. Not all of them, of course; there were those who still ignored the mixed-race couple. Nevertheless, Junius was proud of the boy and glad that everyone thought Abraham was his child. Eventually, Abraham got tired and fell fast asleep, only to wake up afresh with another set of questions. Junius marveled at the boy's intense curiosity. *He could be my son,* he thought.

He must be my son.

At last they reached Gadsden and greeted everyone fondly.

"It's so wonderful to see you again! And my, how everyone has grown. Why, Lizzie, you're a pretty young lady now, aren't you?" Ruby said.

And, of course, there were two additional children in the Hart family household, five-year-old Della and two-year-old

Radolfus Junior. Junius thought that even Sarah Anne seemed relieved to see Ruby back, especially because of how she delighted in talking to the children.

Abraham was shy at first, but gradually, the others came to accept him. Radolfus would comment about little Avram, and Junius tried to correct him at first but decided that if his father wanted to think of Abraham as Avram, that was perhaps a good thing. Only Sarah Anne seemed hesitant to embrace the child as one of the family.

As Junius watched Ruby talk with the children, and especially with Lizzie, he remembered how she used to enjoy listening to him play the fife from her vantage point in the cabin she had shared with Jim. She would mimic his playing and smile when he played a tune she particularly enjoyed. Junius wished he had his old fife and not just the half he had kept. The broken fife. The one that he used to play to Ruby whether she knew it or not. He would have loved to play it for Abraham.

But the fife had been broken, and he had lost half of it, and in any case, it just wasn't the same now that the war was over. Even the one that the army had purchased for him brought back memories still too raw and brutal to contemplate.

Instead, he took walks with Abraham to show him around the town. Abraham would grab his hand whenever he saw something new or unusual and force Junius to come to a complete stop until he answered the unspoken question that he had. Junius took him down to the river and told him more about his grandfather.

"Your grandfather taught me to swim. I'll bet he could do the same for you if we could convince him to live here with us," Junius said to Abraham. Regardless of who Abraham's father was, it was certain that Jim was his grandfather.

As they walked back to the Hart household, men Junius recognized would tip their hats to him, and Abraham would make a show of responding in kind as if he, too, had a hat to doff in their direction, then he would giggle.

Junius wanted Abraham to call him Paw but didn't suggest it because he wasn't sure how Ruby would react. The little boy didn't have any problem calling Radolfus Pappaw, though, despite the fact that he wasn't necessarily the boy's grandfather.

When Ruby finally asked about Jim, he was surprised she hadn't done so earlier.

"I didn't know how to since I was afraid something bad might have happened to him during the war. Do you know anything?" she asked.

"Yes, I do. I have learned from my correspondence with a certain businessman who is also acquainted with him that he not only survived the war but has returned to New Orleans," Junius said.

Ruby repeated the name of the city under her breath several times, gradually smiling as she said it more loudly. "Why are you in touch with a businessman in New Orleans?" she asked. "What kind of businessman?"

"His name is Monsieur Peychaud, and he knew Jim prior to Paw acquiring you and Jim when we were both young. I think he may even have known your mother." As soon as he said the word *mother*, her eyes lit up, and she looked as though she had seen a ghost.

Thinking he had made a terrible mistake, he started to apologize, but she shushed him by putting her hand over his mouth.

"No, it's fine. I am just so curious about her and about my life before Alabama and Missouri that I would truly love to hear more. I've never really had the chance to even express that, but now that you say there is someone who knew her ..." she said.

"I understand. Maybe we will have that chance if my plans develop," he said.

"Your plans? What plans?" she asked.

"The reason I was in Toronto was to meet with Mr. Heintzman. I don't see myself working in what amounts to a clothing store under my father for the rest of my life, Ruby. I've seen too much to be satisfied with that. I want to sell pianos. I have been thinking about New Orleans as the place to set up business. Or, once I am established in Gadsden, expanding to New Orleans or simply moving there."

When she didn't respond, he studied her carefully and realized yet again how beautiful she had become, and he could picture her so easily in society in New Orleans.

Several more weeks went by as Junius continued to refine the plans he had made with Heintzman. His thoughts were given additional impetus as he observed Ruby settling into life in post-war Alabama. While she seemed reasonably comfortable in the Hart household, Junius detected that she wasn't entirely at ease being back in this part of the South, where her memories of being a slave boiled just below an otherwise relatively calm exterior.

On one occasion, he saw her flinch when she saw a White man looking at her for more than just a second or when anyone tried to talk to her.

"Ruby, is everything all right?" he asked.

"Don't pay any attention to me. Just keep walking and don't stop to talk to those men, please," she said. As they passed by the men, he turned his head around to see that they were indeed staring either at both of them or perhaps simply at Ruby.

The time came for Junius to put his plans into action. To do that, he had to go to New Orleans.

"Junius, I so want to go with you," Ruby said, trying to hold back the tears Junius knew were just below the surface when he informed her of his plans to go to New Orleans.

"I know you do, but as Paw says, this time, it's for the best if I go alone. I won't stay in New Orleans any longer than necessary. I promise," he said. "It's important that I be able to concentrate fully on the business at hand down there, and I'm afraid Paw is right; if you were along, I dare say I wouldn't be able to do that!"

She made sure that no one could see them even though they were just outside the Hart home and hugged him for what must have been a minute by his reckoning, until he pulled her arms slowly from around his neck and kissed her delicately on the cheek.

"Your Paw and Sarah Anne don't suspect anything, do they?" she asked.

"No, I don't believe they do, and it's best they don't, at least for now," he said.

"Can I at least go to the train station with you?" she asked him through her tears.

"No, you know that's not wise, not just yet anyway. It's better if we say goodbye here, away from prying eyes who wouldn't understand," he said.

She nodded in a way that suggested to him that she wasn't prepared to quarrel over it. He kissed her forehead once more.

"Take care of that boy while I'm gone. He means a great deal to me."

Ruby stepped back and looked at him wide-eyed. She nodded at him, took his hands to her lips, and kissed them both. "Yes, Junius, we're both in your hands now. Regardless."

"Regardless?" he repeated.

"Yes, regardless of what happened or whatever will happen. Now, go before I decide not to let you go."

As much as he hated to leave Ruby behind in Gadsden, Junius

was excited about the trip to New Orleans. On the train ride, his mind wandered between what he hoped to accomplish there and his thoughts of Ruby. He had to focus on the business at hand. And that would mean hours of laying the groundwork. Maybe it would be better if Ruby and Abraham stayed behind in Gadsden a while longer until he could get things up and running.

While in New Orleans, he could investigate how well they would be received if they were to move there and set up a home together with Abraham. Even if, for some strange reason, she decided that she shouldn't marry him, they could still live together. With any luck, maybe he could even find a two-story building with a main floor large enough to accommodate the pianos and sheet music he hoped to sell with an upstairs where the three of them could live comfortably.

And, of course, there was Jim. Monsieur Peychaud's telegram informing him that Jim was indeed alive and well was welcome news. He couldn't wait to give him the news about Ruby and Abraham. Not only was his daughter alive, but he was also a grandfather to a fine young man. He might wonder why Junius hadn't brought them with him, and Junius would explain that they were just getting adjusted to life in Alabama after what had been a difficult experience and trip back from Dawn. Of course, he would promise to bring them along the next time, and with any luck the next time would be permanent.

Suddenly, Junius realized that this part of the trip wouldn't be easy. He had kept what actually happened under wraps for so long that he had forgotten others didn't know why he had enlisted on what became the Confederate side. The side that would have kept Jim and Ruby slaves if they had won the war.

It didn't matter now, though. The war was over, and they were free, both of them. All of them were free. And he and Ruby would start building a life together. He was sure Jim would be pleased with that development. How could he not be? They had become good friends before the war, and Jim was well aware of how well he and Ruby got along too.

Chapter 34

When Junius arrived in New Orleans, Monsieur Peychaud met him at the train station and escorted him to the accommodations he had secured for him in the French Quarter. They were to have dinner together that night and discuss the plans for the next day when Junius would see Jim for the first time in seven years.

After they had been speaking for a while, Monsieur Peychaud said, "I know Jim must be looking forward to seeing you. He still talks about what you did to get Ruby to safety before the war began."

Heat rose in Junius's cheeks. He wondered what, if anything, Jim knew about what had really happened.

"Do you have any news of Ruby at all? Have you tried to find her since the war ended?" Monsieur Peychaud asked.

What could he say? He didn't want to tell Monsieur Peychaud anything before he saw Jim. "I have some news of her, which I'll share with Jim when I see him tomorrow," Junius said.

"Of course, that is certainly appropriate," Monsieur Peychaud said. "Meanwhile, I must tell you about Jim so that you aren't surprised when you see him. After your family was forced to leave Harrisonville by General Grant, they went to Fort Scott, and Jim accompanied them there," Monsieur Peychaud said.

"Jim enlisted in the Union Army, in the U.S. Colored Troops, where he served with distinction, even though he was severely wounded at one point in a battle. After the war ended, he was able to land a position with the Freedman's Bureau in Arkansas, but he became tired of that after a while when he saw how ineffective the federal government was, and he decided to return home to New Orleans. I know he wanted to try to find Ruby, but I think the war had worn him out so much that he didn't have it in him to undertake any search that would lead to disappointment or to interrupting her new life, wherever that might have been."

Junius hoped Jim would appreciate knowing that he had found Jim's daughter and that Junius would be bringing her with him to New Orleans soon, probably to live as man and wife. After all, Radolfus had told him often enough that such unions were common and accepted in New Orleans.

"Jim's happy enough, but I know there is a sadness that he carries with him constantly," Monsieur Peychaud said.

The next morning, Junius got an early start and visited several shipping companies, being careful to avoid the one that Monsieur Peychaud said Jim worked at, to see what, if anything, he could arrange concerning the shipment of pianos from Toronto. He didn't want to surprise Jim with his presence in New Orleans until he had concluded his other business and was ready for what was sure to be an emotional meeting.

He was able to assess how much the initial shipment would cost and figured that Heintzman would find it acceptable based on their discussions in Toronto. The first shipment wouldn't be arriving for several months, so he still had time to investigate further if need be, but in the meantime, he was satisfied that the basic proposal was workable.

The following day, Junius and Monsieur Peychaud waited until lunchtime, when they knew Jim would be on a break from his work at the shipping office that employed him.

They were surprised to see Jim leaving the building as they were about to enter it. The first thing Junius noticed was how much older Jim seemed. Then he saw that Jim favored the left side of his body, but Junius couldn't see what the problem was. Plus, Jim had some gray around his temples. As Jim drew closer, Junius could make out his eyes and was relieved to see that familiar intelligence and curiosity which he had so admired years ago. How would Jim react to seeing him after all these years? At least Jim didn't know what had really happened to Ruby on that fateful day.

Junius couldn't help but be aware that Jim might judge him harshly for having joined the Missouri State Guard instead of the Yankee Army. He would have to explain, if Jim would let him.

"Hello, Jim," Junius said, reaching out his hand to shake Jim's.

Instead of returning the greeting, Jim said, "Why have you come here?" narrowing his eyes.

I joined the Missouri State Guard. Not the Yankee Army. It bothered him terribly.

"I wanted to see you. And to bring you news," Junius said.

"I'm listening."

Ruby was alive. However guilty Junius still felt, he hadn't failed. Not entirely, anyway. But he still owed Jim the truth about what had happened all those years ago.

"It's Ruby. I found her in Canada. She's alive," Junius said.

Tears welled in Jim's eyes. Monsieur Peychaud started to approach him, but Jim waved his hand at him, then closed his eyes and went down to his knees.

Junius stepped forward and crouched down next to his old friend, who remained silent.

"I knew she made it there thanks to her letter. I'm so glad she is still alive. Thank you. For finding her," Jim said as he stood up.

"I also have news for you that I think you'll appreciate, but I'd rather tell you in private."

Junius anxiously awaited Jim's reaction. There was relief

in Jim's face, but not the kind that Junius had expected to see. It was as if nothing else mattered once Junius told him that Ruby had survived. But there was so much more to the story.

"Let's meet later when you have time. Perhaps you'll dine with me tonight or when you are free? I can tell you the whole story then," Junius said.

"I would like that. In the meantime, have you been able to reunite Ruby with her family?" Jim asked.

Junius was taken completely off-guard by Jim's question and couldn't answer him at first. Gradually, he gathered his wits about him and asked, "The Harts? Yes, I suppose you could call them her family," Junius said.

"They are as much family as the girl has ever had, aren't they? And maybe now her father can do right by her after all this time," Jim said.

Junius felt the air go out of his lungs in a rush. He tried to reach out for something to brace himself before he stumbled but found nothing yet managed to stay upright. What was Jim suggesting? Someone else was Ruby's father.

"What do you mean?" Junius asked.

Jim shook his head slowly and then covered his eyes with his hand, looking down at the ground. "Oh, lord, so it's true," Jim said. "I always wondered."

"Wondered what?" Junius asked.

"I wondered if my sister had told Radolfus the truth before she died. She debated about it for weeks before she got sick and then even more after the doctors told her she didn't have long. She was a good woman, and she didn't want to hurt anyone if she didn't have to, so I was never sure whether she had told your paw the truth about Ruby," Jim said.

Now Junius's head was spinning. He had come on a mission to tell Jim the good news about Ruby, and instead, he feared he was going to learn a truth that would upend his life.

"I guess maybe it's true then," Jim continued. "Maybe your paw doesn't know that he is Ruby's father," Jim said.

For a moment, Junius couldn't hear anything. Then, he was aware of the world around him coming back to life, and a great weight pressed on his heart. Had he heard Jim correctly? Could it be true? If it was, this changed everything. For him and for Ruby. And for Abraham.

"I guess this is a shock," Jim said. "I'll tell you the rest over dinner."

The story that Jim told Junius at Antoine's that night was one that he, at first, found incredible, but as Jim explained, Junius began to see how it had developed and evolved.

"Your father fell in love with my sister Corinne the first time he laid eyes on her while here on business. I say she's my sister because we grew up together after her father died," Jim said. "Once her father died, things became difficult for our mother, and she gave Corinne up for adoption and then simply disappeared."

"Who was Corinne's father?" Junius asked.

"Everyone thought he was a pirate. His name was Jean Lafitte, and he took our mother, Catiche, a free woman of color, as his mistress not too long before he died."

"So, Ruby's mother wasn't a slave? She was born free?" Junius asked.

"Yes, and she and your father fell in love," Jim said.

"But my father already had a wife in Alabama, in La Grange, my mother, Elizabeth," Junius said, uncertain as to how much of Jim's story could possibly be true.

"Your father married his wife after my sister turned him down," Jim said.

"How did my father come to know Corinne, Ruby's mother?" Junius asked.

"They met on one of Radolfus's first business trips to New Orleans while he was setting up his business in La Grange. He even tried to convince her to come to Alabama with him, but she refused, knowing what it would be like for a woman of her color to live there. No one would have accepted their marriage. That's when he decided to marry your mother."

"Then how did you and Ruby come to live with us in Alabama and then in Missouri?"

"Your father came back to New Orleans again on business. But I think he really came back to see Corinne. Unfortunately, she died of yellow fever, leaving Ruby behind. I had a wife of sorts, a woman named Fanney, but she was an escaped slave, and she was recaptured."

"So, Paw brought you back to live with us and Sarah Anne?" Junius asked.

"No, with your mother, Elizabeth. Your sister Lizzie hadn't been born yet, and no one knew your maw was sickly yet."

"But you weren't slaves here in New Orleans? And then you were in Alabama? I don't understand."

"Your father saw a lawyer here who prepared papers saying that Ruby and I were slaves because he knew that Negroes would never be considered free in Alabama. So, we simply pretended we were slaves all those years," Jim said.

"But if you only pretended to be slaves, why did you let me take Ruby to Quindaro?" Junius asked.

"Times were so strange back then. We didn't know what was going to happen. Weren't sure whether Missouri would stay in the Union or secede like the other states in the South were doing. Just seemed like the smart thing to do at the time. Remember, the only thing worth giving up is the thing that is worth having in the first place. And it worked out, didn't it?"

Junius knew this moment would arrive eventually for him to have to tell Jim what had happened to Ruby, but he still didn't know how. As he tried to figure out his next steps, he kept returning to the fact that the woman he loved was his sister. Why hadn't Jim ever told him the truth?

Junius was unable to contain what he was feeling any longer. He didn't know whether to be upset with his father or Jim or Ruby and how to tell her the truth.

One thing he did know was that he couldn't tell Jim the truth about what had happened between him and Ruby on the way to Quindaro. What good would it do for Jim to know that anyway?

Chapter 35

Jim wasn't Ruby's father.

Radolfus was.

Junius and Ruby shared the same father. The woman he loved and had slept with all those years ago was his half-sister. No wonder it was so easy for them to become so close despite their differences. And Ruby wasn't a slave, nor had she ever been. It was all a fictitious story to protect Jim and Ruby from becoming slaves, one which, carried to its extreme conclusion, had almost cost her life.

Worst of all, they could never again be together. They would never be man and wife, let alone lovers. At best, they might become good friends but even that seemed highly unlikely given what he now knew.

And he had to be the one to tell her that and tell her why.

And Junius had to confront his father as well. Their father. Did Radolfus know he was Ruby's father as well as his own? How could he have lied all those years without even blinking an eye, even when Junius brought her back from Canada, as if nothing out of the ordinary had occurred to his own daughter?

Junius took the train back from New Orleans through Mobile and on to Gadsden. He kept hoping something would happen to delay the next leg of the journey. Not for a long time, of course, rather just long enough for him to be able to gather his thoughts about how to explain to Ruby what he had learned from Jim. He would need to speak to her first before confronting his father, and he had no idea what to expect from her. The news would be devastating, especially coming so soon after the elation they had both felt upon rediscovering each other only a few months earlier and making such wonderful plans for their future.

She could stay in Gadsden, of course, and probably would do just that. She would be safe there and be in the midst of family, although not the family that she had anticipated. Not the one that he had anticipated! Once he told Radolfus what Jim had revealed, he hoped that he would accept Ruby and Abraham and that she wouldn't be cast out without anywhere to go. After all, regardless of Abraham's parentage, Radolfus was the boy's grandfather.

Junius was the one who would have to leave Gadsden, for Ruby's sake.

He would start his business in New Orleans and, once in a while, return to Gadsden for family affairs. Would it be too painful for them to see each other? Painful and awkward? But he yearned to watch Abraham grow up. Maybe Abraham would come to think of him as his uncle, and Abraham would never have to know the truth, whatever it was.

How ironic, he thought.

What if Ruby met someone there in Gadsden, fell in love, and got married? How would that be for him? How could he accept another man, a stranger, loving Ruby and raising Abraham as if he were his own son?

It was too much to think of right now.

Right now, he had to just absorb as much of the shock as he could and tell Ruby everything as soon as he arrived in Gadsden. It wouldn't be fair to her to let her think they could be together one day longer than necessary. No matter how much it hurt. And there had to be a way to make everything work somehow. He just needed time to think.

Chapter 36

In Gadsden, Junius hired a hansom cab to take him to the Hart family home. Paw was still at the store since it was midday, and Sarah Anne was in the kitchen washing the morning dishes.

"Junius!" she said. "I didn't know you were coming back already!"

"I got things accomplished quicker than I expected, so I decided just to come on home as soon as I could," he said. He didn't really want to spend any time with her, trying to answer any other questions she was certain to ask. He just wanted her out of the way so he could focus on the difficult conversations he was going to have to have soon.

"Where is everybody? I suppose I should say hello before going to the store to see Paw," he said.

"Everyone else is at school or at work, Junius." She stopped washing the dishes as she spoke, holding a washrag in one hand and a bowl in the other. "Except for Ruby, that is. You know that girl has become a part of the family just like it used to be."

"Oh, is Ruby here?" His stomach twisted. Could he face her so soon? "I suppose I could say hello to her before I head to the store." Sarah Anne was more accepting of Ruby than he thought she would ever be. This would just make what was going to happen soon even more difficult.

"No, she went to buy some fruit and vegetables for me. She won't be back for a bit, probably."

Good, that would buy him some time before he had to face

her. He still didn't know how to tell her. He could feel Sarah Anne's eyes drilling into the back of his neck as he walked through the house toward the staircase. Without turning around, he asked, "Has Abraham gotten settled in school yet?"

Sarah Anne said something unintelligible as he reached the staircase, and he returned to the kitchen to ask her what she had said.

"You know, it's sort of a blessing that you found that girl and the boy the way you did. I never really paid too much attention to her in Tuscumbia or in Harrisonville, her being a slave and all, but now that she has been liberated and endured whatever it was she went through, I've taken a liking to her. I guess it took what we all went through during the war for people to wake up to how we should treat those who were our slaves, and I, for one, have learned that. Nothing can change the color of her skin, of course, but still, she is a fine young woman regardless."

Junius couldn't believe what his stepmother was saying. He couldn't have imagined her thinking changing the way it obviously had.

Sarah Anne continued without looking at Junius.

"I said that it seems like Abraham is adapting to his new school quite well. That's a bright boy, that young man. I know his mother is sharp, and I would have to think that the boy's father—whoever he is—is clever too."

Junius watched her in wonder as she said this. He wondered how she would react when she learned the truth. He could tell that Sarah Anne was looking at him, expecting him to continue, but he couldn't think of anything else that he wanted to add, and anything he would say would simply be a lie anyway.

"I probably should head down to the store to see if Paw needs any help with anything."

"I think you could wait to do that. You must be tired from your journey. Why don't you take a nap and then decide what to do? Besides, you still haven't said hello to Ruby yet."

"I expect that can wait a bit. I want to fill Paw in on what I learned during the trip. And to tell him about seeing Jim."

"Jim! How is he, Junius? Is he well?"

"Yes, he is." He put his foot on the bottom stair, hoping Sarah Anne would take the hint.

But she didn't. "I imagine he was thrilled when you told him about Ruby. And about Abraham!"

Junius cleared his throat several times before he answered. *What can I say?* "He was. Surprised more than anything."

"It would be wonderful if he could see Ruby again and meet his grandson, too! Did you discuss that with him?" she asked.

"No, not really. It was all a bit much for him so suddenly. Well, I'd best be getting on," he said.

Instead of continuing upstairs, Junius turned around and headed to the front door in an effort to shut down any further talk about Jim, Ruby, or Abraham. He was halfway to the door when he heard the door open and Ruby call to him.

"Junius, you're home!" she said, rushing toward him and only catching herself at the last second as he faced her.

She was smiling as broadly as he had ever seen her smile. Then her smile disappeared, and he realized that the way he looked at her was probably responsible for that. Regardless, she was beautiful. He tried to see some resemblance to Radolfus in her eyes and couldn't. Was that because he didn't want to or because there was none?

"Ruby, it's good to see you," he said, struggling for control over his voice. "Sarah Anne says that Abraham seems to be adjusting to school well." He dared not take a step closer to her.

"He is," she said, her eyes searching his, full of questions.

Questions he couldn't answer right then. "Well, I should head down to the store to see if Paw needs me. We can catch up on the trip and Jim and all when I get back, maybe after supper."

She pursed her lips, and he thought her face reddened. Then she stepped aside as he walked past her out the front door, but he thought he heard her screaming silently at him.

Chapter 37

Rather than go to his father's store, Junius walked around the town, trying to clear his head. When he returned home after an hour, it was clear that the children were home from the noises he heard inside the house. He stayed across the street, just a little way away from the house, and waited. After several minutes, Ruby emerged, and he guessed she was looking for him as her eyes scanned the street. He stepped forward so she could see him, and she hesitated briefly before dashing across the street to meet him.

She started to approach him, but he put his hands up in front of him, motioning Ruby to stop.

"Oh, you're right. No one should see us, at least not yet. I'm sorry. I was just so anxious to see you," she said.

When he tried to speak, he couldn't. Instead, he felt his eyes welling, and he choked down the bile that was building in his gut. He felt like he was about to be sick and fought to control himself. He couldn't falter now. He had to tell her the truth without hesitation, or things would only get worse. The question was how.

"Ruby, my dear," he said. That was a mistake. "I have news for you," he said. He had to tell her.

"News? What news? Please walk with me a little so no one can see us and hold me. I need to kiss you, Junius. But you don't look pleased. What is the matter?"

They walked off a ways together, out of sight of the house and anyone passing along the street. Ruby reached out to take Junius's hand. He held it briefly, patted it, and let it go.

"I talked to Jim. He told me things," Junius said.

"What kind of things?" she asked. "Tell me!"

Junius wanted to be anywhere but where he was. He stopped walking to face her squarely. He couldn't hear anything but his heart pounding. He wanted to grab her and hold her and kiss her, but knew that would never be possible again.

"Junius?"

"Jim told me things about us," he started. "Things I didn't want to know, but now that I do, I have to tell you."

The confusion in Ruby's eyes was unbearable. He couldn't tear his eyes away from hers, knowing she would never look at him the same way again after he told her the truth.

"What things?"

"Ruby, we ... we are brother and sister. We have the same father. Radolfus is your father and mine."

She gasped. For a moment, she didn't move. "That's not possible. You're lying. Jim is my father!"

Tears started into her eyes and Junius could bear it no longer. He wrapped his arms around her, letting her sob into his shoulder. "I wish it wasn't true, but it is. There can be no doubt. It's a long story. My father fell in love with your mother in New Orleans before you were born."

She pushed herself away from him and stepped back. "No, no, no ..." She shook her head. Then she slowly turned around and started walking away toward the house with her head down. He called out to her several times, but she simply walked away all the faster.

He stood there for what must have been half an hour. He'd done it. He told her. Now, he had to figure out how they were going to live with those facts.

At supper that night, the family asked all sorts of questions about New Orleans, and Radolfus, in particular, was keen to learn what his impressions were. Lizzie asked about Jim, and

Junius was relieved he could report that Jim was in relatively good health and seemed to be happy to be back where he considered home. Abraham listened intently when the subject of Jim came up, and Junius could tell he was curious about the man he believed to be his grandfather. Both he and Ruby had spoken fondly of him on the trip from Dawn, and he appeared to remember virtually everything they had told him. "Tell me more about my pawpaw," he said repeatedly.

All through dinner, Ruby ate silently, her eyes cast down at her plate. Junius knew better than to say anything to her and did his best to be interested in the conversation.

Exhausted from the effort of telling Ruby and pretending to the rest of the family that all was well, Junius decided the confrontation with Radolfus would have to wait until the morning.

"You haven't yet discussed what you found out with your father, have you?" Ruby asked Junius the following morning on the front porch once all the children were off to school and Sarah Anne was busy in the kitchen.

"You mean our father, Ruby. No, I haven't. I wanted to talk to you first. I thought it only right to tell you before I talked with him."

"There really isn't anything else to say, is there? We can't possibly have the future we imagined now." Her voice trailed off, and the despondent look in her eyes pierced Junius.

He said nothing for a while, imagining that she was in turmoil, just as he was. But they had to figure things out, decide how to move forward—if there was any way to move forward.

So Junius took a deep breath and asked the question that had been in his heart ever since his conversation with Jim. "What will you do, Ruby? Will you stay here, or will you leave Gadsden?"

She looked into his eyes, searching them for something—

an answer, maybe. All Junius could see in hers was hurt and confusion. "I don't know. I was so sure of everything, and now I don't know anything. It's like our future has been ripped away from us because of our father's past."

Junius bit his lip. He had to stay strong, for Ruby's sake. Ruby's eyes were red. Perhaps she'd cried everything out overnight and was ready to go forward. She was strong. She had to be, given everything that had happened to her ever since the Jayhawkers took her on the way to Quindaro. Then why hadn't what he had seen in the war prepared him to face the destruction of his dreams any better?

He took a deep breath. "I've lost, no, we've lost so much. Through no fault of our own. And there is no way to get it back," he said. No turning the clock back to a time before they knew what they now knew.

"None of this is your fault. It had to happen, and it had to end this way. I don't know why, but it did," Ruby said, tears streaking her face.

"I wanted to be Abraham's father. And your husband," he said.

"I know that. Of all people, I know that best. I was hoping that would be you, but that can't be now." She took a long, shuddering breath and wiped her face clear. "We should go back. They'll wonder where we have been."

Junius reached out to take her hand, but she crossed her arms over her chest, turned, and walked back toward the house.

Chapter 38

That night after dinner, once the plates were cleared and Sarah Anne, Lizzie, and Ruby were getting the children ready for bed, Radolfus motioned for Junius to step outside onto the front porch. The sun was just starting to set as Radolfus took out his pipe and offered his tobacco pouch to Junius, who declined.

Junius struggled with his thoughts, unsure how to begin the conversation he knew he needed to have with his father. He couldn't remember a time when they had had cross words between them since he came back from the war, and hardly a time back in Harrisonville either. But his father saved him the trouble of opening the conversation when he suddenly spoke.

"Did Jim tell you?" he asked.

Junius put down the snifter he had just filled and said, "Tell me what, Paw?" *Is he going to tell me the truth? After all these years? The whole truth? A truth that should never have been hidden from him or from Ruby. A truth that, if known, would have answered so many questions that he didn't have, that he didn't even know existed. A truth that would have prevented so much heartache.*

"The truth about Ruby. Surely, he must have said something to you," Radolfus said.

Yes, indeed, Junius wanted to scream. *Jim certainly had told me something.* That much was certain. And that something was profound and would have been life-changing had he known it earlier.

Junius thought his father must have been struggling with

what he had to say next, but instead, he appeared as calm as could be. How could he be so calm with what he had to acknowledge now? What he had to admit to?

This wasn't the father Junius had known, not before the war or since he had returned from the war. That man would never have let this unfold the way the story had. Radolfus had always leveled with his son, even when it hurt him to do so about whatever he thought. When Radolfus spoke again, Junius realized he had been lost in thought for probably several minutes while his father must have been waiting for him to answer.

"Well, what about it? Does Ruby know, too?" Radolfus asked.

Junius's cheeks began to flush, and he had difficulty keeping his voice from rising. He forced himself to speak slowly and distinctly. "Yes, I told her," Junius answered. He waited for his father to react, but Radolfus merely nodded and returned to his cognac yet again.

"Why didn't you tell me? You could have, should have, told me years ago," Junius said.

Radolfus looked up at Junius with shock in his eyes.

"Tell you? What would that have changed? It didn't really matter when you found out, did it?"

How could he believe such a thing? The fact that he and Ruby were brother and sister didn't matter to him? This didn't make sense.

"You don't think things would have been different if Ruby and I knew the truth?" Junius asked.

Radolfus smiled.

"Ruby? She was better off not knowing the truth. Imagine if she had learned that her real father didn't care about her and had left her mother to her fate without a backward glance. How would that have made her feel? No, it was better that she grow up thinking that Jim was her father," Radolfus said.

"But how can you say that?" Junius said. "You knew her

mother, and you were there when she died. She told you that—"

"That's true. I was there. She told me she wanted me to take care of Ruby as any father would any child. I agreed readily since I loved her long before I met your mother or knew of Ruby's existence. She was very beautiful, you know." A faraway look came into Radolfus's eyes.

But Junius wasn't going to let him go without pushing him. "But, Father ..."

"Ruby's mother trusted Jim. He was her half-brother by a different father. I thought that he and his woman, I think her name was Fanney, would make good parents to Ruby, but then Fanney was recaptured by one of those scoundrels who got paid for rounding up escaped slaves."

Then Radolfus told Junius the story of how Jim and Ruby came to be with him in Alabama—most of which Junius already knew from Jim's account. After he'd explained it all, he said, "I knew it was risky bringing Jim's woman along with us since she was an escapee and the man who wanted to buy her would be after her, but I couldn't leave her behind. I had already seen more than enough of how slaves were treated in my years peddling here in Alabama. It was even worse, much worse, than the way people treated Jews in Germany. The way my own father was treated and murdered, with no one being held accountable. I could only imagine how much worse it would be for little Ruby, who had already lost her own mother, if Fanney had been recaptured in New Orleans. What would Jim have done with a two-year-old daughter and nobody to look after her?"

He paused to sip his cognac. Junius was on the point of prodding Radolfus again when he spoke. "I thought we were fortunate to find an attorney who would prepare false papers for Jim and Ruby and Fanney saying they were my slaves, lawfully purchased, that would let me bring them to Alabama safely. And he was a prominent attorney in New Orleans. And a Jew, but he wasn't one of us. He was Sephardic, Moroccan, polluted by generations in Africa, not one of us from Europe. I should have known not to trust him, but by then, it was too late."

Junius watched his father closely while he related his story. It was so implausible that it had to be true. His father couldn't have invented it, yet there was still something missing from the tale. It only made complete sense if Radolfus knew Ruby was really his daughter, so why did he keep refusing to acknowledge that? Why was he so reluctant to admit it?

"How did my mother take it when you and Jim and Ruby appeared?"

Radolfus didn't answer immediately, but instead examined the contents of his brandy glass. After a long moment, he sighed and looked up again.

"When we returned to La Grange, your mother, Elizabeth, died just after giving birth to your sister Lizzie. She departed this world, leaving you and Lizzie in the care of her cousin, Sarah Anne. I found myself with two children, and Ruby had no mother, so the only sensible thing to do was marry your stepmother."

Despite everything else going on in his mind, Junius saw that this made sense. But the two of them had yet to discuss the main issue.

"So, my mother died not know anything about Ruby? Not even of her existence or of who her father was?" The man had kept this secret for so long that Junius wasn't sure his father's memory wasn't betraying him.

"How would she have known about Ruby? And why should she have known anything of a child that wasn't ours?" Radolfus asked.

"No, Ruby wasn't her child, but at least my mother died not knowing Ruby was your child," Junius said.

When he saw the look on his father's face, he felt as if time had stopped. Radolfus's eyes and mouth opened wide, and he said nothing for a while. When he spoke, his voice came out in a ragged whisper.

"What did you say?" Radolfus asked.

"You heard me. I said at least my mother died unaware that Ruby was your daughter."

With that, Junius watched as the color drained from his father's face.

"My daughter? Ruby?" Radolfus took off his glasses and bowed his head.

"You truly didn't know," Junius said.

It all made sense now, even though nothing really made sense anymore.

Junius tried to understand and forgive his father. But after all that had passed, he knew it would take some time.

The next morning, the sun was already bright as Junius took his first cup of coffee outside to the porch. There had to be some sort of solution that would at least make sense to everyone. He racked his brain, trying to think of something, but kept coming up short. As he drained the last bit of his coffee, the door opened behind him.

He turned and saw Abraham standing by the doorway with his eyes wide open. He started to reach out to him when Ruby appeared suddenly with a valise in her hands.

"What are you doing, Ruby?" he asked, even though he knew what her answer would be. He frantically tried to think of something he could say that would change her mind but knew whatever he said would be pointless. She had taken the decision out of his hands and there would be no arguing with her about it.

"Abraham and I are going to take a little trip," Ruby said.

He couldn't stop her. Moreover, no matter how much it hurt, he knew he shouldn't.

"I see. Where to?" He reached out for Abraham's hand, but the little boy stayed close to his mother.

"Dawn, I suspect. No place else to go, really."

"Have you said goodbye to anyone else?"

"No, that would just be too painful and invite too many questions neither of us wants to answer."

She was right. But how could he simply let her walk out of his life? And with Abraham.

"How will you get there?"

"I have my mother's ruby."

"So, this is goodbye then?"

"Yes, Junius, it is. It has to be."

She was right. But how could he just let her walk away? With Abraham?

"Ruby, wait," he said and hastened inside. When he returned, he handed her something he had wrapped in a piece of cloth. "Open this when you get to Dawn. You should have it."

With that, she took Abraham's hand and walked away. Junius's eyes followed them as far as he could, until they turned the bend that led to the train station. She never looked back, but Abraham did several times.

Chapter 39

Janaury 1879

The years went by, and Junius moved to New Orleans, where he set up shop and became very successful. He was able to purchase a building at 191 Canal Street, near the ever-expanding downtown area. He could walk to Antoine's in under ten minutes, and the store's location at the intersection of Canal and Burgundy was close to Rampart Street, which drew in a great many customers.

Not only did he succeed in marketing and selling pianos, but he became a pioneer in selling sheet music of the latest music crazes. Cuban jazz was a reliable source of income, as it was sweeping the Southland, particularly New Orleans. He also was able to parlay his musical connections and enticed the Mexican Army band to tour the United States with him as the tour organizer and stateside manager of the band.

He continued to prosper and was able to employ Jim as his assistant store manager when he was away touring. Both he and Jim shared memories of Ruby on occasion, and both wondered what had happened to her. Junius told Jim about Abraham. Junius met and married Mattie Edwards, and they had a daughter.

Then yellow fever swept the city in 1878—the disease that had taken Ruby's mother, Corinne, years earlier. Junius decided to send his wife and eleven-year-old daughter, Mattie Lena, to Mobile to visit Sarah Anne, thinking they would be safer there.

But the fever followed them to Mobile, where both were taken ill and died within days of each other. It seemed he couldn't save those who were near and dear to him no matter what he did. Maybe he was the one who was the curse that others had to deal with until they died.

Junius plunged back into his business even more assiduously. He spent most of his waking hours at work, rarely taking time off for anything outside of his business. He kept imagining new ways of expanding the business beyond what he was already involved in and realized that sheet music held the key to his success.

Even though he was disappointed that the deal he had struck with Heintzman hadn't materialized for a multitude of logistical reasons, he had been able to secure arrangements with Chickering, Hardman, Emerson, and Vose and Sons, all of which were proving lucrative. He had even started selling Story and Clark organs as his business expanded.

Then, one day, while he was busy at his desk reviewing his inventory in Junius Hart Pianos, he heard a commotion downstairs. Jim walked into his office with a look on his face that Junius had never seen before. It even seemed like Jim had been crying.

"Jim, what is it?" Junius asked.

Barely able to get the words out of his mouth, Jim said, "There is someone here to see you." He looked down and steadied himself on the arm of the chair nearby. Junius started to get up from his chair, but Jim waved him off. "It's fine. I'll be fine. Just give me a second."

"Who, Jim? Who is here?" Junius asked. It was unusual for Jim to seem so uncertain about a visitor. Probably a potential customer.

Jim looked at him as if he had seen a ghost. Then he stood aside from the door to Junius's office, and a young man who must have been about seventeen years old entered the office. He was well-dressed and carried a thin leather case in his left hand. Something about him struck Junius as being familiar, but he couldn't place it at first. Junius stood in order to greet him in the customary way.

"Yes, young man, may I help you?" he asked.

"Yes sir, I believe you may," the young man said. He looked all around the office, seeming to want to take it all in as fully as possible.

No sooner than he had asked how he could help the young man, he realized that the young man bore an uncanny resemblance to someone he used to know. It was something about the way he smiled, the way he imagined him tossing his head back in laughter. He could even tell that the young man would have as confident an air about him as she had so many years ago. He tried to force memories of that fateful night away and couldn't do so. His efforts just made the memories stronger.

"My name is Abraham. Abraham Fontaine," he said.

Ruby's son! He's come back! To New Orleans, of all places! Why? Does he know about him and his mother?

Junius tried to stay calm and said, "What brings you here, Abraham?"

"I am here to see if you can help me with a legal issue," he said.

"A legal issue?" Junius asked.

"Yes, sir. I need the services of an attorney, and my mother told me she was sure you could help me find a good one."

"Is Ruby—your mother here with you? She hasn't sent you here alone, has she?"

Abraham shuffled his feet and looked back at Jim, who stood stockstill. "No, sir, she died a year ago. In Paris."

Ruby was dead. Junius wanted to know if she had died alone. Had she been in pain? Had he been with her when she died? What was the cause? Had she ever spoken of him? Did she try to impress memories of days gone by on him? He wanted to ask why she had decided to go to Paris, but that all seemed irrelevant now.

He needed to concentrate on Abraham, who bore such a

strong resemblance to his mother and perhaps less so to his father, whoever that really was.

"I am sorry for your loss, Abraham. Truly sorry." He didn't know what else to do with the boy who had grown up into such a handsome young man. He looked just like Junius imagined he would.

His Ruby was gone, and she had sent her son, Abraham, to him for help in a legal matter. "Why would she have sent you to see me, young man?" he asked.

"My mother told me you would gladly assist me in changing my name to my father's name," Abraham said.

"She told you what your father's name is?" Junius asked. He couldn't believe what he was hearing.

"Yes, sir, she did. Just before she died."

"What name is that?" Junius asked and held his breath.

"Hart, sir. Junius Hart." Abraham smiled just the way she did when he said that. It was the same smile she had given Junius when he played the fife for her.

Could it be true? "Are you certain?" His voice came out in a whisper.

"Yes, sir, you're my father. She also said that you were the only man who really loved her," Abraham said.

Junius hesitated before responding. He wanted what Abraham was saying to be true, but how did he know? Had Ruby really known?

"I wish that to be true, Abraham. But your mother wasn't sure that was the case when I last saw her and you. What made her so sure before she passed away?"

With that, Abraham smiled. He opened his satchel to reveal a piece of cloth that looked familiar and spread it out. It took a moment before Junius realized that what was inside wasn't just an old piece of wood.

Then, Abraham placed a leather case on Junius's desk and opened it to reveal a beautiful fife. Without hesitation, he picked up the instrument, put it to his lips, and began to play.

Postscript

Initially, this story was meant to be a biographical sketch of my paternal great-great-grandfather, Radolfus Hart, who emigrated from somewhere in Germany to the U.S. in about 1836 when he was twenty years old. He may have worked as a peddler in Alabama before accumulating enough capital to open his own store in La Grange, Alabama, by 1846, where he acted as an agent for Williams' European and Domestic Fashions. By the following year, he opened a shop in Tuscumbia, Alabama, where he and his family lived until the early 1850s.

Junius was born in February 1843. Elizabeth, Junius and his sister Lizzie's mother, died after giving birth to Lizzie in 1846 and was described as being his consort in her brief obituary. Radolfus married Sarah Anne soon thereafter, and together, they had seven children. Junius attended La Grange College, a preparatory school, as late as 1852. By the mid-1850s, Radolfus had moved the family to Harrisonville, Missouri, near the Kansas border, possibly anticipating a further move to California to capitalize on the California Gold Rush. La Grange College was later destroyed by Union forces during the Civil War. Sarah Anne lived until 1914.

H.W. Younger, the father of fourteen children, including Thomas Coleman, nicknamed Cole, later of the James-Younger Gang, was the mayor of Harrisonville by the late 1850s. H.W. was murdered while returning from Kansas City to Harrisonville in 1862, probably by a Union officer, an event which prompted Cole to take up a life of crime. Junius would have been schooled in his teen years in Harrisonville, and he and Cole Younger were only a year apart in age. Junius worked as a printer at the *Cass County Gazette*, previously called the *Western Democrat*, until joining the Missouri State Guard as a musician with the outbreak of the Civil War in April 1861.

At some point during the Civil War, the Hart family left Harrisonville, perhaps after Union troops burnt the town in 1863, and returned to Alabama, settling in Gadsden, where Radolfus opened another store. He drowned in July 1872, just before his fifty-sixth birthday, apparently a well-respected man of the community.

Junius was present at and participated in numerous battles during the war, was wounded three times, and served as an orderly to a colonel during the Battle of Shiloh. The Confederate States Army bought a fife for Private Junius Hart of the 15th Alabama Regiment in May 1863 for five dollars. After the war, Junius joined his father's business in Gadsden and traveled to Cincinnati before eventually settling in New Orleans, where he owned Junius Hart Pianos on Canal Street, selling pianos and sheet music in the 1880s and into the 1890s. He served as an honorary pallbearer to Jefferson Davis's funeral in 1889. He is listed as being a prominent Jew in New Orleans by the early 1890s, shortly before his death in New York City in 1893. His daughter, Lena Cecile Hart Demack, was my paternal grandmother.

Reverend Josiah Henson, sometimes considered Harriet Beecher Stowe's model for Uncle Tom, was an escaped slave who established Dawn outside of Toronto to assist runaway slaves.

Clarinda Nichols was an outspoken abolitionist who resided in Quindaro, Kansas, in the late 1850s and assisted escaped slaves in reaching the Underground Railroad.

Both Jim and Ruby are fictitious characters who would have been great to meet and get to know, as would Abraham have been.

The receipt for the fife purchased for Junius Hart by the Confederate States Army in 1863.

The Junius Hart Piano House in New Orleans.

Sheet music produced by Junius Hart.

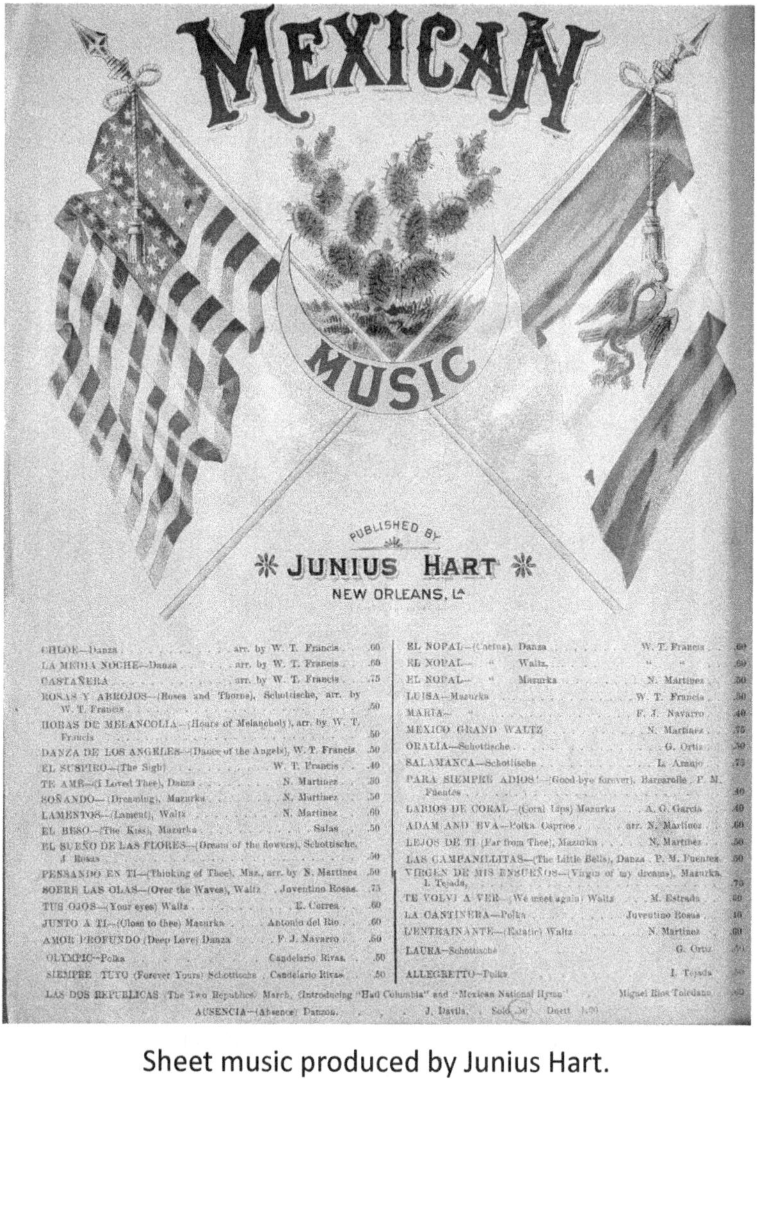

Sheet music produced by Junius Hart.

Junius Hart and his daughter Lena Cecile Hart in September 1886 shortly after her mother died in a fire.

Acknowledgments

I couldn't have written this book without the assistance, greater or lesser, of numerous individuals over the course of the past several years.

Among those, three individuals in particular stand out.

The first is Janet Stroup Fox, a classmate of mine at Kent School in the late 1960s, who read the initial draft of what has become this book after we reconnected at a class reunion several years ago. She encouraged me to continue writing, instructed me in word processing, reviewed my work, and recommended me to a colleague of hers who became my book coach.

Susanne Dunlap became my book coach three years ago and guided me through learning how to write historical fiction and writing in general. Without her assistance, this book would never have seen the light of day.

In order to try to get a sense of what Junius and Ruby, and countless others, must have gone through, I visited Kansas City, Kansas, in 2021. I was fortunate to meet Reverend Stacy Evans, Pastor at Allen Chapel AME Church in Quindaro, who listened to the tale I wanted to tell and guided me through a tour of Quindaro's ruins.

About Atmosphere Press

Founded in 2015, Atmosphere Press was built on the principles of Honesty, Transparency, Professionalism, Kindness, and Making Your Book Awesome. As an ethical and author-friendly hybrid press, we stay true to that founding mission today.

If you're a reader, enter our giveaway for a free book here:

SCAN TO ENTER
BOOK GIVEAWAY

If you're a writer, submit your manuscript for consideration here:

SCAN TO SUBMIT
MANUSCRIPT

And always feel free to visit Atmosphere Press and our authors online at atmospherepress.com. See you there soon!

About the Author

GARY C. DEMACK

A native of southern California, Gary graduated from Duke University, Florida Atlantic University, and the Naval War College. He first embarked on a career teaching Political Science, and then served as an intelligence analyst with the National Security Agency for thirty years in various capacities at home and abroad. After retiring, Gary moved to central Florida where he enjoys writing, golf, and swimming and lives with his wife Tracy. He has combined his life-long interest in genealogy and Civil War history in *The Broken Fife*, a historical novel loosely based on the life of his paternal great-grandfather, Junius Hart.